FIRST SPOUSE
OF THE UNITED
STATES

D1738896

J.R. STRAYVE JR.

Debbie —
It has been
great knowing to know
you. Thank you for everything.
Enjoy the Read!
2023

Cover designed by Carson McDonagh

This book is a work of fiction. Names, characters, places, and incidents either are products of the author's imagination or are used fictitiously. Any resemblance to actual persons, living or dead, events, or locales is entirely coincidental.

J.R. STRAYVE, JR.
Visit my website at www.jrstrayvejr.com

Printed in the United States of America

First Printing: March 2019

ISBN-9781090261007

CHAPTER 1
1992: MEDAL OF HONOR

Marine Corps Captain Ricardo Chambers stood at attention on the dais, watching President Lindsey Tanner commanding everyone's attention as he entered the White House East Room. The Marine Corps Band, uniformed in their crisp blue tunics and white trousers, played "Hail to the Chief." The white-walled, gilded room was jammed with enough people to invite any fire marshal to toss at least fifty from the space. Everyone rose from their seats as the 55-year-old recently elected Republican president headed toward the dais. Tanner was way too conservative for Rocky and entirely too handsome for a Republican. *Shit, better watch what I am thinking and where I look. Damn good thing I'm at attention,* Rocky thought to himself.

Rocky forced his eyes steadily forward. He looked past those assembled to honor him and his now famous heroics. He stood ramrod straight, chin up, and arms to his sides. *How the hell did I get here?*

The president approached the dais. The Chairman of the Joint Chiefs of Staff, Marine Corps General Mendoza and the Navy Chief of Staff, Admiral Chao, flanked Rocky. They too stood at attention, eyes forward. On either side of these men stood the Secretaries of Defense and Navy. Their posture was lacking, but at least they were standing, paunches forward.

The Captain's family, the first lady of the United States, and the senior Pentagon brass occupied the front three rows facing the dais. The first lady was looking directly at Rocky. He affected the glassy look that one embraces when trying to avoid direct eye contact.

Rocky Chambers had done his research on this woman. Mrs. Josephine Tanner was a statuesque beauty. She stood taller than most women. Her demeanor and self-confidence commanded respect. She was reputed to be warm and friendly, but he sensed she had the ability to unmask him. Her reputation was that of being politically savvy, astute and fiercely protective of her husband. She was the power behind the man. Chambers would do all he could to avoid her. She was certain to discover his Achilles' heel.

Rocky continued to contemplate who and what he could see in the East Room. There were plenty of White House staff and politicians for sure. Bureaucrats and politicians annoyed Rocky. He was a fighter pilot. And he was gay. The warrior had no time for political games. The gay man knew he was always vulnerable to discovery, which would end his flying career.

President Tanner stood in front of Rocky. They were the same height and had similar builds. He stuck out his right hand to shake Rocky's. Rocky wasn't accustomed to rendering anything other than a salute while at attention. He awkwardly took the president's hand as their eyes connected in a steely stare. In a flash, they both recognized an exchange of sensual energy. The president slowly took his other hand and firmly grasped Rocky's strong right arm, lingering a little more than was necessary. Rocky wondered if the president would ever release his arm and hand. Thank God, President Tanner began to speak. There was entirely too much electricity passing between them

"Captain Chambers, it is indeed my and the nation's pleasure to host you here at the White House."

"Thank you, sir."

The president then moved on to the others assembled on the dais. Rocky returned to attention.

Pleasantries were exchanged between the

president and those standing on the dais. This gave Rocky some time to regain his composure. *Did the President of the United States just come on to me?*

He was grateful for the tiresome and annoying bureaucratic prattling and political garbage as it gave him a moment to collect his thoughts and composure. The dignitaries were acknowledged, everyone was thanked, and the president got back on topic.

"We are gathered here today to honor an amazing American. An American hero! This young man has served his country with phenomenal courage and skills as an aviator. He is an Air Ace of historic proportions. His skill in the air, quick thinking and flawless judgment..."

The president went on and on to detail Rocky's heroics. Rocky was relieved the president would have to drape the Medal of Honor around his neck from the back. The prospect of encountering those knowing brown eyes again was disarming and caused him to feel a bit weak and vulnerable. Chambers never felt weak or vulnerable. His nickname was Rocky for a reason.

As the president completed his remarks, he approached the medal recipient from the front. They stood less than a foot apart, facing one another. Carefully avoiding eye contact, Rocky executed a perfect military about-face. Rocky was in position, his back to the president. He began to perspire. His parched throat felt as if it were closing. The president gingerly took the ends of the ribbon holding the magnificent medallion and draped it around Rocky's neck, where it came to rest on his chest. Rocky did not know if the palpitations emanating from his heart could be heard by those standing nearby. Surely the medal would move as the force of his heartbeat must be visibly pulsing through his uniform. Was it the reality of receiving the medal or the proximity of the man whose eyes had disarmed him?

The president firmly secured the ribbon's clasp, and then rested his hands-on Rocky's shoulders, pressing firmly against the starched dress whites. This sent a scintillating chill coursing through Rocky's body. Now Rocky had to turn and face President Tanner. As he executed a sharp about-face, he met the president's eyes again. They stared at each other as they shook hands a final time.

"Congratulations, Captain Chambers."

"Thank you, sir!"

More pleasantries were exchanged as the ceremony came to a close. Eventually Rocky made his way past the dignitaries and headed toward his family. He hugged his parents, brother and sister. From behind him, he heard someone speaking.

"Captain Chambers, the president and first lady would like to invite you and your family to join them in the residence."

This was totally unexpected. Rocky was not sure this was a good idea, but he turned to the adjutant with a warm smile, and then to his parents. He could tell that the family was thrilled with the prospect of spending time with President and Mrs. Tanner. "No, thank you" was not an option.

"We would be honored to accept," replied Rocky.

They were escorted to the elevator. Arriving on the residence floor, Rocky and his family were met by the butler and escorted through the long, exquisitely furnished center hall. They arrived at the columned entry to the west sitting room, a somewhat formal room furnished with comfortable sofas and chairs. Tables were conveniently placed, much as a family room might be arranged. The first lady stood at the far end of the room, her back to the magnificent arched Palladian multi-paned window that spanned the width and height of the room.

"Welcome to our home. Please come and make yourselves comfortable. My husband will join us in a moment. Again, Captain Chambers, congratulations on receiving our nation's highest honor."

"Thank you, ma'am, I appreciate the honor and your hospitality."

Mrs. Tanner made the family comfortable as she bade everyone sit and relax. Refreshments and a selection of beverages had been prepared and placed on the large, low table surrounded by Rocky's family, seated in comfortable chairs and sofas. Rocky gave no indication that he was nervous and wished he was anywhere but where he was. The Chambers family was educated, well-traveled, and socially astute. The hostess and her guests were thoroughly conversant and heartily enjoying their banter when ten minutes later, they were interrupted.

The butler reappeared. "Excuse me, Mrs. Tanner. The president is unavoidably detained. He has asked that Captain Chambers join him in the Oval Office." A cold sweat broke out on Rocky's neck.

"Captain, why don't you go with Mr. Matthews? He can show you to the Oval Office. I'm thrilled to spend more time here with your family. We have a lot to talk about. I want to learn all about you and it will be so much easier to get the truth if you are not in the room!" Mrs. Tanner joked. His parents laughed, and his siblings chuckled, as if some family secrets were about to be divulged. Once again Rocky felt a little nervous. His family knew his secret and they loved him unconditionally. Could they withstand what he was certain would be a very nimble inquisition by FLOTUS? His trepidation and awkward rise from the deep seat went unnoticed, as all were engrossed in conversation and contemplating what they would say next.

As Rocky prepared to follow the butler, he addressed his kin. "Okay family remember all my foibles are state secrets and no one in this room has the proper clearance or the need to know!" They all laughed as he exaggerated a bow and winked. Once again, he expertly executed a crisp about-face, leaving the first lady and his family to their own devices. Was Rocky escaping one trap only to be ensnared by another?

Rocky walked alongside Mr. Matthews down the center hall, descending the steps to the first floor. They made their way out of the mansion and onto the outdoor promenade leading to the Oval Office. Entering the Oval Office, they found the president sitting alone in one of the wingback chairs, sipping a cocktail, a roaring fire crackling behind him.

"Come in, Rocky. May I call you that, Captain?"

"Yes, of course sir, please do. My friends call me that and it would be an honor to count you among my friends, sir"

The president smiled and asked the butler to poor a scotch for Rocky. Matthews made quick work of the request, handing the drink to Rocky and exiting the office, leaving the two men alone in the most important room in the world.

"Rocky, please sit," said the president, pointing to the opposite chair.

"Thank you, sir."

"You know Rocky, when I was your age I, too, played football. I would have loved to have flown aircraft but did not have the prerequisite eyesight. So I settled on politics. I think having better eyesight would have saved me a lot of grief." Both men chuckled, seated in the wingback chairs facing one another at an angle. "My nickname back then was Hammer."

"Okay, Mr. President, dare I ask how you got that name? Was it politics or street fighting?" *Shit! I just flirted with the president.*

The president replied, "I would like to think that it had something to do with sex."

President Tanner's directness caused Rocky to take an oversized gulp from his glass, almost spilling it on his immaculate white uniform. He used a sleeve to nervously wipe his still spotless military jacket.

"Captain, I have finally caught you off guard. God, that makes me feel good. I have been so nervous asking you to meet with me privately."

"You, Mr. President, nervous?"

"By the way, as I know you will not do it unless I order it, you will call me Hammer when in private."

"Mr. President, I can't do that."

"Amuse me and obey my order, Rocky."

"Yes, Mr., I mean Hammer." They had both quickly drained their drinks.

"Rocky, give me your glass."

He handed over the glass, engraved with the presidential seal and stood up as the president headed toward a concealed shelf holding several bottles of expensive scotch. As he watched the president and looked around the Oval Office, Rocky was dumbstruck with the reality of being there, alone with the most powerful man in the world. He felt aroused. It was now very obvious the president was hitting on him.

President Tanner handed him his drink. "Here's a toast acknowledging your commendation, Captain." Their glasses clinked as they toasted, and each drank a third of the smoky contents. "Come with me," said the president. Tanner took Rocky by the shoulder and led him to the right of the presidential desk toward the door leading to his private office.

The president closed the door behind them, securing the oversized latch and locking the door. A small corner lamp illuminated the room slightly. There were only shadows.

Both men stood facing each other. Simultaneously, they lifted their scotch-filled crystal glasses in a toast. As he brought the glass to his lips, Rocky noticed a smile playing on the president's lips. Returning the smile, Rocky downed his scotch in a single gulp.

With his empty glass in hand, Rocky moved toward the president. Slowly, deliberately, Rocky leaned toward Tanner and placed the glass on the table behind the president. He "accidentally" brushed against the president, his fingers lightly touching his arm. Rocky made a move that could destroy him instantly. Uncaring, he faced his willing cohort, and with a predator-like grace, leaned in and parted the older man's lips with his tongue. The war hero's senses were filled with the taste of scotch and endorphins, as the president's body demanded more.

Rocky realized the President of the United States had just seduced him.

CHAPTER 2
1982: THE EARLY YEARS

Rocky Chambers was the guy every high school girl wanted, and every boy wanted to be. His height, blonde hair and blue eyes came from his father, William Appleton Chambers. His olive complexion came from his mother, Consuela Bourbon Chambers. His extraordinary athleticism was a product of both. An older brother and a younger sister, Alejandro and Sophia, flanked him. As the middle child, he was naturally accorded less attention and more latitude. This suited him well. His ambitions needed room to flourish.

"Rocky, your father and I are headed to Boston this afternoon. I hope you remembered."

"Yeah, mom!" Rocky yelled as he wolfed down his breakfast burrito.

"We'll be at your grandparents."

"Doesn't sound like much of a vacation for you," Rocky chuckled under his breath.

"It's not, and don't be a wise guy," she said, handing him his lunch bag. "Make sure that you kids look after one another while we're gone. Your father and I know you'll behave as always. Food is in the fridge and spending money is in the drawer in the library."

"Okay, Mom, have a nice trip. Give my love to everybody. Hey Mom, can you remind Grandmother and Grandfather that I'm interviewing at colleges and will be in Boston this summer? I have dibs on my regular room! It is reserved for me and off limits to cousins!"

"Right, I am sure your grandparents will be taking orders from you, young man. Just count your blessings that there's room for you!"

"Ah, c'mon Mamacita, you know they'll do anything for their sweet Rocky!" He flashed her the charming smile.

"Sadly, I think you may be right. Well, anyway, be good, and good luck with the game tonight. And don't forget to let us know how things go. Love you!"

Rocky hugged his mother, kissed her on her forehead, and sped out the kitchen door. With his backpack over his shoulder and car keys in hand, he headed toward the garage.

"Love you, too, Mom. Hi to Dad!" hollered Rocky, leaping and clearing the back steps and railing.

It was a big day for Rocky. It was Friday, and the football game of the year at La Jolla High was scheduled for 7:00 p.m. As the quarterback, he would be fully engrossed in the game. He also had a trig exam and a biology paper to complete. On top of that, the student body officers were meeting. As president of the junior class, he thought he'd better show up.

* * *

"Hey, Umberto! Get those scrawny legs over here!" Rocky hailed his friend and teammate.

"These scrawny legs will have to work overtime tonight trying to catch the wobblers you throw with those pencil arms!" retorted the stellar wide receiver.

Umberto Castañeda had four full scholarships waiting for him when he graduated next year. Rocky wished he had the same opportunities Umberto had. Rocky just wasn't sure what he wanted to do or where he wanted to go to college.

Umberto added to both their reputations as exceptional athletes. Rocky was a talented quarterback with obvious potential, but he knew he needed more experience and time on the field to hone his skills. Umberto was simply exceptionally gifted. They complimented one another on and off the field and realized one could not succeed without the other. They read each other's minds. They could anticipate each other's moves. The two were the stars and backbone of a winning team.

"Umberto are you taking Joanne out after the game tonight to celebrate?"

"Of course, mi amigo. She would have my balls if I didn't. And you would not like that," teased Umberto.

"That's true, but then there are oceans of *bolas* that could replace yours if she took them," scoffed Rocky.

"Okay smartass are you tied to the lovely Belinda *esta noche?*"

"Yep, she informed me that we are going down to some jazz place in the Village. Sounds interesting, so I said okay. My folks are out of town. Are you up for an 'after date?'"

Umberto looked sideways at Rocky. "That depends if we connect on the field. It would be nice to celebrate the victory, yes?"

"Sì," Rocky snorted. Both he and Rocky always looked forward to a couple of beers on the beach after a good game after they took the girls home.

* * *

Rocky and Belinda had started dating at the end of their sophomore year. They enjoyed being together. There did, however, come a time when he felt that he should break it off and go on to someone else. He really didn't care if he dated. He just did it because it was expected. One day he was hanging out with his teammates in the locker room as they bragged about the sex they were having with their girlfriends. They started baiting him about his relationship with Belinda.

"None of your business, assholes!" He gathered up his gear and stormed out of the locker room.

The next day, Belinda and Rocky were in her room doing their homework when Belinda stood up and walked over to him. She grabbed his hands and put them around her hips. She began kissing him. Her hands moved toward the bottom of his T-shirt, whipping it off his chest in an instant. Rocky replied by relieving her of her tube-top. He could feel himself grow hard in his board shorts. Shaking a bit, he ran his hands down each side of her tanned neck and on down her sides, resting them on her hips. She looked into his eyes.

"I heard that you defended my reputation in the locker room yesterday. Thank you."

"Um, uh, you're welcome." He gulped. His hard-on was now pressing against her abdomen.

She pushed him down and straddled him. One of her hands found him inside his shorts. "You know, I can think of a much better way to say thank you."

* * *

Rocky stared up at the ceiling. Admittedly, the first time was clumsy. Finally, it was over. *God*, Rocky thought. *I thought it would be better than that. She's probably laughing at me. Next time we do this, I hope it's better.*

It was one of the few times in his life Rocky felt he was not in charge. He felt embarrassed. He gently rolled toward her, took her face in his hands and kissed her. Getting out of bed he dressed silently, packed up his books and slipped out of her room. He did not say goodbye.

Belinda and Rocky barely said hello the next day. That weekend she went out of town with her parents. Rocky was relieved. He threw himself into school and sports.

After another awkward week, they got back together. Rocky didn't want to hurt anyone, especially Belinda. He cared for her and tried to convince himself that he loved her. He tried to convince himself that they were meant to be. But something was missing. The sex was just sex.

* * *

That night at the game, Rocky and Umberto didn't disappoint the crowd as they executed the choreographed throwing and receiving that led to the victory over their rivals. Two more recruiters from two colleges indicated they were eager to throw scholarships at Umberto. Rocky could not understand why he had not received at least one firm offer. He did realize that Umberto was magnificent. *Oh, what the hell. I don't even know what I want to do, or where I want to go,* thought Rocky.

After the game, Rocky and Belinda went down to the jazz club in the La Jolla Village. He would have preferred to be out celebrating the victory with Umberto and his friends. He liked Belinda. She was a terrific girl. She was beautiful and smart. But he didn't feel about her the way she felt about him. He was not sure he had really felt that way about any girl. He liked girls. It seemed the natural thing. But tonight, Rocky was bored. He felt let down by the dark jazz venue after the big victory. He wanted to do something to celebrate.

Rocky took Belinda home and headed back to his house. His real celebration was sitting in a car parked in front of his house.

"Get in, Umberto."

Umberto jumped in Rocky's car and they sped down the street toward La Jolla Shores. They were only three blocks away, so it took less than a minute for them to reach the sand, strip down to their shorts, grab the cigarettes and beer from the trunk and head toward the water. The beach was dark, with the moon hidden by a light cloud cover. A storm down in Mexico had sent warm, humid breezes to the southern California beach.

Umberto put two cigarettes between his lips and lit them simultaneously. He handed one to Rocky. It was weird but thrilling, and the move kind of turned Rocky on. They started walking down the beach and eventually found a spot out of the way between two small dunes out of sight of the houses along the shore. They spread out the large, soft blanket and sat facing each other, their legs crossed. Umberto opened two beers, handing one to Rocky.

Not much was said as they made themselves comfortable. They were physically inches apart.

Umberto lay back on his side of the blanket. Rocky looked at his best friend and saw what looked like a hard-on growing beneath Umberto's shorts. Rocky was in unfamiliar territory. He couldn't find a comfortable way to lay back and relax.

Before Rocky could speak, Umberto motioned for the pack of cigarettes that had fallen between Rocky's legs, just above his knees.

"Should I help myself, or will you give them a toss?"

Feeling bolder and more curious (and also feeling his own cock beginning to respond), Rocky retorted, "Get them yourself."

"I don't mind if I do," replied Umberto as he reached for the cigarettes, brushing the inside of Rocky's thigh, sending an electric charge through Rocky's body.

Having retrieved the smokes, he once again lit two. Umberto sat up, leaned forward and placed the cigarette between Rocky's partially opened lips.

A little shocked by this overt come-on, Rocky gasped slightly. He inhaled a bit more than normal and stifled a cough. Umberto resumed his reclining position as they both downed another beer and finished their cigarettes.

"So, Mr. Wide Receiver, how was your date?"

"It was okay. Nothing special. I didn't get laid. Really didn't care. I wanted to celebrate our win with the guys, but I was stupid and went on a date. Jesus," whined Umberto.

"Me, too," said Rocky. "Why didn't we celebrate with the team? I wanted to hang with the guys." He shrugged and pretended to pout.

Umberto was just drunk enough to pose a question he had wanted to ask Rocky for a long time.

"Have you ever had sex with a guy?"

Rock's heart kicked up. He thought about the question. He was curious as to where this was going.

"No, have you?"

Umberto didn't answer. He broke out their fourth beer. Rocky felt a stirring in his shorts. He looked out at the breakwater.

They had another cigarette. They finished their fourth beer and started on the fifth. Rocky refused to speak until Umberto answered the question.

Umberto leaned over inches from Rocky's face and said, "Have you ever heard the joke, 'How do you turn a Latino gay?'" Umberto's breath ghosted Rocky's face.

Rocky, startled by the warm moist breath and the erotic feeling welling up within, laughed nervously. He sat up facing Umberto.

"Sure, make him drink a six pack!" Rocky paused and then teased, "Is that really true, Latino Man?" Umberto retrieved their sixth beer, handing one to Rocky.

"Do you want to find out?" Umberto winked, licking his upper lip with the tip of his tongue. They had just started the sixth beer when Rocky got his answer. He liked the answer just as much as Umberto liked answering the question.

Umberto moved closer to his handsome quarterback. He placed his moist, full lips against Rocky's mouth and kissed him hard. Umberto ran one hand down Rocky's bare chest, exploring each muscle, curve and ripple.

Rocky, emboldened by the sensations that Umberto had unfurled, began to touch his friend, too.

The sex was different, rougher and more passionate than with Belinda.

Rocky wondered if it was Umberto's first time with a guy. He doubted it. He really didn't care. But as they headed home, he thought, *what just happened? Fuck! That was hot!*

* * *

The next afternoon, Umberto showed up at Rocky's home unannounced. He had run the two miles from his house to sweat out the hangover and the anxiety from the previous night's activities on the beach. Rocky had the house to himself and was standing in the kitchen in his boxers, getting a glass of water. He had just completed some laps in the family pool for all the same reasons Umberto had gone out for a run.

Umberto was glistening with perspiration on his neck, chest and forearms. His shorts were soaked through and were stuck to his brown thighs.

Rocky paused a little too long, staring, and said, "Hey Umberto, good to see you. I don't know about you, but I'm a bit hung over and embarrassed. Glad you're here so we can talk it out, I mean work it out."

"What do you mean, man -- work it out?" asked Umberto.

"Well, I just thought that you might be pissed at me. You know, the gay thing and thinking that I am some sort of fag."

Umberto started to deflate. He looked away from Rocky, and down at the floor. "Really, I thought that you would think the same thing about me."

Rocky looked at Umberto. "I do think the same thing about you. You're a flaming Maria!" Rocky teased. Umberto stood shocked.

"Umberto, what's wrong? I was only kidding!"

Hurt and pain covered Umberto's face. He faltered. Rocky reached for him and pulled him close, wrapping his arms around him. Umberto was dead weight. "I'm so sorry. I didn't mean anything."

Umberto looked devastated. Rocky guided him to a kitchen stool. "Umberto, you're my best friend. I was teasing you." He cupped Umberto's face in his hands and brought their lips together. Umberto did not respond. Rocky kissed him harder as he pulled Umberto up off the stool.

They held each other for several intense moments, their bodies slowly warming to one another as Umberto's perspiration covered Rocky's torso. Rocky gently raised Umberto's chin from his chest toward his gaze and looked into Umberto's soft brown eyes, kissing him as Umberto melted into him. As their passion grew, Rocky grabbed Umberto's hand and led him up the stairs to his third-floor bedroom.

The two boys spent the afternoon making love and exploring the reality of their new relationship. Their desire was undiminished by their inexperienced clumsiness. There was no shame, no guilt. They felt freed by genuine affection and youthful passion for one another. Was this love? It didn't matter. They had opened themselves up to a new world, one that felt just right.

CHAPTER 3
CLOSETED

Over the next year, Rocky and Umberto developed a routine. They continued to distinguish themselves on the football field. They were an unbeatable team. Although they continued to date Belinda and Joanne, they also found time for each other. It was not difficult. Their sexual energy fueled their lives on and off the field. They had plenty to spare.

They were careful. They were the star athletic duo in a small school in a small community. The fall of their senior year was about to come to a close. Umberto had continued his stellar pace on the field. He would accept a scholarship to a top college team. No one was surprised about that. But everyone was surprised with the sudden avalanche of multiple full-ride offers Rocky started to receive during his senior year as quarterback. Rocky and Umberto's new closeness and awareness had refined their skills and improved their performance on the field.

Rocky was comfortable having sex with someone he could trust. Umberto was devoted to Rocky. People teased them for spending so much time together. However, no one, as far as they knew, suspected how deep their relationship went. Absolutely no one wanted to jinx the magic the two performed on the field. Umberto's early success, followed by even greater success during his senior year, had created a mythical reputation. While Umberto was confident in his abilities, he developed an insatiable yearning for more and more validation on and off the field.

Rocky had become increasingly more comfortable with his growing reputation as a prospective college-quality quarterback. He focused more on his studies, his family, athletics, and Umberto. He yearned for Umberto and somehow felt sure they could continue their football magic and their personal relationship. Rocky loved his family. Why couldn't he have that same love with Umberto? Times were changing. The Stonewall riots in New York and all kinds of stuff in L.A. and San Francisco made it look like gays might be accepted one day. Weren't they making headway? Maybe. Even the more conservative Latino community would come around, right?

* * *

"Umberto, I've been looking all over for you! We were supposed to go over next week's plays."

"I know Rocky, sorry, I was at the beach and lost track of time."

"Which beach? I went to the Shores and no one had seen you. I jogged up and down and halfway to Scripps Pier and didn't see you. You know, you *do* stand out in a crowd, particularly on white sand!"

"Very funny, Rocky. You just didn't jog far enough. If you'd kept going past the pier you would have found me at Black's Beach."

"Black's? Are you out of your mind? If anyone got wind of you carrying on at that beach bare ass naked, you could lose your scholarships!"

"Relax, I was jogging in running shoes and shorts. Well, until I got to the other end. You know, the North End. Where the boys are. I gave them a little show."

"You have got to be fucking kidding me!" roared Rocky. "That's insane! Why? Why would you put yourself in that position? After all we've done to protect one another. It doesn't make any sense!"

Rocky paced the sidewalk in front of Umberto's home. Umberto sat on the retaining wall. He wasn't looking at Rocky. He was slouched and observing his calf muscles, periodically flexing them.

"Listen, Rocky, I know you like my body. Hey man, I wanted to see what the gay dudes would think of it. You know, share the wealth. You know it takes a lot of work to look this good, and well, I guess I wanted someone to show me a little appreciation."

Rocky could not understand what he was hearing. It still made no sense to him. His breathing became rapid and shallow. The hair on the back of his neck bristled. He could barely contain the fury that consumed him. He felt nauseous. He blurted out, "I guess I'm not enough for you. I guess I don't mean enough to you. I guess all we have worked for together doesn't count!"

Surprised and alarmed, Umberto stood up, got into Rocky's face and shouted, "No, you drama queen! This is not about us. It's about me. What the fuck is wrong with you? Where is your head?"

Umberto turned away from Rocky, paused, then turned right back in his face waving his finger inches from Rocky's nose, "No one has worked harder than me to make it to the big time. Now I'm there! I want to have some fun! I want to enjoy myself! All I do is study, work out, practice, and do it all over again. I want more! Now back off and leave me alone." Umberto, shaking, turned to walk away, only to whirl back around, shouting, "You are such an unrealistic dreamer, gringo! Do you really think my family and community would ever accept us two together? Now, get out of here!"

Umberto sat back down on the wall and leaned forward, resting his elbows on his knees and his head in his hands. Rocky stood staring down at Umberto. His eyes were moist and his chest sunken. He finally summoned up enough strength to mumble, "We'll study the plays tomorrow when we both calm down."

Umberto didn't respond. He stood and walked toward his house, leaving Rocky standing there, trying to digest what had just happened. Why was Umberto risking everything for what seemed to Rocky like meaningless validation from some guys looking at his naked body? This wasn't like Umberto. Umberto was always careful. He didn't take unnecessary chances. Umberto was the ultimate cool guy. This was not cool.

An uncomfortable pit formed in Rocky's stomach.

* * *

The last game of the season was coming up. Rocky was determined to win this one. After they won the championship, Rocky planned to sit down with Umberto and make things right. They would win the game next week and he would talk to Umberto that evening. They always had their own special celebration after partying with the team.

They barely spoke the following week. They never had their game-planning meeting. The coaches and team members sensed something was wrong between the two stars, but no one could figure it out. The offensive team was only hitting on nine of its eleven cylinders. Every effort was made by the coaches and team members to help get the juice flowing. Rocky went through the motions. Umberto acted like nothing was wrong and missed the entire last practice. Someone said they had heard he went to the beach.

The night before the game, Rocky was in his room studying. He wasn't really studying, but he didn't hear his father come into his room.

"You know, Rocky, if I had been Umberto, you would have heard me coming up the stairs."

Rocky regained consciousness, "Hey Dad, sorry. I was just thinking."

"Son, I just got off the phone with the coach. He's very concerned about you. He doesn't think your mind is in your studies or on tomorrow's game."

"It's not, Dad."

"Well, where is it?"

Staring blankly out the window, Rocky said, "It's Umberto. He's doing some stupid things and I'm worried about him. He just seems different and I think he might get himself into trouble."

There were a few moments of silence as his father took a seat on the bed next to the table where Rocky was studying. "Well then, have you spoken to him about it?"

"Yes, Dad, I have. I told him the truth. It was like I was talking to a stranger; and now he's shut me out."

"You love him, don't you, son?"

"I do. I love him. I want to help him."

Rocky's father stood up, rested his hands on his son's shoulders and said, "When you love someone, you go the extra mile to help them. You do all you can to meet their every need, regardless of the consequences. Love is unconditional. Much like the love your mother and I have for you." Gently squeezing his son's shoulders, he turned and walked out of the bedroom, gently closing the door behind him.

The next morning was game day. Rocky drove by Umberto's house to see if he wanted a ride to school. The Castañeda's housekeeper told Rocky that Umberto had spent the night with a friend and was going directly to school from his friend's house. Rocky stood staring at the housekeeper. Her comments did not register. He thanked her, turned and walked back to his car. He sat in the driver's seat face forward, both hands on the wheel. Gripping harder and harder, he pounded the wheel, yelling "On the night before a game? That's bullshit! What the fuck is going on?"

When Rocky arrived at school, Umberto was nowhere to be found. He missed homeroom and when he showed up in chemistry class, he looked disheveled and exhausted.

"Umberto, I've been trying to find you all morning. I even went by your house this morning on the way to school. Where have you been? You look awful!" Rocky sounded just like he had several days earlier, the last time they had talked. That conversation had not ended well.

Again, Umberto was in no mood to talk. Rocky went to his next class.

The morning was endless. Teammates and coaches kept coming up to Rocky asking what was up with Umberto. They were concerned and nervous. As the morning classes dragged on, Rocky imagined scenarios he might find himself in during the game. For the first time, he envisioned Umberto not being *Umberto* on the field. Rocky was scared.

Later that morning, one of the student aides in the principal's office told one of his friends that a football player had been arrested and thrown in jail the previous night. The story spread like a California wildfire.

The whispering caught members of the football team off guard. Players and fellow students focused on the gossip, not their studies. Teachers and coaches caught the fever, most abandoning their planned lessons. Customary conversations in the hallways during class changes were replaced with speculation and gossip. Cheerleaders abandoned their spirit cheers in the halls. They were too busy catching up on the hearsay. Finally, it was lunchtime. Everyone headed to the cafeteria.

During the last class before lunch, Rocky hadn't seen Umberto in his customary classroom across the hall from Rocky's trig class. His seat was empty. Typically, they went to lunch together. Today, they did not.

Coach Thomas and the assistant coaches showed up at the players' table in the cafeteria. Normally Coach avoided the table, giving the players time to have fun and let off steam before a game. One by one, each team member noticed Thomas and his staff standing quietly next to their table. This was not going to be a pep talk. Coach's face looked old and haggard. His shoulders stooped. His chest looked sunken and his stomach pooched out more than normal. The other coaches were looking down at the floor.

The team didn't fidget or make jokes. They sat stoically still. Most looked down at the table, contemplating the crazy rumors that had raced through the student body. As Coach Thomas spoke, the entire cafeteria went dead silent. No coughing, no shuffling, no murmuring. Just deafening silence. The eerie hush startled the coach. None of the onlookers was surprised. All were frozen. Students and school staff stared at the coach.

"The coaching staff and I are aware of the many rumors that are spreading throughout the school." Thomas, who had been focusing primarily on the football players, stopped speaking. He raised his head and surveyed the large room. There was no commotion or movement anywhere. Cafeteria workers abandoned their posts in the kitchen and walked into the room. Teachers and staff left their private dining room to join those in the cafeteria.

"Excuse me for a moment." The one-time star athlete turned coach moved to a central part of the room. He thought it best to address everyone, so all could hear. The customary spring in his step had been usurped by a slow shuffle.

"Okay, let me start again. I ask that you show respect as I share with you a very serious message. It is with great sadness that I announce that one of our star players, one of our best students, one of our most cherished students, was arrested early this morning. I do not have any other details on the charges to share with you. The student is out on bail, but the charges are serious enough to have forced the school to expel him."

The collective gasps and profanities exploded. Rocky knew instantly whom the coach was speaking about. His chest tightened. He had to find Umberto. Rocky sprang from his seat near the cafeteria exit. He burst through the double doors and flew toward the locker room.

CHAPTER 4
UNFORGIVABLE SIN

Rocky raced down the corridor toward the gym. Umberto had to be there. It was the only place he would be; it was his sanctuary. His heart pounded as he flew down the hallways, barely pausing to negotiate a series of turns and closed doors. Inwardly panicking and screaming *Umberto! Please, please don't do anything stupid!*

Reaching the gymnasium, he catapulted toward the boy's locker room. Terror filled his chest, constricting his breathing. As his head grew lighter he forced himself to breathe. He burst into the locker room shouting as best he could, "Umberto! I'm here. Where are you?"

He careened about the catacomb-like lockers, ducking in and out of the spaces. The silence surrounded him. He came to a jerky stop. He heard running water in the therapy room spilling onto the floor.

"No! No! No!" He ran toward the closed double doors, splashing through the rose-tinted water pouring from the therapy room onto the locker-room floor. Careening into the room, he lost his balance and fell into the scarlet-colored water, skidding across the tiled floor. His breath was knocked out as he crashed into the source of the flowing water. In pain, he turned to his side; he looked up from the floor at the flow pouring over the sides of the stainless-steel therapy tub.

A waterfall of blood-infused water cascaded onto Rocky as he attempted to find his bearings. Rocky's mind and body throbbed. He feared facing what he knew he would find in the steel tub.

Gasping for air, he splashed and churned in the water falling directly on him. Rocky reached up with his right hand and gripped the lip of the tub. Anticipating what he might see, Rocky broke into uncontrollable sobs. "No, Umberto, no, Umberto. No!"

His cries turned to wails as he lifted himself with both hands. Peering over the lip, he found his lover and friend immersed in bloody water. Howls of pain rose from deep within Rocky's soul. His screams, amplified by the hard surfaces of the room and hallways traveled into the crowded cafeteria, taking a vice-like hold on the students. The sound was more like a wounded wild animal than that of a sorrowful teenager.

Rocky's howls subsided as the coach and staff followed his wailing to the therapy room.

As he lifted Umberto's head and torso above the water line, Rocky began to sob again. Rocky covered Umberto's face with kisses, sobbing, "No! No! No!"

Rocky was oblivious to Coach entering the room. He didn't notice when the water was turned off just inches from his head. His face was buried between Umberto's neck and shoulder. Coach motioned the onlookers out and then turned and left the room, closing the doors behind him and leaving Rocky alone with Umberto.

The authorities and medical units began to arrive. Rocky's father came into the room twenty minutes after the coach had closed the doors.

"Rocky." Rocky did not move. "Rocky, I'm so sorry. I'm so sorry. Let me help you."

Rocky removed one of his hands from around Umberto's lifeless body. He grabbed his father's hand and pulled his father alongside.

"Dad, I don't understand. Dad, he left me. I loved him, and he left me." Rocky looked up at his father, his face inches away. "I'm so scared."

At that moment the doors opened. Four paramedics entered with a stretcher in tow. Rocky was still holding Umberto. He finally moved aside to allow the paramedics to take hold of his dead lover's shoulders and head.

The water that had collected on the floors had disappeared down the drains. Only a bit sloshing from the therapy tub remained. Someone had opened the tub drains. The eerie gurgling echoed as the tub continued to empty.

Rocky half sat on a stool. He stared blankly into nothingness.

Umberto's body lay on a stretcher, the outline of his body showing through the wet sheet.

Rocky felt as though he might be able to stand and walk but then Umberto's mother entered the crowded room. The paramedics turned and froze in place.

She walked quickly across the wet tiles, then stopped mid-stride. She focused on the stretcher. Her complexion blanched. Her dark eyes framed by her now ghostlike face seemed to enlarge and leave her body. She appeared to have abandoned breathing. Her arms reached for her son's lifeless body. She fell onto Umberto, covering his body with hers. Rocky's father caught him as he fell to the floor.

CHAPTER 5
REJECTION

That Friday evening, what was supposed to have been the most important football game of the year was cancelled. A prayer vigil for Umberto and his family was held in its place.

The public remained puzzled as to the reason for the suicide. Rumors abounded, and gossip took hold. Loss and grief changed to fascination and speculation. Rocky missed classes the first two weeks in December. Every time Belinda delivered his assignments to his house he refused to see her. Rocky would stare at his homework, unable to grasp what he was supposed to do with it. He rarely left his room.

* * *

Consuela Bourbon Chambers was firmly rooted in the old school. Pride, raising her children to be good Catholics and her place in La Jolla society were her life.

She was strong, compassionate and supportive, but she had boundaries.

Rocky's father watched and waited, afraid of how she might react as it became apparent that Rocky was mourning more than just a friend. Would she be able to comprehend his broken heart and the loss that reached into the depth of his soul? He hoped and prayed his wife could handle the reality with unconditional love. He doubted she could.

* * *

"I am here for you, son. I love you. I am afraid for you. You must pull yourself together and get out of that room." Consuelo was speaking gently to her son through the closed and locked bedroom door. Rocky had not left his room for days. His mother had faithfully placed meals at his bedroom door. He had picked at the meals and left the partially emptied dishes outside his door.

"Okay, Mom."

"'Mom' is not going to work this time, Rocky. It has been over two weeks since you have been to school."

"Okay, Mom, please leave me alone."

"Rocky! Open the door!" Consuelo lost her patience. "You will open the door now!"

"Give me a minute."

"*Madre Mia*, Rocky! If you do not open this door I will have your father break it down!"

Consuelo heard a click.

"The door is open."

Consuelo grasped the doorknob and slowly turned it. Opening the door, she braced herself for what she might find.

She had anticipated a room as disheveled as his emotions. Walking into the room she surveyed his customarily neat and organized room. It was more orderly and oddly emptier than she had ever seen it. Her attention was drawn to large sealed black lawn bags placed neatly by the door. Then it dawned on her, all his junior high and high school pictures, plaques, and trophies had vanished. He had stripped his room of memories, painful memories.

Rocky sat on the side of his bed and looked up at his mother. His gaunt face reflected exhaustion. Dark circles framed his eyes. He was stoop shouldered. His schoolwork was nowhere to be seen. He appeared dressed to leave the house.

"Mom, I'm headed to school. Will you write me a note?"

"Are you sure that is what you want to do?"

"You're right, Mom, I have to get myself together."

"Okay, Rocky, would you like me to drive you?"

"That's so sweet, Mom, but I can drive myself."

Consuelo remained standing, looking at her son. This was not the same boy. Something had changed. He looked *wounded*. She walked over to him. Taking both his hands in hers and pulling him up to her, he stood. She wrapped her arms around him, drawing him to her.

His height dwarfed hers. He rested the side of his face on the top of her head as she began to tremble and cry. Rocky had never seen his mother cry. They wept and held each other tightly.

Still embracing her, Rocky said, "Mamacita, I cared deeply for Umberto. He was the love of my life."

Consuelo's back stiffened. She made a faint attempt to pull away but stopped. "Surely, you do not know what you are saying. You are so young and inexperienced. You cannot mean or know of what you speak."

Rocky attempted to remain calm. A trembling from deep within reached for the surface. "Perhaps you are right, Mamacita. But we were lovers in every sense of the word. He was everything to me."

Consuela slowly looked up into Rocky's eyes. She stepped back. Mouth open, eyes wide as saucers, she teetered, then fell backward.

Rocky lunged forward and caught her as she fell, lifting her and placing her gently on his bed. He flew to his bathroom, quickly returning with a cool cloth for his mother's forehead.

Moments later, she stirred. As she opened her eyes her lashes fluttered. Her dark eyes looked hollow as they focused on his, sending a deep chill coursing through his body. "Go, get out of here. Leave me alone. I do not, nor do I want to, know you. You have wounded me. Go!"

His mother's words sliced into his heart. He knew there was nothing to say. He had witnessed a dark side of someone he never dreamed could have anything but love and compassion for him.

Rocky stood ramrod straight. "Very well, Mother. Have it your way. We won't speak about this again."

Rocky picked up his backpack and walked out of the room. He did not see his father, brother or sister as he passed them in the kitchen and walked out of the house.

* * *

Rocky knew that returning to school would be difficult. He anticipated encountering stares and snide remarks. He anticipated questions and he was sure many would connect his friendship with Umberto and Umberto's rumored sexuality. Rocky was determined that the first guy who confronted him would be met with a fist straight to the jaw. But the first person he saw walking up to him as he got out of his car at school was the perfect person for his plan.

"Hi Rocky, I've missed seeing you. Why haven't you returned my calls? I left five notes at your house for you. Are you okay?" Belinda nervously rattled off the words at a higher than normal pitch. She wanted to hear directly from Rocky what was happening. She had been his advocate as rumors flew around the campus. She defended him. "I know firsthand he is not queer!"

Rocky stunned her by dropping his backpack to the ground, wrapping his arms around her and placing a passionate kiss on her lips. She returned the kiss with equal passion.

"I'm so sorry, Belinda. Please forgive me."

"Of course, Rocky. There is nothing to forgive. I'm here for you. I love you."

"I love you too, Belinda. Thank you for being here for me."

Rocky was now in survival mode. For the remainder of the school year, he would focus on their relationship. They were a couple. They had to be.

His return to school and the remaining school days in December appeared to go smoothly. Most of his friends expressed sorrow and gave their condolences for the loss of his best friend. Rocky was astute enough to realize who was sincere and to catalog the names of those he thought insincere or suspected his sexuality. He would deal with them later. No one appeared to want to challenge him openly. Not until George.

* * *

"Hey, Rocky! I heard you were a widower!"

Rocky and Belinda were in the cafeteria a month to the day after Umberto's expulsion had been announced to the student body. Chatting hand-in-hand they walked toward the football team's lunch tables.

George Raton stood with his back to the football team as he taunted Rocky. He was a smaller player who had always been jealous of Rocky. Rocky knew his future depended on his answer to George.

Rocky's body became taut as his face reddened and the back of his neck bristled. His muscles tensed beneath his thin polo shirt. He tossed his lunch tray at a table of students next to him, splattering several with mashed potatoes, meatloaf and gravy.

Rocky launched himself into the air less than three feet from George, at the same time cocking back his throwing arm. Descending on his target, he thrust his fully loaded fist forward, catching a bewildered and frozen George Raton square on the nose. George landed on top of several of the players at the table behind him, with Rocky now on top of him.

Rocky was the first to stand. A bewildered George using his hand to explore his bloody, now crooked nose looked up at Rocky. Toppled players began to upright themselves.

Rocky looked around the silent room, his fists still clenched at his sides.

"Are there any more of you assholes out there who want to fuck with me?"

Rocky stepped away from George. He walked over to Belinda, gathered both their books, wrapped one arm around her shoulder, and walked her through the crowd.

"Let's get the hell out of here!"

CHAPTER 6
1984: I'LL SHOW YOU

It had been his and Umberto's plan for Rocky to follow Umberto to whichever college Umberto chose ᴛᴏ accept. Now Umberto was gone. Rocky had to make other plans.

For weeks now, mail had collected on Rocky's bedroom desk, unopened. Four envelopes from four different colleges: one from the University of California, two from Ivy League schools and one from the Naval Academy.

The week between Christmas and New Year's, Rocky finally opened them. Three contained offers of a full scholarship as a member of their football teams. The Naval Academy wanted him as a cadet. Football was not mentioned. Rocky assumed that to play football at the Academy, he would have to start at the bottom as a walk-on.

Rocky began to ponder his options. *Which school will take me away from my past and offer me a new future?* He knew the answer.

Six months earlier, Coach Thomas had encouraged Rocky to apply to the Academy. His father had assisted with letters of recommendation. Coach Thomas had shepherded the paperwork through the school, speaking with other coaches, teachers and staff. Rocky had been diligent on his part, preparing his statements and papers. Coach Thomas, Rocky's father and Rocky had teamed up and had worked well together. Rocky embraced any project that included his father and Coach Thomas.

Rocky perked up a bit, particularly when he opened the Academy school catalog. Page after page of strong, proud men in incredible uniforms. *Would I fit in? Going to the Academy would be my gig, not Umberto's and not my parents,* he mused. *The Academy is far enough away, too. A first-class education, financial independence, a career, maybe even some football.* Graduating from the Academy would also give him a chance to go to flight school, a boyhood dream. Energy flowed in his veins. He stood straighter. He slept soundly.

* * *

Accepting the appointment to the Academy required his immediate attention. Completing the physicals, releases and miscellaneous directions was time sensitive and time consuming. Rocky was on a mission. He was going to get away from his mother's judgment and his past. He wasn't really into Belinda that much. She was someone who kept him safe at school. And maybe this "queer thing" was just a phase. Maybe he just needed to be around *real men* and get his head on straight. By the end of January, Rocky had submitted his Naval Academy Cadet Enrollment package.

* * *

Rocky avoided his mother and became adept at not revealing his hatred for the way he felt she had betrayed him. He left for school when he thought he could avoid seeing her. He rarely came home for dinner. He excused himself with study groups, practice and social activities. Rocky left notes on the kitchen table making excuses. When forced to spend time with her, he was merely polite. No one else appeared to take notice of the divide. She, too, avoided interaction whenever possible.

Consuela also spent increasing amounts of her time away from home. She immersed herself in charity work and social activities. She traveled to Spain for a month. Family dinners and meals became a thing of the past. She went to Mass by herself more often. Destroying her relationship with Rocky clouded her relationships with other members of the family. Only mother and son knew why. Neither mentioned their confrontation. Both counted the days when Rocky would leave for the United States Naval Academy.

* * *

"Rocky, I had a conversation with your mother. My guess is you know full well what I mean. I have to tell you, I am not impressed with the way in which either of you have handled this situation." Rocky sat looking at his father across the table at the La Jolla Country Club. Rocky had just finished a round of golf with some high-school chums. He was delighted when his father met him on the 18th green, asking him to join him at the "19th Hole."

Rocky's voice rising and growing agitated, "Well Dad, what did you expect me to do? She was the one outside my door asking me to trust my emotions with her. When I told her the truth about Umberto and me, she cut me out of her life. She said she didn't want to know me! She is the one who asked me to leave."

"Calm down, Rocky, we're in a public place."

Rocky sat up straight in his chair, glaring at his father. "Really, Dad? What a brilliant idea to confront me in a public place where your friends might find out your son is a faggot," Rocky whispered.

A look of disbelief was all over his father's face.

"I agree with your mother, Rocky. It's a good thing for everyone that you are leaving next week. You're ripping us apart."

"*Is* it me? Or is my mother that bitch ripping *me* apart?"

Chambers stood up and slapped Rocky across the face.

Running his hand along his jaw, "Nice slap, Dad. Feel better?"

His father's anger would have gotten the better of him if two of his golfing buddies hadn't hauled him over to the other side of the room. Rocky left the bar, gathered his things from the locker room and drove off.

Arriving home, he went upstairs to his room. He had packed for his trip to the East Coast weeks ago.

Rocky piled everything in his car and headed to Belinda's. He had nowhere else to go. As Rocky had made his plans to attend the Naval Academy, he and Belinda had agreed to break up. She knew his heart wasn't in their relationship, but they remained friends.

He hoped that her parents would allow him to stay at their house for a couple of days until graduation.

* * *

Graduation day came without incident. Rocky sat with his classmates. He was recognized as one of three valedictorians. A special mention was made of his Presidential Appointment to the Naval Academy. His classmates cheered enthusiastically. Rocky was still their number-one guy. His parents did not appear to have attend the ceremony, but his brother and sister were there.

"I am going to miss you so much, Rocky." Sophia hugged Rocky as other families congratulated their graduates. "I know something horrible happened between you and Mom and Dad."

Rocky pulled her tight. "Not to worry, sweet sis. Things will be okay. You have to remember to write to me when I send you my new mailing address. I love you so much and I'll miss you, too."

Sophia stifled her sniffles. She took hold of Alejandro's hand and pulled him toward them.

"Well, little brother, do us proud! Go Navy!" Rocky and Alejandro hugged each other for moments, not wanting to release one another. Rocky then pulled their foreheads together.

"I want you to promise me to take care of our Sophia. If you don't write, you are an asshole!" Rocky laughed.

"You're right, I'm an asshole. I won't write, but I might call!" Alejandro clapped him on the shoulder and drew Sophia into a group hug.

Alejandro and Sophia took Rocky directly to the San Diego airport.

Rocky boarded a flight that afternoon for New York.

CHAPTER 7
A LIFE REMEMBERED

Anticipating lifting off from Lindbergh Field was surreal. Boarding the plane, Rocky looked down at his boarding pass to check his seat number. It indicated he had a first-class seat. This was a mistake. He had purchased a coach ticket.

"There's a mistake on my boarding pass," Rocky told a flight attendant.

"Let me check, sir." The attendant pulled out the flight manifest.

"Are you Ricardo Chambers?"

"Yes, ma'am."

"It says here you're in 2-B. Please go to your left and head towards the front. Your seat is on the aisle, second row back."

"Wow. Thanks!"

"My pleasure, Mr. Chambers. May I get you something to drink while you get settled in?"

"Sure, how about a Coke?"

"A Coke it is. I'll have it for you shortly."

"Thanks!" Rocky made his way forward, a bit giddy and with a spring in his step.

This was the first time Rocky had ever purchased his own plane ticket. *If this is how I'm going to screw something up, this is the way to do it!* He was not new to first class. Several trips at his grandparents' expense to visit them in Boston over the years had spoiled him. He had been disappointed to see what the fare was when booking his own trip. He liked first class. Maybe the upgrade portended good things for his future.

Rocky smiled with anticipation as the jet ascended over Point Loma and the Pacific Ocean. The aircraft began to bank gently north, then northwest. Rocky gazed out his window past a passenger sitting next to him. He watched as altitude and clouds diminished the shoreline and ocean. The plane continued to circle back, heading east. Climbing through the light, puffy clouds to thirty-five thousand feet, the aircraft leveled off.

Rocky felt the weight he had borne for months begin to vanish. "Finally," escaped his lips before he could stop it. His remark caught the attention of the passenger in the seat to his left.

"First time flying, young man?" a smooth, warm voice asked.

Rocky turned to see a youthful-looking, middle-aged man. The stranger had deep green eyes above an aquiline nose. The light facial stubble complimented his expensive, sophisticated attire. The button-down pastel shirt accented a smooth, deeply tanned face and hands.

Rocky remarked, "Naw, I've just said good riddance to my past and I'm seizing my future. *Carpe Diem!*"

"Well, congratulations, son. I wish you the best."

Rocky nodded, not sure what else to do. "Thank you, sir." *Who is this guy? He seems nice. Maybe some conversation will kill time. Surprise #1, first class. Surprise #2, a pleasant person sitting next to me.*

The tanned man ordered two beers. The flight attendant handed both to him. As she disappeared into the galley, he handed one to Rocky.

"Thank you, sir!"

"You are very welcome. My name's Jack." He held out his hand; they both shook. Tanned man had a firm but not overwhelming grip.

"My friends call me Rocky." Rocky sipped his beer. Man, it tasted great. It was exactly what he needed. Halfway into a second beer they were well into small talk.

"Aren't you that quarterback from La Jolla High School headed to the Naval Academy?"

Rocky sipped hard on his beer. His stomach felt a bit uneasy and his neck muscles tightened. "Yeah, I am. I'm on my way to Annapolis, a couple of weeks early. Summer school starts in July."

"Congratulations on your acceptance to Annapolis. That's a huge honor and opportunity. You certainly have the athletic talent and ability. Are you planning on playing football?"

"No, badminton," he joked.

"Better choice," Jack returned.

Rocky liked to talk about himself. He began to relax. The queasiness in his stomach subsided. "I do plan on playing football, but they don't know it. I'm planning to walk-on. Regardless, I *will* be their first-string quarterback one day." Rocky surprised himself a little with that bold and presumptuous statement. He had not heard or felt himself talk with such confidence since Umberto had died. He thought to himself, *things must be looking up!*

"This may surprise you, but Umberto was a friend of mine. I am sorry for both our losses. I cared for him deeply, too."

Rocky felt his stomach collapse into his seat. All the color drained from his face. He stared forward and did not speak; he focused on breathing. His right hand, holding his beer, began to shake.

Jack nudged him gently. Rocky continued to shake a bit, trying to regain his composure. He remained facing forward and downed what was left of the second beer. He took a long, deep breath, sat up straight and placed his finished beer on the tray in front of him. Looking at the beer, Rocky said, "We have a long flight. I'm going to give you some money and you are going to keep these beers coming."

"Have you forgotten? Drinks are complimentary in first class."

"Shit. Excuse me, sir, you caught me off guard with that thing about Umberto. My apologies."

Rocky remained looking forward. He wiped a tear before it could drop. Fighting the overwhelming, slow creep of claustrophobia, not knowing what to say or how to react, he turned to face Jack. The tanned man returned his gaze.

"How did you know Umberto?" Rocky asked.

"We frequented a coffee shop in Old Town. We knew each other long before you two hooked up."

"Really?" gulped Rocky. "So, I guess you know more than anyone else in La Jolla." He looked at the back of the seat in front of him. The color returned to his face and he felt his stomach return to where it belonged. "Jack, what do you think happened with Umberto and me?"

"I thought the two of you were lucky."

"What? Lucky?"

"Yes, lucky."

"That makes no sense to me. You have to know what happened. That wasn't lucky."

"No, the end was not lucky, but there never was going to be a happy ending. Umberto was never going to allow there to be a happy ending. Umberto could not see himself having a happy ending. Family and culture bound him. He couldn't visualize the possibilities. Unfortunately, he lacked a certain courage."

He understood what Jack was saying. He, too, knew Umberto had been his own worst enemy. Umberto could not believe their love would ever be accepted.

"You're right about that. He left me. I don't think I'll ever forgive him."

Rocky was relaxing as the third beer mellowed him. He felt pleasure and a release talking about Umberto. Finally, Rocky had someone with whom he could speak freely. Someone who was not part of his life and really didn't matter. And, apparently, someone who was gay.

"It seems like you are making an excellent choice, getting out of town and starting a new life. You may not know this, but Umberto was afraid to leave home and go to college. He talked a big game, but he wasn't ready to sprout wings and go for the big time. His acting out at Black's Beach and getting caught in the bathroom with another man was the act of a boy overwhelmed. Overwhelmed with life and afraid of losing you."

"Why did he share all of this with you and not with me?"

"I guess it was because he and I were close before you and he were lovers. We became friends, trusting friends."

Rocky did not want any more surprises. Enough was enough. He reclined his seat and relaxed. He hadn't reacted to Jack's revelation. *It all made sense. Umberto had guys before him. This was a bit weird.*

Twenty minutes later, Rocky turned slowly and said, "It's not a coincidence you're on this plane and we're sitting side by side, is it? You had me upgraded to first class in the seat next to you."

"No, it's not a coincidence. It's premeditated and meticulously planned. I listed you as my nephew on the manifest. Enjoy the ride!"

Rocky and Jack sat silently and tugged on their beers. Rocky began to get more comfortable with the older man. A familiarity and comfort continued to draw them closer.

"How did you arrange it? You couldn't know my plans. Only my family, my ex-girlfriend and her family knew my flight info."

"I'm a pilot with this airline. It was easy to check the manifests. It was common knowledge the star quarterback at La Jolla High had turned down full rides to top schools to attend the Academy. The local papers announced your plans. Everyone knew you were headed out of town soon. I must admit, I'm glad I started checking airline manifests early. Most high-school grads don't leave the day they graduate. I had to rearrange my flying schedule a bit, but this was important. I wanted to help you adjust. I thought you might be confused about your affair with Umberto. I felt I owed it to Umberto to fill some of the void he left behind."

"You've gone to a lot of effort to put us together. I understand your wanting to do something for Umberto, but there has to be more to it."

"There may be. Are you open to some new options?"

Rocky speculated on what options might be presented. He had two weeks before he was required to report to Annapolis. This could be interesting. With the beer starting to have a strong effect, Rocky found himself aroused. He decided to take charge. He leaned over, his lips inches from Jack's ear, and whispered, "So, you like younger guys?"

Jack, in mid-sip, gulped hard, laughing and gasping as beer exploded from his nose and mouth onto his lap. Rocky removed a white, linen napkin from his tray, placing it squarely on Jack's lap, pressing down slowly and firmly on Jack's crotch. Jack stared at Rocky, considering his own options.

Rocky removed his hand, leaving the imprint of his hand on the napkin covering Jack's cock and balls. He sat back and smiled, congratulating himself. Jack began to clean himself up.

"Sir, would you like another napkin?" The female flight attendant looked past Rocky at Jack.

"Yes, please."

Now looking at Rocky, the attendant asked, "Sir, would you mind passing me that napkin?"

Rocky couldn't hold his laughter back any longer. "I would be happy to, ma'am.

Rocky snatched a corner of the napkin quartered in Jack's lap and handed the dangling, moist linen to the grinning woman. The attendant, enjoying Rocky's amusement and Jack's predicament, presented a new napkin to Rocky. "Sir, would you please hand this to the gentleman?"

"Yes ma'am."

By now, Jack was simultaneously amused and irritated. He no longer felt in charge of the scene, but he also felt attracted to the younger man he had decided to "adopt." The mess cleaned up, the green eyes turned to look directly at Rocky.

"Young man."

"My name is Rocky and yes, I am a hell of a lot younger than you," teased Rocky.

"You did not answer my question. Are you open to some different options?"

"Yes, I'm game."

"Then buckle up and get ready for the ride of your very young and inexperienced life!"

CHAPTER 8
RIDE OF A LIFETIME

Jack and Rocky's flight landed late that afternoon at JFK. Jack told Rocky to meet him at baggage claim. Rocky was feeling a little less confident as the beer wore off and he headed to pick up their luggage. With Jack's encouragement, he had changed his plans and would not be going directly to Annapolis. Was he taking a chance with Jack? Deep in thought and not concentrating on the task at hand, he found himself at the wrong baggage carousel. The big city and imagined adventures were also on his mind. Gaining control of his wits, he located the correct carousel and retrieved their bags. Jack headed his way with a bounce in his step and a warm and exuberant smile splashed across his face.

He handed an envelope to Rocky, "Okay, young stud, here's the updated ticket for your flight to DC ten days out. Picking up his bags Jack exclaimed, "Now, let's head into the city."

"Sounds good but let me make a phone call first. I need to let my family know I made it to New York. That's all they need to know, it shouldn't take more than a minute." Rocky headed to the bank of payphones on the opposite wall. He mentally crossed his fingers that no one would be home to take the call. The now independent Rocky wanted, above all, to remain that way, in charge of his life. Letting his family know he was okay would keep them at bay. Taking hold of his thoughts, he paused, braced himself and made the call. The phone rang on the other end, once, twice, three, four and five times. On the sixth ring, the answering machine picked up. He flinched when he heard his mother's recorded voice.

"No one is available. Please leave a message."

"This is Rocky, I am safe and sound in New York. The flight was great, smooth and relaxing. I have a slight change in plans. Feeling good and want to do some exploring. Wish me luck. Hugs to everyone, talk to you in a week or so. Bye!"

Placing the phone back in its cradle, Rocky stood more erect. His shoulders pulled back. His heart pumped stronger. He chuckled to himself, broke into a grin and started to hum the Broadway tune *New York, New York!*

Jack saw a brighter, carefree Rocky approaching. "You must have had a brief but happy chat with the family!"

"Nope, well maybe," grinned Rocky. "It was brief, I left a message and didn't have to talk to anyone. That made me happy!"

"I believe you are more mature than I originally thought you were."

"I'll give you a chance to find out," grinned Rocky.

It was the latter part of rush hour and thank God the traffic was mostly headed in the opposite direction. Wired, Rocky sat straight up, leaning forward, looking out the cab windows, pummeling Jack and the cabbie with questions about everything he saw.

"You know, Rocky, you don't have to figure out the city in one cab ride!"

"Yeah, but I sure can get a good start!" he said, playfully nudging Jack in the ribs.

Jack moved a little closer to Rocky. "So, what do you want to do tonight?"

"Hell, I don't know, Jack. Party? I want to go to the places that you and Umberto might have gone. I'm still mad at him for leaving me but we can drink to – new options!"

Leaving the cab, they approached a Lower West Side walk-up. They climbed two flights of stairs and Jack used three different keys to unlock the door's three heavy locks.

"Jesus, this apartment is small," Rocky said as they entered. "My bedroom is bigger than this entire place."

"This is New York. This *pied à terre* is considered luxurious and is very expensive. You are in one of the choicer neighborhoods in Manhattan."

"I like the neighborhood, but you have got to be kidding me. This will take some getting used to. Is this your place?"

"No, it belongs to a fellow pilot on vacation in Thailand. He lets me use it when he's not in town."

"There's one bedroom and one bed. I guess I'll be on the couch?" Rocky stood, arms hanging down in front; one hand atop the other just below the beltline. He cocked his head a bit to one side, making an effort to look innocent.

"Suit yourself, but you don't have to. It's a small place, but the bed is full size, like me!" Rocky laughed, then smiled as he let Jack take him by the hand and draw him close, beginning Rocky's initiation into the New York gay scene.

* * *

New York City was hot and humid. Both men dressed in jeans, t-shirts and comfortable shoes. Chelsea had the action Jack wanted Rocky to see first. The Meatpacking District would come once Rocky was more comfortable with gay nightlife.

"New York is definitely different from the little town on the beach I come from. Glad we took a break and got some rest. I never thought of heading out to party at midnight."

"I've found disco naps to be a good idea, particularly after a romp in the hay, right?" teased Jack.

"Yep, I guess you're right. I think I wore you out, old man. I'm sure you needed some sleepy time to recuperate," Rocky teased him back. They both chuckled, holding hands as they walked in the gay-friendly neighborhood. Rocky loved holding hands. He particularly liked it in public. He felt a cozy warmth throughout his body. Yet, his head felt like it would explode with anticipation. He felt alive in a way he never had before and experienced a surreal contentment. New York City, midnight, out on the vibrant streets and holding hands with a guy. Jack's attention and proximity helped Rocky feel safe. Rocky had not felt safe since his father had slapped him. *Just please keep holding my hand, Jack. I like it.*

Jack brought them to a halt in front of a storefront sandwiched between a small convenience store and a dry-cleaner shop. No lights were on in the two flanking businesses. *Of course, it's after midnight*, Rocky thought to himself.

The two men climbed the six steps to the landing leading to double doors. There was some sort of rumpled covering on the windows on each side of the solid wood portal. A dim light framed the outer edges of the coverings. There was no signage. "This place must be a hundred years old," Rocky quipped.

"It is. Let's get inside," replied Jack.

Jack entered first. The smell of stale beer and clouds of smoke permeated Rocky's lungs as he stepped inside. His eyes began to water and the desire for breathing faded quickly. The dimly lit bar obscured his vision. He saw fans whirling, but the air was hot and still. His t-shirt grew damp with sweat.

Rocky noticed the low-lit colored lights. Christmas lights in June, draped along the back of the bar, resting on what were surely mirrors. Mirrors that had once reflected images when last cleaned years ago.

Bare-chested men flaunted perfect abs, six-packs and even a couple of eight-packs. Clean-shaven, no sign of chest hair. Muscular, almost naked men. Very tight, sweaty short-shorts kept it barely legal. Rocky was hypnotized by what he saw. He ogled the bartenders as they poured generous drinks and laughed with the patrons. Everyone seemed to be finely built.

"Rocky!" called Jack. "Rocky!"

Jack walked back to his straggling friend, grabbing him by the hand. "Hey, California Dreamin', pay attention. I called you twice." Rocky stopped fixating on the bartenders and laughed. Sporting a huge smile, he followed Jack.

"Wow, did you see those guys? They're all...hot!"

"Every time I'm here. Take a seat," Jack pointed at two stools near the middle of the bar.

A sharp whistle and then a catcall came from somewhere in the smoke-filled room. "Hey blondie, come over here and sit on my lap. I've got something for you!" Rocky looked in the direction of the voice. He couldn't distinguish who had whistled or hollered. He did hear a bunch of laughter and more whistles. He assumed he was the target. Rocky enthusiastically plopped down on the closest bar stool. Jack ignored the catcalls.

"Hey Frank, how about two drafts here?" Jack called out to the handsome man behind the bar.

"Sure thing, Jack. And who is that cutie sitting next to you? Is he some of that California meat you like so much?"

In a jocular tone, Jack spouted back, "That will be enough out of you. Just give us the beers." Rocky sat grinning, taking it all in. Frank brought the beers, smiling at Jack, and ogling Rocky.

"Welcome to the Big Gay Apple! It's obvious this is your first time here. Those deer-in-the headlights eyes are a dead giveaway." Frank stuck out his hand. Rocky reached over the bar to take it.

Frank grabbed his extended hand and pulled Rocky closer saying loud enough for everyone to hear, "When you get done with that old man next to you, come and see me. I can show you how it's done with men closer to your own age."

Jack half stood up, playfully pushing Frank away. "Stay on your side of the bar and leave this youngster alone!" chortled Jack.

Frank blew Rocky a kiss and went back to work.

Jack moved his stool a little closer to Rocky. "Listen, these boys are always on the prowl for fresh meat. Keep your cool; limit conversation to those you know and trust. Frank's all right. He's just a real horn dog."

They clinked their mugs of cold, frothy beer. Taking a couple of tugs, Rocky spun around on his bar stool.

The bar appeared old and not well kept. Toward the back of the room stood what appeared to be some cigarette vending machines and more. "Christ, it's smoky in here."

"Rocky, there are a couple of things you need to know. Kind of like getting a pre-game briefing."

"Okay, cool. What 'ya got, coach?"

Jack leaned his forearms on the bar and faced Rocky, "There is this sickness or disease going around. Not much info has reached the streets on exactly what it is, but a lot of gays and druggies are getting really sick. Some are dying."

"Yeah, Jack." Both men turned solemn, looking at their own beers. "I heard something about that. It's kind of scary. I didn't know it was that bad, guys dying. I thought it was more like the flu."

"That's the problem, Rocky. It starts out like the flu."

Jack hollered out to Frank, "Hey, how about two bucks in quarters?" Jack exchanged bills for quarters with Frank.

Frank smiled at Jack, "Teaching the kid the facts of life?"

"You know what, Frank? You can be a real pain in the ass, and not a good one!" Jack said, getting up and heading toward the back.

Frank stood, leering at Rocky. "Shit, boy, you sure do have some muscles on that body. Why don't you take that shirt off and give me a look-see?"

Rocky ignored the comment as he watched Jack walk toward the back and put money in what looked like a cigarette-vending machine.

"I didn't know Jack smoked."

"He doesn't, he gave that up years ago."

"Then what is he doing?"

"Oh, that. He's probably buying you some *armor*, like protection. He's a good guy, even if he is stuck on you young'uns. I like Jack. Listen to him. Then come and look me up for some real fun!"

Frank gave Rocky a playful slap to the side of the head. Swinging his ass, he sauntered off towards a customer clamoring for service.

The spinning ceiling fans did little to eradicate the perspiration pouring off Frank's back, soaking his shorts-clad rear and revealing well-toned cheeks. Rocky was transfixed. Once again, he sprang back to consciousness as Jack handed him a couple of condoms. "What are these for?"

"Rocky, really? Don't you know what those are?"

Rocky laughed, pushing them back to him. "I only use those with girls. Somehow, I don't think they're on the agenda."

"Okay, dumbass. Remember what I told you about the flu?"

"Yeah, of course."

"That's what this is all about. Use these or die!"

"Oh, okay." Rocky sputtered. He looked down at the condoms, then at Jack. Jack watched Rocky scan the room. Rocky bit his lips shaking his head. He sighed. Grudgingly, he grabbed the packets, burying them in his back jeans pocket.

Jack gulped down his beer and ordered two more from another beauty behind the bar. This one was taller than Frank. He had to be 6'4". His tight muscles framed a warrior-like body. Rivulets of sweat ran from his long neck, between his very large pecs, cascading down the washboard abs. The flow puddled, then disappeared inside his sheer shorts. The sodden shorts left nothing to the imagination. Rocky sighed.

The beers were slammed down on the bar. "'Sarge, meet Rocky. Rocky meet Sarge." There was no handshake. Sarge and Rocky locked eyes. Rocky lit up inside.

Sarge leaned over the bar, stretched out his neck and kissed Rocky square on the lips. Not to be outdone, Rocky rose up before Sarge could pull back too far. He clasped Sarge by the back of his head pulling him to his open mouth, tasting Sarge with his tongue.

Those in the crowd that had seen Sarge kiss Rocky were amused. Those that saw Rocky's move on Sarge went off like fireworks! Cheers, laughter and applause broke out simultaneously throughout the bar. Hands pounding on the tables, "More! More! More!" rang out from the crowd.

Rocky had made no point whatsoever other than that of being a gamer. He sat down. Sarge, looking directly at Rocky, ran his long, thick tongue the circumference of his lips then feigned a swallow. More banter erupted.

Rocky sat up and leaned against the bar, as if he had made some sort of conquest and looked over at Jack. Jack clasped his head with both hands, elbows on the bar.

"I have unleashed a monster!" He sat up, took his beer in both hands and finished it, placing it firmly on the bar. "Rocky, you are definitely in for the ride I promised you!"

* * *

The next morning Rocky slept until noon. Jack was not in bed. Only the hum of the city punctuated his thoughts. Rocky looked up at the popcorn ceiling, rolling over the previous night's activity in his head. *That was fun*, he mused to himself. He drifted in and out of a light sleep as he continued to mull things over. *This New York nightlife is amazing. I can't wait to see what Jack has in store for tonight.* Stretching, his hands above his head, he realized he was naked. Double-checking and verifying the sensation, he ran his hands the length of his body. It felt sexy and liberating not to wear shorts in bed, another advantage of not being home. He rotated his body as if on a spit. He laid flat on his stomach, and dreamily recalled he and Jack falling into each other's arms about 5:00 a.m. He grinned, satisfied, and fell back asleep.

* * *

"Rocky, are you going to be spending the entire day in bed? Jack was sitting on the side of the bed, rubbing Rocky's shoulders, and then the full length of his taut physique. He luxuriated in Jack's masculine hand rubbing and stroking his calves, thighs, ass and shoulders. Dreamily, Rocky thought, *please don't stop.*

Jack, following his own hand caressing every inch of Rocky's body murmured, "You might want to get up. Remember the promise you made when we agreed you would stay in New York? Have you forgotten?"

Rocky felt a sudden tinge throughout the length of his body. He rolled over, threw off the sheet, jumped out of bed and stood up.

"Nice!" chortled Jack. His eyes drank in the well-built young man before him.

"Shit! What time is it?" Rocky exclaimed, as he rubbed the palms of his hands across his face and through his hair.

"About two in the afternoon."

"Christ! I should've been running and working out hours ago! Crap!"

Jack rested back on the bed on his elbows. He grinned, taking in Rocky's frustration and surprise. His tousled hair, his well-defined chest, abs, thighs and calves shimmered in the afternoon sun leaking through the half-opened blinds. He reclined slowly on the bed, showing Rocky exactly what he had in mind.

"Don't get any ideas, Jack. From the looks of this place, you got all you wanted last night. I mean this morning." He perused the room, searching.

"What can't you find?"

"My clothes, my workout gear. I've got to get with the program. I can't lose a day. Less than nine days and I am dead meat if I'm not in shape."

"Rocky, get it together and calm down. It's early afternoon. You have plenty of time to work out. Your stuff's in the living room, remember?"

Rocky left the room, his body catching Jack's attention as he went out the door.

"Jack," Rocky hollered from the other room. "I have this workout routine perfectly planned. It takes several hours each day. If we have rain days, I'm fucked. I'll lose momentum, so I gotta stay with it!" Rocky rummaged through his things; his frustration manifested in cussing.

Still in the bedroom, Jack called out, "Listen, young man. I need go back to work tomorrow afternoon. Tonight, will be our last night out together for about four days. My schedule is taking me to South America. You'll be on your own. A set of keys is on the kitchen table."

Rocky popped back into the room, half-dressed, carrying his shoes and shirt. He plopped down on the bed next to Jack. He leaned over and gave Jack a kiss. "That sucks! I have no clue how to get around if you're not here. Besides, I like being with you."

Rocky struggled with his socks and shoes as his impatience and frustration, along with Jack's news, distracted him.

"You'll be fine. Tonight, I am going to show you around. We're going to drop by some of the clubs you can explore while I'm gone."

Rocky paused, looked up from tying his shoes, smiled and finished knotting his shoes. "Thanks!" Again, he gave Jack a quick kiss.

"Ok, I am out of here! I have a long run and a workout ahead. I'll see you in a couple of hours. Shirt in hand, he bounded out of the room, grabbing the keys on the table, and exiting the apartment, slamming the door behind him.

CHAPTER 9
AWAKENING

Exiting the West Side apartment, the suffocating humidity hit him hard. Rocky gulped for air. The sun beat down like a sunlamp.

His pace slowed as his initial run decreased to a quick jog. Soon he was walking. The pavement seemed to throw heat back up at him. Rocky took note of the addresses and cross streets as he began what was now a slow jog. He headed south. He crisscrossed streets and intersections in search of less congestion.

Thirty minutes of dodging people and traffic was frustrating and exhausting. His lungs fought back trying to reject the inhalation of wet, heavy air. The airflow could not move fast enough to oxygenate his body. His legs fought back. They didn't want to exert themselves, much less run. Labored breathing and tingling in his lower calves brought him back to a brisk walk, then a slow walk. Rocky consumed water at every water fountain he could locate. Walking for another hour brought his workout to an end. Drenched, lightheaded, his heart beating hard, he was done.

Entering the apartment, he showered, dressed in shorts and a t-shirt and donned a pair of flip flops. He ventured outside in search of an athletic store. Locating one several blocks away, he bought an athletic fanny pack, one capable of holding two water bottles. It had a pocket for food bars and little else. He purchased a case of water containing electrolytes and a 24-pack of nutritious food bars.

Paying for the items, he asked the cashier, "I was wondering if you or someone here could help me. I am visiting New York for a week or so and need to train daily. Is there anyone that can point me in the direction of a decent gym and some running routes?"

"Sure, no problem. See that guy over there in the multi-colored running clothes? He's one of the owners and competes in Iron Man competitions. Talk to him. He knows everything," replied the cashier as he handed Rocky his purchases.

"Thanks! I'll leave my things over here while I talk to him." Rocky said, placing his packages on a nearby platform.

Iron Man and Rocky bantered back and forth for twenty minutes as he outlined his fitness program.

The conversation over and feeling more empowered, Rocky left, armed with a detailed jogging map. He also snagged a certificate for one week's free membership at a nearby gym. Retrieving his water and food bag, he carried the heavy load four city blocks to the apartment.

Rocky showered a second time. *Jesus, it's still hot and humid!* Downing two sports drinks and some leftovers in the fridge, Rocky wrapped a towel around his waist and plopped down on the bed for his disco nap. He fell asleep instantly.

* * *

"Rocky! You in bed again?" teased Jack. "I've put together something to eat. It's on the table. Come join me."

Rocky rubbed his eyes, "Okay, thanks. I'll be right there." Feeling refreshed, he climbed out of bed, his towel falling to the floor.

Jack playfully pushed Rocky back on the bed, climbing on top of him. A couple of hours later, the room now dark, Rocky rolled over and gave Jack a playful slap on the butt. "Hey old man, can we have that meal you promised?"

Like the previous late evening, the two of them set out in jeans and t-shirts. The night's humidity and heat weighed on them. Neither commented on the obvious as sweat plastered their shirts against their torsos.

"Tonight, I am going to show you some off-the-wall places."

"What do you mean, 'off the wall?'"

"Well, these places are a bit different. I want you to know everything that's out there in the gay scene, so you can decide what you like and what you don't like."

Rocky felt his crotch begin to tingle.

"Okay, I'm game."

"Nice thing about you is that you're always game."

Rocky looked at Jack, smiled, puckered his lips and tossed him an air-kiss.

The night's events proved to be an unsettling revelation. Jack had been correct. Rocky could never have imagined the underground gay nightlife. The visit to the Haymarket on 47th and 8th Avenue was an appetizer. Rocky felt sorry for the desperate young gays being "bought" for as little as twenty dollars by older men. It made no sense to him.

The Cat's Bar on 48th was a dive bar, but full of clean-cut dudes looking for rough trade. They found it. It was mesmerizing. "I guess opposites attract," murmured Rocky as they finished their beers and exited the place. "Jack why are we going to places like this?"

"What do you mean?"

"I mean these places are not a lot of fun. I was looking for more of the dancing and drinking and good times. These places might be fun for some, but they're depressing. A lot of these guys are really fucked up."

"You mean they're not like a high-school dance?"

"Knock it off, you know what I mean," Rocky stopped in place, his head hanging down. "You're trying to scare me off since you're leaving town tomorrow. Right?"

"Granted, this isn't the gay life you know about. It's new to you. It really is another world. Most gays never see it. It's just an experience. Think of it as a learning experience. Treat it like a cafeteria line; take what you want."

Jack faced Rocky. They stood in silence. Jack placed his right hand under Rocky's chin. Lifting the square jaw, their eyes met. "Rocky, I'm your friend. I want to make sure you're equipped to venture out on your own. I'm preparing you to stay safe. That is all this is."

Jack hailed a cab. Sitting in the back seat, they scrunched together. "Next stop, The Anvil!" Jack whispered into Rocky's ear. The erotic sensation created by his hot damp breath on his ear caused a scintillating vibration throughout Rocky's torso.

Both jumped out of the cab. "Rocky, this place will knock your socks off!" quipped Jack, putting his arm around Rocky's shoulder. He ushered him toward the entrance.

"Cool!" Can't wait, let's go!"

Rocky had never seen drag queens, much less full-blown drag performances. "Crap, these guys look like real women! They could fool anybody." Eyes wide open, gawking at the performers, Rocky's jaw dropped when he looked toward the bar. "What the shit?" Men were suspended over the bar in different positions, held by ropes tied in exotic knots. Some moved around, some just hung there.

"You ain't seen nothin' yet. Follow me." Jack grabbed Rocky by the hand, pulling him away from the dangling men. Neither could miss the acrid smell of sweat, stale beer, smoke, and urine. Wafts of cleaning agents occasionally penetrated nostrils. Men were packed together. Sweat mixed with sweat as the shirtless men made no attempt to avoid physical contact. Rocky endured a thousand hands fondling him as they coursed through the crowd. His nipples were pinched, his ass slapped, and dozens of men of all shapes and sizes tried to kiss him. Rocky released

Jack's hand to fend off a muscular dude trying to undo his jeans while sliding another hand down his backside.

"Christ, Jack! This place is nuts!"

Jack shouted back over the loud disco music ringing in their ears, "It sure is! Keep up!" Rocky did his best, fending off the men checking out the "fresh meat."

Descending the stairs, the stench increased as the music grew weaker. Rocky heard moans and screams. The men traipsing between rooms were barely clothed, if at all. Many carried sex toys of varying descriptions. Rocky stopped and looked into a room and saw four men in the room. Three of them were dominating the fourth suspended in a sling. Rocky gasped. His heart pounded as he took in the scene. He felt aroused and embarrassed at the same time. He kept watching as they strolled by room after room, each one a scene from the rough S&M trade.

Rocky tried to convince himself he hated everything he saw. But he slowed his pace and lingered while peering into every open room. Weirdly, he didn't want to miss a thing.

Finally, having seen enough of the underground gay scene, Rocky shouted to Jack over the din, "I want to get out of here!"

Looking for a quick escape, he spotted a door that he prayed was an exit. He pulled away from Jack and headed toward it. The door opened. It led to another room where more violent and abusive acts were taking place. Rocky gagged and headed toward another door. He pushed against it. It didn't budge. Jack came from behind and threw his full body weight into the door. It forced open half way. Jack slithered through the opening, pulling Rocky with him. A rusted metal stairway reached up three flights to the street level. Jack and Rocky trod up the dangling structure. It creaked and groaned as they carefully made their way up and out.

"See that fountain over there?" Rocky pointed through a line of trees clustered in the dimly lit park. "Let's go for it!" Rocky hollered. They ran across a 40-yard expanse of grass and jumped into the fountain. Exuberantly they surrendered themselves to water cascading from the upper levels of the large fountain. The cool water beat heavily upon them, water penetrating bodies and clothing, forcefully removing filth and stench, both real and imagined.

They stood still, arms stretched out to the side, refusing to leave any part of their body or a stitch of clothing unwashed. Jack removed his T-shirt. He wrung it out several times under the crashing waterfall. He put the shirt back on. Rocky followed suit. Rocky took off his shoes, then his jeans. Nothing remained to remove. Ass naked, he scrubbed his jeans and shirt in the water and against the granite fountain.

Jack stood aghast. "Rocky! You never cease to amaze me!"

Rocky turned facing Jack, a big grin on his face, clothes in hand, "What's going to amaze me Jack, is if you think you are going to walk down the street smelling like you do. Take off your pants and scrub them inside and out!" Jack did as he was told.

Dressed and refreshed, the two walked barefoot through the park. Jack was headed for The Mineshaft. "If you thought The Anvil was something..."

* * *

Rocky woke up at noon the next day. *I love sleeping naked. Chances are they don't do this at the Academy.*

Jack was gone, gone for four days. Four days to explore and have fun. And work out!

Rocky's second day running in NYC went better. He was slowly acclimating. The day was also a bit drier and not as hot. He made it to the gym for a light workout. Later that afternoon, he skipped the disco nap and headed to a local library. There he looked for anything he could find on the Naval Academy.

Researching the card files and microfiche, he found stacks of material. His search centered on summer school. The material was limited, but some existed. He spent hours digging through articles and Academy literature. The pictures in the material provided a lot of food for thought.

Only when his stomach was rumbling for dinner did he think to look up from his research. It was 9:00 p.m. The library would close soon. He checked out a couple of items and headed back to the apartment. Rocky opened the kitchen cabinets and refrigerator looking for something to quell his hunger. Not much there. Taking stale bread and preserves from the fridge, he located a half-empty jar of peanut butter in a cabinet. This would have to do for dinner.

Rocky plopped down in the recliner and pulled out the material he had checked out from the library. Reading for another hour or so, he nodded off. His focus was slowly turning toward his future.

The next morning, he placed a call to his family. It was Saturday and his father picked up the phone on the second ring. "Bill Chambers here."

"Hey Dad, it's Rocky."

"Rocky, how are things going? Where are you?"

"I'm in New York."

"What are you doing there? Are you with someone?"

"I am staying at a friend's place. I have been exploring the city, working out, and studying up on summer school."

"Sounds interesting," his father paused. "So, not to pry, but who is your friend?"

Rocky gulped. "A guy I met on the plane to New York, a pilot. He hasn't been here much. He's flying to South America or somewhere. He's letting me use this place while he is gone."

"That was nice of him. Is he affiliated with the Academy?"

"Nope, but he did learn to fly with the Navy. He knows all kinds of cool stuff to tell me about flying."

"So, have you reached out to your grandparents since you left? You know, they are not that far away and would love to see you."

"Naw, I haven't talked to anyone. How's everyone at home?"

"Everyone is doing fine. It's different not having you around. Your brother and sister asked if you called, and to say hi if you did."

There was more silence. "Okay, Dad, say hello to everyone for me."

"Rocky, the reason I mentioned your grandparents is that they are worried about you. Frankly, they are more than disappointed you have not reached out to them. Do you think you could call them?"

"Sure, Dad. No problem. Do you know if they are in Boston or at the Cape?"

"They are leaving for the Cape tomorrow. Try to give them a call before they leave if you can."

"Yeah, sure. And you Dad, how are you doing?"

"Not so good. I'm very sorry about the way we left things. It hurts."

Rocky could hear the hesitation and sadness in his voice. "Dad, I love you, and I'm working through it, too. Thanks for everything you've done for me, especially making it possible for me to get into the Academy." Rocky took a moment to collect himself, then said, "Dad, thank you for being there for me when Umberto, when he..."

His father heard him cry softly. "Son, I will always be there for you. Please forgive me for slapping you." His dad covered the phone.

"Dad are you still there?"

"Yeah, I had to sneeze."

"Yep, there's some sneezing going on here in New York, too."

Both mixed a chuckle in with their sadness.

"Dad, that's okay, you didn't hit me that hard," Rocky said, faking a laugh.

The phone line was silent for a few minutes.

"Okay, Rocky, I think we should hang up now."

"Okay, Dad. I love you!" Rocky lowered the receiver into its cradle. Wiping the tears from his eyes and the runny nose on his bare arm and went to the bathroom to wash his face.

* * *

"Grandfather, this is Rocky!"

"Hey there, Rocky. I am so glad to hear from you! Where are you?"

"I'm in New York checking out the babes running through the park!"

"That's my grandson! Good job! Keep up the great work! How about joining your grandmother and me at the Cape before you head to Annapolis?"

"That would be super, Grandfather. When would you like me to come?"

"How about I send the jet for you and pick you up at LaGuardia tomorrow morning, say around 11:00 a.m.?"

"Really?" exclaimed Rocky, almost shouting into the phone.

"Really!" retorted his grandfather almost as enthusiastically. "I will have a car pick you up tomorrow morning at 9:00 a.m. It will take you to the corporate terminal, and we'll meet you at the Cape. How does that sound?"

"Well hell! I mean sure! Let me give you my address in Manhattan."

* * *

After a vigorous run and strenuous routine at the gym, Rocky found himself packing for the next morning's departure. It did not take long for him to put his stuff in his bag. Most of it was dirty. His grandparents had an efficient and helpful staff. They would take care of the dirty laundry, no questions asked. He was looking forward to a good spoiling by his doting grandparents.

Now, what to do about Jack? thought Rocky. It seemed cruel to be running off to the Cape without saying goodbye. *I'll leave a note and explain that I had to go. I can blame it on my father's request and aging grandparents. That should do the trick. I'm going to miss Jack. I'm not going to miss New York. I've had enough of what I saw of it.* Rocky shuddered to think of his last night out on the town. His head spun a tad as he recalled the action at The Anvil and The Mineshaft. *I have to get out of here before that life takes hold of me. Thank God, Dad had me call Grandfather.*

Rocky penned Jack a note. He detailed his conversations with his father and grandfather. He finished the letter with: *Jack, you are the best. I cannot thank you enough for all that you have done for me. Your friendship and mentorship (not to mention the sex) was sensational. You taught me how to fish and to realize that some fish can be tossed back into the sea. I plan on keeping only good ones. You're one of them. I'll never forget you. Thank you for the education. I really hate leaving you like this but know you will understand. Play safe, Rocky.*

That night Rocky did not sleep well. He kept playing over and over in his head the experiences he had the last night out with Jack. Jack had done him a huge favor in exposing him to the not-so-pretty side of gay life. *I like men. I want to be with a man, but not like that. I know it is okay for some, but I don't think that's me.*

* * *

By 3:00 a.m., Rocky had slept two hours. Tossing and turning, he crawled out of bed. He packed and repacked his bag, then turned on the TV. There was only so much news and reruns he could watch. He dozed off in front of the television.

Partially awake, adjusting his position in the uncomfortable chair, he was startled as he noticed the library items on the table. *Shit! I've got to get those to the library before I leave. What time is it?* The clock read 5:15 a.m. Fishing through his bags he found the running shorts, shoes, and socks he had used the day before. They were damp and smelly, but that was all he had to wear. Everything but his khakis and polo shirt were dirty, and he was saving those for his flight. The soiled clothes felt gross as he pulled them on. He gulped down two health-food drinks and chewed on a food bar as he dressed and picked up a little around the apartment.

Rocky reached the Library by 5:45 a.m., depositing the items in the overnight drop box. Rocky then set course for a two-hour run, planning on ending it with a 45-minute workout at the gym. A quick shower and getting dressed would take no time. He was back on his plan. Grandfather's jet and the Cape awaited!

CHAPTER 10
GRANDFATHER'S SECRETS

The buzzer from downstairs rang inside the apartment. Rocky depressed the button, "Yes?"

ı'm the driver for Mr. Ricardo Chambers."

"Okay, I'm on my way down."

"Do you need help with bags sir?"

"Nope, got it, thanks!"

Rocky regretted not taking the driver up on his offer. He had to make two trips to transport his bags and the almost full case of water and food bars. He wasn't sure what he would find at the Cape. Somehow, he had to survive the East Coast heat and humidity. The Cape had a nice breeze but could be sticky in the summer.

The Lincoln was new, shiny and well appointed. The seats were made of the finest leather. Refreshments in the small bar tempted him. *It's too early for a beer*, he thought. He reached for a Coke; poured half of it into a crystal tumbler and added ice from the bucket. Rocky succumbed to the assortment of chips and nuts.

The ride in the Towne Car was uneventful, full of stop-and-go traffic. It gave him time to think. He thought a lot about his family, Umberto, Jack and his crazy time in New York. It was time to leave that all behind. Grandfather and Grandmother would spoil him. The rest of the time would be spent getting in shape for summer school. He had less than a week to go.

Observing the traffic and people, he leaned back, pushed a button and the seat reclined a bit. The driver broke the silence about twenty minutes into the ride. "Mr. Chambers, the jet is waiting. We've been given access to the tarmac and the jet. There will be no need to stop at the corporate terminal."

"Thank you. That's sure convenient. Do you have any idea how long the flight takes to the Cape?"

"Which Cape, sir?

"Oh, Cape Cod."

"I'm not certain, sir. My guess is between 90 minutes and two hours, just a guess."

"Thanks."

The Lincoln pulled into the small terminal's parking lot. Rocky brought his seat up into the upright position. The car was waved through the gate and made its way toward a line of shimmering planes. Corporate aircraft of every size were lined up as if on parade for all to see. Their sleek bodies, swept wings, and markings were designed to impress. Owned by those choosing to flaunt that they could afford the best. Convenience, speed and luxury draped the tarmac. This is where the rich and powerful kept their toys.

Sitting on the edge of the seat ogling these winged beauties reaffirmed Rocky's desire to become a pilot. Every plane was lined up uniformly. Each was shiny clean, reflecting the late morning sun. His chest tightened with anticipation. The reality of being part of this very special world boggled the mind.

The car slowed as it approached a twelve-passenger Lear. On the tail in maroon was painted "CE." The upper part of the fuselage read: Chambers Enterprises, also painted in maroon. The aircraft number was in black letters.

The driver drove the Towne Car to the front of the silver bird. A substantial and elegant length of steps lead up to the aircraft's forward hatch. Someone who appeared to be the pilot descended the stairs to the tarmac.

The driver opened Rocky's door. "Sir, we will take care of your things. Please feel free to board your jet."

Rocky stopped when he heard "your jet."

My jet, his mind repeated. A crisp but brief chill grabbed him as he approached the plane and stairs. *I guess it is sort of my jet, at least it's Grandfather's. I'm his grandson. That's so cool.*

The man he thought to be the pilot followed him up the stairs into the aircraft, stowing Rocky's items in a forward luggage compartment concealed behind elegant doors.

"Welcome aboard, sir."

"Thank you. Are you the pilot?"

"Yes, one of two on board. I am the First Officer; the Captain is in the cockpit. Feel free to introduce yourself. Follow me if you please, sir."

Rocky held out his hand, "I'm Rocky Chambers. It's a pleasure to meet you. What is your name?" Introductions made, Rocky followed the First Officer toward to cockpit.

Rocky never left the cockpit. He sat on the folding seat between the pilots for the duration of the flight. Take-off, the flight, and the landing fascinated him. "I'm going to be a pilot, a Marine pilot, one day," he must have told the two pilots a half-dozen times.

* * *

One of the Chamber's Rolls Royces was waiting for the jet to come to rest inside the hangar.

"Good morning, Master Rocky, it is good to see you. Welcome to the Cape. Your grandparents can't wait to see you!"

Rocky recognized the family's chauffeur immediately. Howard had been with them forever. Howard had looked old all of Rocky's life. He had been Rocky's father's playmate when they were young boys together. Howard's father had run the stables and then the garages for the Chambers.

"Howard!" Rocky gave him a huge hug. "I am so glad to see you!"

"Me, too, Master Rocky. Ready to head to the compound?"

"You better believe it!"

Rocky, comfortable knowing that he was once again in arms of the Chambers household, inquired about his luggage. "Master Rocky, everything is in good hands," offered Howard.

"You're right. My apologies, Howard. It's been a while."

As was his custom when Howard picked him up or took him to the airport, or anywhere over the years, he jumped into the front passenger's seat. Howard was like an uncle. Rocky loved and cherished his time with him.

"How's Grandfather?'

"Well, only because I know you won't rat me out, I'll bring you up to date. He is not quite his old self. As you know, your Uncle Tommy, er...Thomas is not well."

"I heard Uncle Tommy wasn't well. What's the problem? I mean, is he sick?"

"Yep, sick, but not so you'd notice much. But he's real sick."

Rocky, feeling as if had been sideswiped, his head pounding, peered hard at Howard. He hesitated, then burst out, "What the fuck's wrong with him? Why hasn't anyone told me?" He clenched his fists.

Howard sat up straight, jerked with a start, and took his eyes off the road. He glared at his passenger. "Listen here, young Master Rocky, you better not use that kind of language around your folks! Humph. As far as you not knowing, that is not my business!" He turned his attention back to the road.

Rocky sat staring at Howard. *Not Tommy. How could this be? I shouldn't have spoken to Howard like that.*

"Sorry, Howard. It just sorta shocked me," stammered Rocky. "You know, what you said about Uncle Tommy."

Howard had returned to his cool, calm and sophisticated manner. "Now keep what I said to yourself. You know, I don't miss much. Your grandfather is going to be talkin' to you serious- like.

Act surprised when he does. Listen and don't talk so much. Think before you say something or cuss. Don't swear!"

"OK, thanks. Got it."

"Now, go ahead and tell me all about your dad, Alejandro and Sophia. I heard you and your mother are at odds, so you needn't get into that."

"Is there anything you don't know, Howard?"

"I sure hope not!" Howard chuckled. "Hurry up, talk. We don't have far to go."

* * *

Rocky got out of the car. His grandparents were already waiting patiently. They stood at the bottom of the stairs leading from the main house at the center of the two-acre beachfront compound.

The three-story white clapboard structure had been in the family for two-hundred years. The bold façade commanded the bay and ocean before it. Clad in golf attire, Grandmother was in her plaid below-the-knee skirt and contrasting blouse and sweater. Grandfather loved his knickers, Argyle sweater, vest and tam. They looked so cute together. It was obvious they had started their game early this morning to have finished and returned back to the house before noon.

"Hello there, Grandmother, Grandfather!"

"Hello, son," his grandfather returned with a hug.

"Hi Rocky! We're so glad you're here. Come and give us a hug," chirped his grandmother.

After exchanging hugs, the older couple placed Rocky between them as they walked hand-in-hand toward the towering house. Howard followed behind with Rocky's things.

"Now, Rocky, everything is ready for you in your room. I hope everything suits you."

"Thanks, Grandmother. I'm sure everything will be perfect as usual."

Entering the house, Grandmother turned to Rocky and took his hand. While patting it, she looked lovingly into his eyes, "Go upstairs and change."

His grandfather added, "The three of us are headed to the yacht club. We're taking the sixty-footer out for a sail. Your grandmother has had lunch sent down ahead."

"What? The three of us? Grandfather, you and me sailing that monster by ourselves? It took four grown men to handle her last summer," Rocky exclaimed. "Honestly, you know I love to sail ever since you taught me as a kid. But how is this going to happen?"

"Not to worry, son. Your grandmother has got things well in hand," chuckled his grandfather.

"Rudolph, tell the boy how we do it!"

"Not on your life. He's got to see for himself. Go change, son!"

* * *

They took the golf cart down to the club and out onto the pier alongside their boat. There stood sixty feet of elegant lines and towering masts; the beam a bit wider than racing yachts provided a comfortable ride. The modified rigging augmented a faster sail for similar cruisers of its size. The twin inboard diesels were capable of spanning the Atlantic if one were so inclined.

"Grandfather, something is different. You've changed the mast and reconfigured the lines. Those are heavy wenches. What's up?"

"Come aboard and see!"

"I told you, honey," directing his comments to his wife, "this boy's the smartest one of the bunch."

"Yes, you did dear," she said patting her husband on his arm. She turned and smiled at Rocky. Rocky blew her a kiss.

Climbing aboard, Rocky took note of a complex panel alongside the double wheel. "Jeez, look at that console!" Rocky exclaimed. "Where are all the lines and sheets? They must be hidden below, and the levers. Engraved even! Looks complicated, but not too complicated."

"You like that? That's what allows this ship to sail with only one person on board."

"What? You're kiddin' me. How is that possible?"

"Well, all the sails are controlled here on the console. They're powered by individual electric motors manipulated by the skipper," boasted Grandfather, his hands now on his hips, chin uplifted, buttressed by his wide smile.

"This is so cool!" the young man purred, running his hands across and exploring the chrome-plated switches, levers and dials.

* * *

The nine-knot wind and lightly rolling seas made for a pleasant and relaxing cruise. The cool breeze and gentle pitch of the yacht relaxed everyone. The three, in and out of their own thoughts, made light conversation. Caressed by the salt air and warm the sun, no one wanted to work at small talk, or any talk.

"You know, Rocky, we're out here so you can have our complete attention. We want to know everything about you. We certainly want news of the California kinfolk, and yes, Annapolis. How was New York?" His grandmother attempted to fill a void that no one else really wanted to fill.

Rocky regaled them with details he felt appropriate. His estrangement from his mother was not broached. His grandparents were not close to Consuelo. They posed only perfunctory questions that might include her. Uncle Tommy was not mentioned. Rocky dared not ask.

"Rocky."

"Yes, Grandfather?"

"When we return home, we'll rest and meet for cocktails by the pool."

His grandmother added, "Dinner will be served in front of the cabana, so you can dress as casually as you like."

* * *

Back at the house that evening, cocktails and dinner passed quickly. The sun was setting behind them and they were soon in shadow. A breeze encircled and cooled them. The table, long since cleared of dishes, held a dessert wine in the family crystal.

"Boys, I am going to head inside. It's getting late. It's late for an old woman who was up early, played 18 holes and spent the afternoon sailing with two handsome gentlemen. Thank you for a lovely day. And thank you, Rocky, for coming to spend some of your time with your old grandparents. You have made me very happy."

Rocky and his grandfather stood as she came around the table. She stood on her toes and gave them each a peck on their cheeks.

"Goodnight, my dear. Rocky and I will head to the study shortly for a nightcap."

"Sleep tight, Grandmother. It's great being here with you."

"Don't stay up too late." Grandmother's light steps appeared to float on air. She was happy, wistfully strolling through the twilight toward the house.

The two men sat in silence, neither of them inclined to interrupt the sound of the ocean, the chirping crickets or the occasional hoot of an owl. Each fiddled with their now empty glasses.

"Rocky, I have some things that I would like to share with you. Would you please join me in the library for a scotch?"

"You bet!"

They passed through the French doors leading from the large foyer into the cherry wood-paneled library. Grandfather headed for the bar.

Rocky walked about the large two-story room. It must have held over a thousand leather-bound volumes, books spanning hundreds of years. There were four mobile ladders, each affixed to the floor and shelves. They could travel the length of their assigned wall. The twelve-foot ceiling was crowned along the edges by a narrow mezzanine providing access to another four walls of bookshelves. More books on more shelves occupied the second story. Rocky wondered if the old guy still climbed the ladders. How long had it been since anyone had accessed the secret panel behind the books on the second floor? Behind the innocuous wall of books, a spiral utility staircase reached to the Widow's Walk high above. It had been great fun hiding amongst the cases, books and hidden panels playing hide and seek as a kid. The cousins had been forbidden to climb the ladders. Nobody listened, and everyone climbed.

"Sit over here, Rocky," said Grandfather, as he pointed to the two heavily stuffed leather chairs. A medium-sized table nestled between the ancient, well-worn chairs. The table held a crystal lamp and a humidor packed with fine cigars. An oversized meerschaum ashtray caressed a cutter and cigar torch. The scent of worn, treated leather, scotch, and cigars teased Rocky's senses.

"I love this room. I love the way it feels. I love the way it smells," hummed Rocky.

"Me too, Rocky. Eight generations of our family have enjoyed this house and this room."

"I certainly hope this place will always remain in the family," said Rocky.

"It will. This house can never be sold. It is entailed in a trust established by your great-great-great-grandfather. Maybe one day you and your family will live here."

"Entailed? What does that mean?"

"Just as I said. It cannot be sold. It must remain in the family. There's a formula for deciding who gets use of it. Let's save that for a later date.

Young man, we need some clarification. There are many things I need to discuss with you. You know your grandmother and I both love and respect you."

"Yes, Grandfather." Rocky moved uneasily in the chair.

The grand old man placed a bottle of Macallan 25 and two lead crystal tumblers on the table. After pouring, he removed two Cuban cigars from the humidor. Cutting them, he handed one to Rocky. He took a seat in the chair next to Rocky. He cut then placed the cigar in his mouth, flicking the large lighter. The light from the flame illuminated the old man's face as he rolled the cigar in his fingers ensuring it was properly lit.

The same flame cast against the dimly lit room accentuated the patriarch's age. The old man's features were stark and brooding.

He handed the lighter to Rocky. This was a first for Rocky. Lighting a cigarette, he could handle. The lighter was so large, and heavy. He fumbled with it, not sure how to proceed.

"First time smoking a cigar?"

"Uh, yep."

"Well, I know you know how to smoke cigarettes. Smoking a cigar is different."

Rocky's caught his breath and looked at his grandfather, mouth slightly open, and eyebrows furrowed. *How does he know I smoke sometimes?*

The cigar aficionado went on to explain the proper and most efficient way in which to cut and torch a cigar. As the experience unfolded, Grandfather's mood softened. Rocky coughed and hacked a bit, but soon acclimated, consciously mimicking his grandfather.

"Thanks for showing me how to do this. I always thought it would be cool to smoke a cigar. I love the aroma, l always have."

Grandfather sat back in his chair, observing his grandson. The young man noticed a twinkle in the old man's eyes. Rocky inwardly speculated his grandfather absorbing, reflecting; taking joy in having his son's son all to himself. At the same time, the old guy emitted confidence and serenity.

"I have a confession to make, son. I invited you here for a purpose. You'll find out later in our talk that I've had this rendezvous planned for some time."

Rocky lost interest in manipulating his cigar. He sat up straight. As he rested the cigar in the ashtray, he took a large gulp from his tumbler. He moved to the edge of the chair, leaning forward, forearms on the top of his thighs, the tumbler clasped between his hands. His gaze angled to the side and upward toward his grandfather.

"You know that this family has been around a long, long time. I would like to see it continue to thrive. The family needs to find someone to help advance the Chambers legacy. Suffice it to say, I was saddled with heading the family by accident."

"There were four girls and three boys in my family. Two of the girls could easily have accomplished what I have done, and perhaps more. Times were different. The girls weren't considered for the responsibility of running the family. My two older brothers were not well suited to assume the mantle of patriarch. One was a drunk, and the other more of the literary type."

Grandfather took a puff of his cigar and sipped his Scotch. Rocky hadn't moved.

"Now comes the hard part, the same part my father had to play when forty years ago he was trying to sort out who would carry on for the family. Times have changed. But the responsibilities have not altered. Let me share some history and details."

"Your Uncle Tom is very ill. He is not in a position to take over the reins of Chambers Enterprises. Your father does not want to run the family interests. Obviously, that puts the focus on the cousins. I am not going to waste your time as to why I have chosen you and not your siblings or cousins to have this conversation. Suffice it to say, I feel you have the most potential. Any questions?" Grandfather waited as Rocky processed what he had just said.

Rocky rubbed his dry lips together, swallowing, trying to moisten his mouth. He sipped more Scotch and resumed his position gazing up at his grandfather.

"What's wrong with Uncle Tommy?"

"We don't know. I suspect it's that 'gay flu.'"

"But, Grandfather, he has kids and is married."

"That doesn't seem to matter," sighed his grandfather.

"My dad, why wouldn't he want to take it on? That doesn't make sense."

"Your dad should have been offered the position a long time ago. Had I known what I know now, he would have been groomed for the position. It's too late now. Your Uncle Tom as the older and equally talented brother was a natural choice."

"When I made the decision in favor of your uncle, your father felt that he had been cheated. He knew of your uncle's varied and prolific dalliances, which obviously have led to his illness. Your father is a man of integrity. He never revealed his brother Tom's secret. Had he done so, I would have removed Tom and replaced him with your father. Your father knew that. My heart aches for your father."

Rocky sat back in his chair, placing the glass on the table. He relit the abandoned cigar. Grandfather watched the young man assume a more confident and mature demeanor. Rocky held the cigar expertly between thumb and index and middle finger. "Maybe that is why my father understands me so well."

His grandfather paused and said, "I think so."

Rocky sat not knowing what to think of what he had just heard his grandfather say. *How much did he know about his personal life? Did he know? Christ!* Perspiration formed on his brow.

"Ever since we became aware of Tom's illness, I have been speaking with your father regularly on this topic. I begged him to come and run the firm. His only comment was, 'That ship has sailed, and I have my life with my family in California now.'"

Grandfather poured scotch into each of their tumblers.

Rocky made himself more comfortable, kicking off his boat shoes. He pulled one foot under the opposite thigh. "Okay, Grandfather, my guess is that my aunts have never been in the picture."

"That's right."

"What do you want from me?"

"If you're to assume the Chambers Enterprises leadership role, you'll have to earn it. To earn it, you must know everything about the family, its history, and its two-hundred years of commerce. Such an endeavor will require passion, discipline and education. You have passion and some discipline. But you still have a long way to go. Take another drink, son. You're going to need it."

Rocky put down what little was left of his cigar. He placed the edge of the three-quarters full tumbler between his lips. He hesitated, then downed half its contents. His taste buds rebelled with the mild burn from the alcohol. His head tingled. He leaned back. He placed the glass on the table next to him.

"As I said earlier, I want to be up front. For the past eighteen months, I have had you followed. A private detective has documented your every move."

Rocky blanched. Both hands gripped the edges of the chair. The tingling in his head morphed into a swirl. Every muscle in his body contracted.

His grandfather nursed his scotch and cigar. Inhaling deeply, Rocky settled in for whatever was coming next.

"I am aware of your relationship with your former girlfriend Belinda and your friend Umberto. I know some of what transpired between you and your mother, through a lot of cajoling of your father. I made every effort to mitigate the problem between you and your mother. I insisted that she visit your grandmother and me on her way to Spain. She sat in that same chair in which you are now sitting. I am afraid that my efforts appear to have been to no avail. Perhaps that will change over time."

Rocky rose unsteadily out of the chair. His taut muscles demanded he loosen them with a walk around the room. His grandfather continued to smoke his cigar and sip his Scotch. Rocky returned to his seat.

"I also had you followed in New York City. Your pilot friend and you seem to have had quite the time. Now, I want to share a little about my youth."

Rocky sprang out of the chair, ran to the sink and threw up. Having completed the emptying of his stomach, he turned on the water. He cupped the flowing water in his hands and proceeded to wipe his mouth. He moistened one of the monogrammed bar towels and wiped his clammy head, neck, and face. Sobered, he returned to his chair.

Grandfather poured more scotch into each of their glasses. "As I was saying, I want to share a little about my youth. When I was about your age, the thirties were booming with jazz and dancing. The city was in a frenzy with WWII looming. Rich, young and foolish, I camped out in the family rooms at the Plaza Hotel. My friends and I ventured into every dark corner of the throbbing city. I had dalliances with women and a couple male musician friends of mine. Surprised?"

This revelation shook Rocky out of his daze. He sat up. He moved forward, his hands on his thighs, focused on the old confessor.

"What?"

"The war changed all that. My time spent in Europe deeply affected me. I returned home more serious, the innocence and gaiety of life diminished. Time heals wounds. I completed my education at Harvard, then stepped into the family business and married your grandmother."

Rocky again rose out of his chair and paced the room. "Does anyone else, like grandmother, know about this?" He continued to pace.

"Well, you know your grandmother, she isn't stupid. It was never discussed. Society back then was much more closely knit. She must have heard about the women. She also was familiar with some of the musicians I ran around with. Now, come, sit down."

Rocky returned to his chair. He felt less frazzled, but still dumbfounded. Picking up his glass and leaning back, "Okay, tell me more."

"I don't know where you're headed with your personal life. As you can see, it is not something on which I care to judge or am qualified to proffer advice. But, I do demand discretion."

"I understand."

"Are you interested in hearing more?"

"Yes, of course."

"In preparation for your availing yourself of these prospects, you must embrace your Naval Academy experience. Distinguish yourself as a cadet, student and leader. I need not go into that much more. As far as your dream of becoming a Marine fighter pilot, that's your decision. Success as a pilot will better prepare you for your career choices, in or out of the Navy."

Agitated, Rocky snapped, "That's eight to ten years of my life removed from the family business. That is a long time. Perhaps you'll find someone else to fill the role in the meantime."

"Perhaps. But during that time, we'll remain in touch. During the third year of your sojourn at the Academy, we'll revisit this. I hope to start educating you on the business. That will include quarterly meetings and discussions between you and me. You will receive monthly reports on all Chamber Enterprises activities. After your graduation, should you appear to be interested and show a talent for business, we will move forward. What do you say to that?"

"Can you give me a minute here?" Rocky didn't wait for an answer. He got out of the chair and walked around the room, Scotch in hand. His head throbbed as he tried to take it all in.

Rocky went over to the ottoman in front of the old man. He took a seat facing him. "Grandfather, this is a lot of stuff." He chuckled, "I'm not sure if I'm drunk or if this is a dream."

His grandfather amused, reached over, patting his grandson on the shoulder. "I understand. But it's real. Why don't you sleep on it?" He sat back in his chair.

Rocky offered, "Just like you said, the decision to commit to the family business is years out. We've over two years before we put this plan in motion, if we do. Let's spend time together over the next few days. I want to learn more."

His grandfather rose out of his chair, pulling Rocky up with him. Rocky saw tears glistening in his grandfather's eyes. They embraced.

"Thank you, Rocky."

His grandfather was exiting the library when Rocky said, "Grandfather?'

"Yes?"

"I know that you are my grandfather, and I respect that. But it seems as if we're always so formal. Would it be okay to call you something less formal, like granddad, pops or something like that?" Rocky stood with both his hands in his pockets, biting his lip.

Rudolph turned and faced Rocky. "Grandfather works for me, son." He gave Rocky a slight smile, nodded, turned and left the room.

* * *

The next morning Rocky was intent on running off the hangover and sweating out the smell of cigars. Leaving the house, he passed by the library. He heard his grandmother humming an old Cole Porter tune. She appeared to be cleaning up the debris left on the library table from the previous evening.

"Good morning, Grandmother!" Rocky cheerfully greeted her.

"Good morning! Going out for a run?"

"Yes, it's a beautiful morning!"

"Yes, indeed, it truly is. Rudy's still in bed." Holding the two glasses nestled atop the soiled ashtray. "You two boys must have been up very late. Did you solve all the world's problems? You must have, as I have never seen him sleep so soundly and so late." She inhaled deeply. Her eyes moistened. Her voice trembled. "Thank you, Rocky."

Rocky read between the lines. Grandfather sleeping better meant our talk gave him hope. Rocky felt a weight trying to seize hold of him.

"Sure, see you later, Grandmother."

CHAPTER 11
SUMMER SCHOOL

Rocky was sitting on his hands, trying not to fidget. He took three deep breaths. *You can do this.* Rocky was perspiring in the back of the air-conditioned limousine.

The Chambers Enterprises jet had delivered Rocky to the Tipton corporate terminal near Annapolis. Grandfather had arranged for a car to deliver the "plebe" to his new home and life's next chapter.

Gazing out the window, he did not see the passing traffic, buildings, trees or people. Deep in thought, he placed his family in one box, his time in New York in another, and in yet another he tucked away his grandparents. The last box, labeled "Naval Academy," was empty. He would fill it.

"Mr. Chambers, congratulations on your acceptance to the Academy!" the driver called out cheerfully.

"Oh. Thanks," replied Rocky.

"Have you been to this part of the country before?"

"No, I haven't. First time. It looks nice." Rocky shifted uneasily around in his seat.

"You know, things are going to be a lot different here than where you came from. There are lots of rules and there ain't no exceptions."

Rocky could see the driver glancing at him through the rear-view mirror. Rocky avoided his gaze and stared blankly out the window, hoping the driver would get the idea he wasn't into small talk.

"Most of the guys showing up on a private plane wash out before summer school is over."

The remark traveled the length of Rocky's body. His head jerked up searching for the drivers' annoying gaze. The driver was looking directly at him in the mirror. Rocky's steely blue eyes locked on to his stare. "Would you mind telling me what you mean?"

"Sure, no problem," the driver said, sounding like he had achieved his goal. "Well, it's like this. It's like these boys suddenly find themselves in a rotten summer vacation. Some are scared, some are cocky, and then there are the few who seem to have a good idea of what they're up against. Most of these guys have one thing in common: they're pretty much spoiled and don't have a lot of street smarts."

Rocky sat up and leaned a little closer. "So, what you're saying is the silver spoon gets in the way and they choke."

"Pretty much."

"So, how about throwing me a couple of tips?"

The driver relaxed in his seat and removed his right hand from the wheel. Resting his arm on the console, he assumed the posture of a sage.

"Tip number one: Keep your head down. Don't attract attention. For God's sake, let me drop you off a block from the Induction Center. Getting dropped off in this car will put a target on your back for a long time. Those 'Firsties' will home in on you fast!"

"Got it. Drop me off two blocks from the Academy."

"Tip number two: Keep your mouth shut and don't say anything but 'yes sir' and 'no sir.'"

"Tip number three: Never, I mean never, volunteer. It's easy to screw up, and if you don't screw up, your classmates already think you're a suck ass."

"Remember, when it gets tough, it'll pass. If you quit, you'll remember it the rest of your life. Stick with it. It'll be worth it. I wish I had." The driver placed his hand back on the wheel and stared forward.

Rocky's ears rang as he realized what the driver had shared. The remaining five minutes of the drive passed in silence.

The car stopped several blocks away from what appeared to be a gathering of young men milling about. "Driver, you don't need to get my things. Just pop the trunk, and I'll get my stuff. And, by the way, I'll never forget what you said."

"Sure, son. Go Navy!"

Rocky grabbed his gear and strode toward the Naval Academy Induction Center.

The driver remained in the car and drew a bottle from underneath the seat. He watched Rocky head down the street, letting loose a satisfying belch. He gulped down the contents of his pint of whiskey then wiped his mouth with his sleeve. Wheeling the car around, he muttered "dumb fuck" under his breath and headed back to the airport.

* * *

Rocky recalled Jack's thoughts on the Academy. "Induction is often a big-time surprise for young cadets. Your first reality will be the loss of self. You're always herded about like cattle. Introductory talks, films and more talks are crammed into your skulls. This shower of information, alongside constant hazing, is designed to intimidate and dehumanize you. The immediate goal is to tear you down, then build you up again over the next four years. Their goal is to build character and instill ethics. The best leaders are those who can infuse ethics and character while making decisions under duress. Uniformity in everything. The short haircuts minimize identity; identical uniforms subordinate the individual to the group. And of course, there's the marching."

* * *

Marching, marching and more marching. Marching to class. Marching from class. Marching to formations and marching to practice marching

Fortunately for Rocky, the act of marching and executing commands was simple and took no concentration. He used that time to think. He reviewed his classwork, drilling himself academically. He was careful to perform well enough on the parade deck, but not to attract attention.

Hours in the classroom, physical workouts and training made up the bulk of every day. Phone calls were not permitted for the first couple weeks. Rocky's first letter was to his family.

Dear Dad, Mom, Alejandro and Sophie,

We're about a week into summer school. I miss you. It seems like forever since we've seen each other. There's

plenty of food if we get enough time to eat it. During meals, Firsties ask us questions about newspaper articles and stuff we were supposed to have memorized. You can't eat when they're asking you questions. That's not fun. We are up at 5:30 a.m. and don't hit the rack until 10:00 p.m. It's go, go, go, all the time. I'm exhausted most days but sleep soundly. Classes are all Navy training stuff. No real academics. As you know, I can memorize easily, so that's a breeze. Academics will get heavy when the Brigade returns for the fall term.

The hazing and screaming are tough. I'm sure glad you guys didn't get in my face and scream like these upperclassmen do. Lots of push-ups and physical fitness, but I was in good shape when I got here so that hasn't been a problem.

I used to hate the marching; I'm okay with it now. I just keep doing it.

The weather here is hotter and more humid than you can imagine. We're always sweating.

I guess one of the reasons I wanted to write was I've been thinking a lot. I have been thinking about how much I love you and miss you. All of you.

I want to apologize for some of the things that I've done and said. I can be a real jerk. I'm sorry, Mom.

Love,
Rocky

Rocky enclosed four Naval Academy bumper stickers in the envelope.

* * *

Afternoons at summer school focused on athletics. In his induction paperwork, Rocky indicated his intention to walk-on for the football team.

"Chambers! Get over here!" An older cadet in a football staff uniform motioned him over waving a clipboard.

Rocky sprinted across the basketball court toward the upperclassman. He halted and came to attention directly in front of the senior cadet. "Sir, yes sir, Cadet Chambers reporting, sir!"

"Okay, Chambers, no need for all that here, we have work to do."

"Sir, yes sir!" Rocky replied. "Oh, sorry sir!" *This is the first time an upperclassman isn't screaming at me. And this guy's pretty cute. I love his wavy black hair. Better watch that. Not the time or place.*

"Okay, Chambers, what are you looking at?

Shit! I sure hope he didn't catch me looking at his crotch. Christ, that's all I need. But didn't he just check me out?

"Nothing, sir!"

"It'd be a good idea if we both focused on why we're here."

The older cadet avoided looking directly at Rocky. He did his best to focus on his clipboard. He was blushing just a little. "Let's talk football. First of all, my name is Jeffries. I will be working with the freshman players."

Together they reviewed Rocky's football background. The more they talked, the more they both relaxed. Jeffries' tone became more personal and engaged. Occasionally, Jeffries would not look directly at Rocky, but past him. Rocky mused to himself, *He looks uncomfortable. Or is he trying to get to know me, to trust me?*

Finally, Jeffries looked up from his clipboard and directly at Rocky.

Rocky's defenses relaxed as their eyes met. He could see Jeffries had collected himself. He seemed calmer. Rocky started to relax and unwind. He focused on Jeffries' deep brown eyes. They projected a warmth and compassion not evident in other upperclassmen. Now it was Rocky's turn to feel a bit uncomfortable.

"Chambers, I'm looking forward to helping you during the summer-school term. Making the team is going to be hard. But I think you can do it."

Still looking into his eyes, Rocky said, "Thank you, sir."

Now more comfortable with each other, they got to work.

Rocky found out there were three other plebes interested in the quarterback position. "As you know, Chambers, there can only be one first-string quarterback and one back up. There are currently four quarterbacks ahead of your class. Can you play any other position?"

"No, sir."

"Well, I suggest you get to work and find a way to qualify for one of the two quarterback positions that we have available for your class."

"Yes, Sir!"

"Make sure you understand what I am saying. You have to beat out two of the other three guys in your class for one spot. Got it?"

"Sir, yes, sir!"

Jeffries reached out to shake Rocky's hand. "Chambers remember to be cool. Let me know if you have any problems."

"Sir, yes sir!"

"Dismissed!"

Whoa, that was interesting, thought Rocky.

* * *

Rocky's second letter was addressed to his grandparents:

Dear Grandmother and Grandfather,

We're four weeks into summer school. This world isn't anything like what I expected. You were right, Grandfather. I have to fully commit to this life to make it happen. I'm okay now with the hazing, the screaming and even the marching. Even cutting all my hair off was okay. And the uniforms are pretty cool, especially the upper classmen'.

The summer classes are pretty much over. The memorization drills were a piece of cake. The challenges were the heavy schedules and all the rules and inspections. We are "on" eighteen hours a day.

As you know, football is pretty important to me, so in addition to all the work and marching, I'm also spending a lot of time at practice. There are four of us guys trying out for the two quarterback slots. I've got my work cut out for me!

I'm looking forward to the few days between summer school and the Brigade returning.

Wish me luck!

Love you,

Rocky

* * *

The few remaining summer school weeks flew by. Rocky breezed through classes and memorization requirements. The afternoon's football practice took every ounce of mental and physical energy he could muster. Jeffries took a special interest in Rocky's training and drills. They studied football plays and the strengths and weaknesses of the other players. Rocky found himself looking forward to the one-on-one time with Jeffries. For some reason, he reminded him of Umberto.

Rocky made a point to arrive at practice early and leave as late as possible. Jeffries was more familiar with Rocky than the other players. When working on positions and drills, Jeffries would often find a way to adjust Rocky physically. Rocky couldn't deny Jeffries' touch sent warm, sensuous sensations throughout his body. Rocky did his best to compartmentalize these erotic feelings. He felt an overwhelming urge to please his mentor by performing well. *The only way I will be able to see more of Jeffries is if I make the team. I gotta make the team.*

"Chambers!"

"Sir, yes sir!"

"Cut it out, Chambers, I told you that you didn't have to say 'Sir, yes sir' when it's just you and me, right?"

"Yeah, sir."

"Really? Smart ass. That one sucked. Try just yes."

They both chuckled. Jeffries put his arm around Rocky's shoulder and walked him over to a secluded area off the field.

"Please, sit down, Chambers."

Rocky turned his head, stunned that he had heard the word *please* from an upperclassman. They sat on the grass.

"Well, I just wanted you to know that I think you're doing a fantastic job. Your heart is in your training. No one tries as hard as you do. I appreciate your efforts. It makes my job easier."

Jeffries leaned back on his elbows. Rocky couldn't help noticing his athletic build was accented by the sweat saturated t-shirt and shorts.

Rocky liked the compliment but was caught off guard by the familiarity. "Okay, thanks. I appreciate your faith in me. It means a lot. Frankly, these practices are kicking my ass."

Rocky saw a slight grin spread across the upperclassmen's face, obviously noticing Rocky checking him out.

"What are you looking at, plebe?" Jeffries murmured. "See something you like?"

* * *

The following weeks were filled with finishing up summer school and anticipating the news as to whether or not he'd made the team. *Did I make it? I've given my best. I know I'm good. I sure as hell hope the coaches thought so, too.*

On the last day of summer school, Rocky entered the athletic facility to learn his fate. As he inhaled deeply, he heard Jeffries call him.

"Plebe!"

"Sir, yes sir!"

"Get over here!"

"Sir, yes sir!"

Rocky followed Jeffries into the locker facility and one of the training rooms. Jeffries waited just inside the door, closing and locking it behind them. The sound of the door closing, and the snap of the lock thrilled Rocky. Rocky noticed a slight bulge in Jeffries' shorts. Rocky inadvertently ran his tongue along the underside of his top lip. "For Christ sake, Chambers, I told you weeks ago to be discreet!"

"Chapped lips, sir!"

"Bullshit! You know if gays get caught they're booted out of the Academy, right?"

"Sir, I really haven't thought much about it. Well, that is until I met you." Rocky realizing what he just said, felt a moment of panic and his knees started to buckle. Jeffries rolled a chair over to him.

"Sit down before you fall down. Jesus, plebe!"

Rocky grabbed the chair and fell into it.

Jeffries went over to a sink and turned on the cold water. Moistening a towel, he walked over to Rocky. "Now, don't get the wrong idea. I'm just trying to make sure you don't pass out." Reaching from behind, he placed one hand on Rocky's shoulder and with the other, gently wiped Rocky's face and neck.

Rocky began to get his color back and felt a little stronger. The hand on his shoulder was warm, strong and comforting. The other hand running the towel across his face and neck began to slow down. Rocky's chest began to rise and fall more quickly. His loins tightened

Rocky closed his eyes and leaned back, letting his head lie against Jeffries' abdomen. Jeffries was now caressing every inch of Rocky's throat, neck and face with slow, sensual movements. He moved in front of Rocky, who opened his eyes and stared at Jeffries.

"So, I guess we're going to do this, plebe," Jeffries whispered.

He took the ends of the towel in each hand, wrapping them once around each wrist to shorten it. He lifted the taunt towel over Rocky's head placing it around his neck. Only inches from Rocky, he pulled upward, drawing Rocky up and toward him. Their moist lips met. Their tongues explored each other. Now standing, Rocky wrapped his arms around Jeffries' back, pulling him closer. Their torsos melded together. Jeffries ran his hand down Rocky's back and under his athletic shorts and jockstrap. Rocky followed his lead and did the same.

Forty minutes later, they dressed and prepared to leave the exercise room. Jeffries placed Chambers' back against the unopened door. He took both hands and caressed the sides of Rocky's face. He whispered, "By the way Chambers, you made the squad." Jeffries didn't wait for a response. He kissed Rocky lightly on his open lips.

Rocky's head spun. His chest tightened as he felt his stomach flip.

Jeffries, now standing with his hands on his hips, growled "Plebe, this is when you say 'Sir, yes sir, thank you, sir!'"

Rocky stood staring at Jeffries, his eyes wide and his mouth hanging open. He couldn't think, but he knew what he'd heard. *Oh my God, I made it!*

CHAPTER 12
MAKING THE GRADE

The first day of summer break, the cadets, staff and service personnel poured out of Bancroft Hall, affectionately known as "Mother B." Only those who had nowhere to go, or had delayed travel plans, remained. Summer school was over and for a week, the Academy grounds breathed a sigh of relief. No screaming, no marching, no drilling, no chow formations. The tranquility enveloped the tree-lined swaths of grass and grand stone structures.

Knock! Knock!

"Enter!" Rang out from the third-year cadet's room.

A figure entered and locked the door. His back against the door and cracking a smile, the visitor winked at Jeffries.

"What the fuck are you doing here?" whispered Jeffries. "Don't you know we could both get drummed out for this? This area is off limits to lower classmen! What are you thinking?"

"I guess that would depend on what we were doing. If we got caught." Rocky remained standing against the door. "So, are you here for the break? I'm here till tomorrow afternoon, then headed to DC for a family get-together."

Jeffries fumbled with the manual he was reading and tossed it to the floor, his eyes wide in disbelief. His bewildered stare only encouraged Rocky.

"So?"

"Who the fuck do you think you are, talking that way to me, Chambers?"

Rocky put his hands on his hips and cocked his head to one side. "Uh, your lover?"

Jeffries' voice was low, calm and quiet. "Just because we screwed around doesn't mean you can show disrespect. This is simply wrong and out of order." His tone was not convincing. Rocky tried to look contrite, but he grinned hopefully at Jeffries.

Jeffries felt a sensation throughout his ass as his cock grew hard. Resigned to Rocky's presence, he sat back in his chair. Rocky hadn't changed his position. He stood watching Jeffries, occasionally running his tongue across his lips.

"So, this is what we're going to do. Meet me in the Mahan Hall bell tower at 2100 hours. It will be dark.

Don't bring a flashlight. If you hear others up there, ignore them. And keep away from them! Got it?"

"Yep, got it." Rocky walked over to Jeffries and whispered in his ear, "Sir, yes sir!" Rocky's tongue flicked out and into Jeffries ear. He reached down and gave Jeffries' crotch a squeeze and exited the room.

* * *

The climb up the stairs to the bell tower was eerily quiet and dark. His steps echoed on the granite steps and the cold, iron railings sent a chill through his tense hand and arm. Reaching the top landing, Rocky opened the door to a large space. The room had only ambient light to distinguish the shadows.

A faint smell of sweat hung in the air. Rocky had expected the place to be deserted, but he heard low moans coming from the far side of the room. Outlines of what appeared to be mattresses and abandoned chairs were strewn about.

"Hey, wanna join us?" Echoed from the other side of the room.

Rocky froze in place. *Jeffries told me to keep away.* Rocky walked a few feet forward. He shuffled his feet a bit. "Maybe next time. I'm meeting someone."

"Come here, let's get a look at you!"

Rocky turned to walk out of the room and plowed into Jeffries. "Shit, I'm glad you're here. Fuck, what took you so long?"

Jeffries didn't say a word. He took Rocky by the hand and led him over to a far corner he had prepared for them. Jeffries pulled Rocky down onto the mattress. A break in the shadows revealed a lustful stare. "Make love to me," Jeffries whispered.

Hours passed. The room had experienced an intermittent stream of men coming and going. Now they were the only two in the room. Jeffries spooned Rocky. They dozed. "You know, Chambers, you shocked the shit out of me when you came to my room."

"Hell, I shocked the shit out of me!" Rocky laughed.

"Thanks for having the guts to do it. I was thinking about you. I've been thinking about you all day." They cuddled closer.

"You know what? I don't even know your first name."

"Nicholas."

"I like it. Do you like it?"

"Yes, it's a family name."

"Are you a czar or something?"

"Sure, and you're my czarina!"

They wrestled and laughed a bit more as they rolled around on the mattress. Their wrestling eventually gave away to more lovemaking.

* * *

Jeffries had rented a car for his drive to Charlottesville the next day and offered Rocky a lift to Washington, DC.

"Okay, Mr. Nicholas Jefferies, what am I going to call you? Nicholas or Nicky?"

"Sir! That's what you will call me!" Jeffries pretended to be serious.

"Fuck you!"

"You did!"

In a resigned voice, Rocky said, "Seriously, when it's just the two of us, I want you to call me Rocky. Will you do that?" His voice had a hopeful tone.

"I'd rather call you honey, or dear, or something like that. But, I guess that won't work. Okay, I'll call you Rocky." He turned to Rocky in the passenger seat, smiled and squeezed Rocky's left thigh. He didn't remove his hand.

They drove on toward Washington. Rocky took Jeffries' hand in his and placed both their hands in his lap.

"Most people call me Nick. I never really liked the nickname Nicky."

Rocky sighed. "Too bad, I love Nicky." Rocky caught himself, and blushed, "I mean the sound of it."

Jeffries chuckled. "Be careful, Nicky might fall in love with Rocky." Rocky blushed again. "I guess you can call me Nicky. But only you."

Changing the subject and trying to gain some composure, Rocky asked, "Nicky?" Jeffries turned and looked into Rocky's eyes squeezing his hand. He turned his attention back to the road. "Nicky. I want to ask you a question. Please be honest with me."

"Okay."

"Did I get picked up by the team because I'm really good, or was it because you like me?"

"Neither." Nick paused. "Actually, you're not that good yet and my liking you had nothing to do with it." That statement sobered Rocky.

"What?" He removed his hand and turned his body toward Nick.

"You're a good athlete with potential to be a superstar, and I like you."

"C'mon, give it to me straight. What's going on?"

Nick inhaled, held it and then exhaled. He pursed his lips and breathed in and out again. "Okay, listen carefully, and please don't interrupt. I'm a man of integrity. I shoot straight. I care for you very much. It may be more than that. We've been working together daily for over a month. I've seen you at your best and otherwise. Not only are you talented, but you also have courage, drive, and most importantly, potential. Nevertheless, in my opinion, you weren't one of the top two candidates for the quarterback position. You were number four; maybe number three. I didn't recommend you for selection."

Rocky's heart crashed. His face blanched.

"The offensive coaches asked my opinion and I told them what I thought. The list came out, and your name was on it. The coaches called me into their offices. They told me they respected my recommendation but were going to give you a chance anyway. I was instructed to inform you of the decision."

The two sat in silence. Washington, DC was only ten miles away.

"Pull over somewhere, please."

Nick found a turnoff and a place to pull over on the side of the road. Both unbuckled their seat belts.

"So, Nicky, where do we go from here?"

Nick ran his hands up and down the length of his thighs. He looked down at his lap and then tented his fingers atop the steering wheel. His head rested against his hands. "I don't know."

Rocky paused before speaking. "Okay, I think I do. Thanks for being honest with me. It helps to know what you really think. I respect you for it. It makes you even more special to me. It still hurts, but I'll get over it."

"I'm glad you'll get over it. It was hard for me. Very hard. But, I did what I thought was right."

"I guess you'll be working with the squad when we get back. You'll continue to train me as if we're not lovers. You'll drive me as hard as you would any other player."

Nick took both Rocky's hands into his. "And we'll remain discreet. We'll find time for each other when we can." Jeffries announced through a wide grin, "And yes, you will still call me sir!"

"I really like you."

"I really like you, too."

* * *

The Brigade returned to Annapolis a week later. Rocky had two new roommates. The three of them were quartered in an upper wing of Mother B.

If summer school was tough, the fall term was worse. Up at 5:30 a.m., rush to shower, shave, dress, read several articles in the newspaper and be ready for formation. If it wasn't your lucky day, you got to stand in the middle of the passage and shout out the menu for breakfast, lunch and dinner, all the while harassed by an upperclassman. When not being dogged during meals or in between classes, cadets had to be on time. They had to be in their seats before the beginning of class, not when the bell sounded. Classwork was demanding. Professors expected disciplined and teachable students. Classes in the afternoon were followed by athletics.

Football practice and games dominated Rocky's afternoons and weekends. Six weeks into the season, Rocky felt exhausted and demoralized. He needed to sound off to someone.

Dear Dad,

I have to tell you, I'm worn out. I just don't know if I am going to make it. Academics, particularly biology, are not going well. I don't have enough time to study and I'm worried about my grades. We're a third of the way into the semester and I'm not sure I'll pass.

I feel like I have to schedule a bathroom break! There's so much to do all day long, I've been studying by flashlight. I've been caught and received demerits on several occasions. *This sucks!*

I love football but lately something always hurts. And I won't even play in a single game this year. It's weird going to a game and being glad I don't have to play so that I can take a break. I always fall asleep when I travel with the team. When I'm not sleeping, I'm studying. It looks like they're assigning me a tutor for sciences. I guess they've figured out that I am sinking fast. How the hell will I fit a tutor in my schedule? There's no time for socializing. Misery loves company, right? There's a lot of that here.

Say hey to everybody and wish me luck!
Rocky

* * *

Dear Rocky,

Thank you for your letter. I am so glad that you took the time to let me know what life is like at the Academy, particularly yours. I shared the letter with your mother. If I hadn't, she would have found a way to get her hands on it. She handed it to me the day it arrived and refused to prepare dinner until we had both read it!

You should have seen her. She didn't want to damage it by studying it too much, so she made a copy and tucked the original away with all your other letters. Then, she started to dissect it. I finally gave up and ordered pizza for dinner.

So, here are some of our thoughts: First of all, we want you to know how proud we are of our son at the United States Naval Academy. We always knew that you were never really challenged in high school, but there wasn't much we could do about it. Everything we enrolled you in, you mastered. We think you need this. Embrace it. We are so excited and can't wait to see how these challenges forge you into a man.

From your letter, it sounds like you are doing everything right. Keep doing it! Never give in to doubt. If you feel physically ill, go to the infirmary. It is not a sign of weakness to go to the doctor. It is a sign of poor judgment if you don't go. It's that simple. Execution of judgment has consequences, good and bad. Never forget this.

As far as your academics, embrace the system. They are there to help you and teach you how to succeed. Be transparent with your advisor. They are chosen to do what they do because they are good at it. Use them as resources.

Stop studying after Taps. You are losing ground when you do that. You have always needed your rest. You need it more now than ever.

Write when you can and keep us informed. It means the world to your mother and me.

We love you and have the greatest faith in you.

Love,
Mom & Dad

CHAPTER 13
1984 – 1988: ANNAPOLIS YEARS

Early one Saturday morning, the two men found a secluded place to sit. The spot, along the Severn River, was not far from the Academy.

"Hey Rocky, I hope you get a chance to play this year." Nick put his hand on Rocky's shoulder, looking into his eyes. "I'm rooting for you."

"Thanks, Nicky. Maybe I'll play today. We're odds-on favored to win the game. Maybe if we pull way ahead, the coach will put me in. I hope so. Sitting on the sidelines is getting old."

Both were dressed in grey Academy sweatpants and dark blue Navy hoodies. Sitting cross-legged on the grass, they sipped their steaming coffee.

"Well, what did you expect? There's lots of competition for the top job," Nick jabbed Rocky's arm. "I want to see my guy play before I graduate. You've got two years to go after I leave."

Rocky looked at the ground. "I wish you wouldn't talk like that. I hate the thought of you graduating and my being stuck here without you." Rocky picked at the grass.

"Me, too."

"You know, Nicky, I want you to see me play, too, at least one game before you leave." Rocky kept his head down, now picking at the cuticles on his left hand.

"Stop playing with your fingers and look at me," whispered Nick. He looked to see if anyone was around. He reached over and gave Rocky a gentle kiss.

Rocky inhaled as he felt the warmth of Nicky's lips on his.

Nick pulled away and took a swig of coffee. "I love being close to you. It just feels right." Nick smiled at Rocky.

"Yep, it does. I'm gonna miss it," Rocky said, smiling and sniffing once, his eyes moistened. He lifted his cup to toast. Nick returned the toast and blew him another kiss.

Nick and Rocky leaned back on their elbows and stared out over the river. Gold and red autumn leaves framed the river. They savored the crisp morning breeze and simply enjoyed sitting quietly side by side.

"Okay, enough of this, let's head back, sonny boy! Let's see what I can do to set you up to play this afternoon!"

"Sounds good to me!" Rocky smiled contentedly as they jumped up and headed back to the campus.

* * *

There were three minutes left in the third quarter. Navy had succeeded in opening a 25-point lead over Army. The second-string quarterback had been playing for most of the third quarter. Navy had just scored another touchdown. Walters, the third-string quarterback, was sent in. He lasted three plays as he was sacked every time.

Nick came up behind Rocky on the bench. "Okay, it looks like Walters is hurt. I just spoke to the coach. Pay attention and don't fuck up."

"Chambers! Get your ass over here!" hollered the head offensive coach.

Rocky had all but given up on getting a chance to play. He sprang up off the bench and trotted toward the coach. "Sir, yes sir!"

"Listen, we're going to put you in to give you a couple of plays. Keep your eyes open and anticipate everything. Got it?"

"Got it, Coach!"

Rocky strapped on his helmet as he sprinted toward Navy's forty-third yard line. He had watched every second of every play, offense and defense. He played quarterback in his head, mentally picking plays he would have recommended if he had been on the field. Most of the time he picked what the team executed.

Just before reaching the huddle, he slowed down and looked back at the coach. *I haven't been given a play.* The coach waved him towards the team huddled on the field. *I guess this one's up to me.*

The center placed the ball squarely in Rocky's hands. Rocky fell back and handed off to the halfback, who was promptly tackled for a loss of five.

On the second down, Rocky again received a perfect hike. He immediately drew back to throw. A receiver was crossing 25 yards downfield directly in front of him. Spying a defensive lineman barreling towards him, Rocky tucked the ball under his arm and sidestepped the mammoth opponent, only to be tackled hard at the line of scrimmage by a player he hadn't seen.

Third down and 15, the ball was on Navy's 28-yard line.

"Okay, Chambers, we can do this. Let's go!" shouted a teammate, slapping him on his shoulder pads.

"You can do it, man!" echoed another player.

"Go Navy!" rang out.

A well-executed hike and Rocky found himself trying to escape three linemen who had broken through the Navy defensive line. This came as no surprise. The Army defense was playing their first squad. Navy was playing their third squad, with their fourth-squad quarterback.

Rocky had the ball and was being chased by two linemen. Wide receiver Henry Johnson magically appeared open and sprinted thirty-five yards down the right sideline. Rocky hugged the left sideline. He drew his arm back as he jumped out of the way of one of the oncoming defensive lineman. He fired the ball across the field. It spiraled as it arched upward and disappeared into the sun. *Oh God, oh God, please get to him!*

Johnson, running full throttle, caught the ball in mid-air, stumbled then regained his balance and was forced out of bounds.

Rocky could not believe what had happened. His heart was pounding and his stomach churning.

First and ten on the Army 37-yard line. In the huddle his teammates were slapping one another on the back with high-fives all around. "Awesome job, hot dog," hollered the center.

"Let's do that again, guys!" shouted another.

Grabbing another solid hike, Rocky fell back then collapsed on the ball as the offensive line gave way and four 230-pound plus monsters surged toward him.

Second and 15. Rocky anticipated the line not holding. His head throbbed. The beefy linemen had pummeled him. Faking a pass, he turned and tossed the ball to the halfback. Navy picked up seven yards.

Third and 8. A Hail Mary pass and another skillful catch by Henry Johnson, who stayed on his feet and ran the ball in for a touchdown. Players, coaches and fans went berserk. The Navy band threw itself into the celebration with the Academy fight song. A line judge threw a flag for no apparent reason. Rocky stopped breathing until the referee declared there was no penalty. Navy scored the extra point.

Nick came up behind Rocky, spun him around and enveloped him in a bear hug, lifting him of the ground. "You did it! I knew you could! You did it!"

* * *

"Hey Chambers, those were a couple of great passes you threw my way!"

"Yeah, Johnson. They wouldn't have been shit without your being there to snag 'em. Thanks!" The team shower room held half the players at any given time hollering and cutting up. A lot of grab ass followed as the team congratulated one another on their win.

Rocky reveled in the respect and adulation his teammates threw at him. He felt elated and bewildered. As the shower room emptied out, he soaped up.

Johnson was three feet away, facing the middle of the shower room. His head was tilted back, eye closed, water cascading down his back. Rocky couldn't help noticing Johnson's six-pack abs. Johnson opened his eyes and looked over at the mildly aroused quarterback. He looked down at his own arousal. He turned and faced the showerhead, smiling as he lowered the cold-water temperature.

* * *

The remainder of second year flew by. Nick graduated in late May. The weekend before graduation, Rocky and Nick traveled to Harpers Ferry, going out to dinner at a cozy pub.

"Nicky is your family coming for graduation?"

"Yep, and not just my immediate family. I've got a slew of aunts, uncles and cousins on the way, too." He took a swig from his beer and placed it on the table. "Even my old girlfriend."

Rocky looked up as his stomach flipped. "Oh?"

"I'd like you to say hi to my folks when they're here. They asked about you. I've told them we're best buds."

"Do you think they've figured out it's more than that?"

"There's no reason to think so."

"How about the girlfriend? What's up with that? I figure she'll want to be serviced right away."

Nick shot a hurt look at Rocky. He pursed his lips and with a clenched jaw said, "Well, that's kind of the problem. I've not been doing a very good job with that. I told her it was nothing, just stress." Nick paused, looking downcast as he folded his arms. "She asked me if you were the stress."

Rocky looked up quickly, immediately alarmed. "Shit! What did you say? Fuck!"

Nick rested his forearms on the table. "I said, what stress? I told her you gave great head." Nick dissolved into hysterics.

"You asshole! You didn't." Rocky started laughing.

"No, not really. I did let her know that you were a special guy, but nothing else. Besides, she's a great girl and I feel like a jerk treating her this way." Nick took a swig of beer and sat back.

"I sure hope you didn't. But I'll bet she knows."

"Maybe."

"Okay, enough about that crap. Let's talk about you and law school. Harvard! I'm glad you won't be too far away. Only six or seven hours by train."

"It'll be great to see you when we can get together." Nick paused. He peered into Rocky's eyes. "Do you think we can handle the long-distance thing? I mean, they say out of sight out of mind." Nick backed away and focused on his beer.

"I don't know, but we can try," Rocky sighed. "It's not like we're married or anything. Don't get pissed, but sometimes I feel stupid about what I'm thinking."

"What do you mean?"

"Shit, this is dumb. Sorry I said it."

"You didn't say anything yet." Nick leaned forward.

Rocky ducked his head. "Sometimes I want to say I love you. But I'm afraid I'll scare you away." Under the table, Rocky pressed his knee against Nick's. The pub was dark, and their table positioned toward the back, away from the crowd. Both focused on their empty glasses.

Nick returned the pressure. "You couldn't scare me away. I love you, too," he whispered. They sat in silence. Nick stared into Rocky's eyes. "But maybe we're just two guys who like sex a lot," grinned Nick.

"Yeah. So, are you saying there might be some fooling around while we're apart?" Rocky fought to keep his voice even.

"Maybe," continued Nicky.

Taking a deep breath, Rocky responded, "Well, if something happens, it happens. No one can help that. But let's not let anything or anyone get in the way of our friendship."

Neither of them could look at the other, only their empty glasses.

The waitress walked up to their table. "Are you two okay? You look like someone died or something."

"We're in mourning," scoffed Rocky, grinning at her. "We're out of beer!" All three of them laughed. Then Rocky and Nick thrust their empty glasses at the waitress.

She called back over her shoulder as she headed toward the bar. "Cheer up! Two more on the way!"

"Make that two each!" called Nick.

"You got it!"

* * *

Rocky spent most of that summer at Quantico, Virginia. Cadets preparing themselves to go into the

Marines had to attend The Basic School or the Bull Pup Program for prospective Marine Officers.

Hey Nicky,

How's it going? I guess you're enjoying the summer break.

I hope like hell I didn't make a mistake going into the Marines. Quantico is in the middle of nowhere and it's tough. It's like we're plebes again. The instructors pound on us all day and treat us like a bunch of kids. I thought that plebe crap was over!

I like the physical stuff. It's more fun than being in class all day. They're always working our asses off. I'm not too worried about it. The Corps is different. More macho than the Navy.

This place is riddled with hard asses. I don't think all of them are playing with a full deck, officers and enlisted alike. They say a lot of stupid things, but surprisingly, I like their "esprit de corps." So, I guess I can put up with the stupid. I just want to be a Marine fighter pilot! OORAH!

Actually, I'm having an okay time. Nothing is as hard as the regimen you put me through the last two years of football. Jesus!

So, what's going on with you? Are you becoming a candy ass sitting all day in class and studying? I bet I could kick your butt these days.

Grandfather said you guys met for lunch at the club. What did you think? He's pretty cool. He said you'd make a decent corporate attorney. I think he's got us figured out. Not to worry, as I said, he's cool.

Have you gotten laid yet?

Let's get together when you get a break in August.

Adios,

Rocky

* * *

In Autumn of Rocky's fourth year, Rudolph Chambers arrived in Annapolis to pay Rocky a visit.

"Grandfather how are things going?" He shook the old man's hand and gave him a big hug.

Rudolph Chambers had a wide grin and twinkle in his eye as he motioned his favorite grandson to take a seat. "Great, Rocky. I hope you don't mind me dropping in like this, unannounced. I was in DC on business and got the Academy Superintendent's permission to spend the weekend with you." Both men, beaming and relaxed, sat down.

"That's cool, but how did you get the Admiral to allow me off campus?" His voice was incredulous. "A lot is going on, and they've pretty much restricted us to campus for most of September. You know, the indoctrination of the new plebes and all."

With his right fist, lightly pounding his chest twice, "The Admiral and I go way back."

Rocky grinned and chuckled, "I wish I would have known that! It could've come in handy the past four years."

"As a matter of fact, he kept me in the loop on how you've been progressing. I like what I've heard. Your academics and leadership skills have impressed them and me." He sat back and crossed his legs. "I know you're not at the top of your class, but that's not important. What's important is that you are ready to move on with your life, be it the Marines, Chambers Enterprises or whatever."

"You've had the inside scoop on me the whole time? Is this a repeat of spying on me in high school and New York?" Rocky said, incredulous.

"Yes."

"Grandfather, that's not cool. It's an invasion of my privacy." Rocky sat back and folded his arms, glaring at his grandfather.

The glare didn't faze his grandfather. Looking at Rocky, he said, "Son, there is no privacy in this world. Besides, as you know, I make it my business to keep track of people and events that are important to me."

"I didn't say anything when you pulled this crap on me before, but it's just not right."

Grandfather sat back, sipping his beer. He slowly enunciated, "It's just business; family and company business. It's called doing your homework. It's the real world, son."

Irritated, Rocky looked down at his beer. "So why are you here? I've been studying everything you've sent me for over a year. I think I've got a pretty good idea of how things work. So, what the hell else should I be doing? I've got a lot on my plate, with classes and graduation and all. And I'm still going to be a Marine fighter pilot."

"You've been exemplary. You have a fair grasp and understanding of Chambers Enterprises. But, so would an investigative reporter."

The cadet inhaled and exhaled. He pursed his lips, returning to his upright position. "Really? That's all? I've given feedback, comments and suggestions. I've also volunteered some ideas on how to maximize company interests. Didn't you read the stuff I sent you?"

Grandfather leaned forward, placing his elbows on the table. He lowered his voice. "Don't be impudent. It's obvious your experience at the Academy has not honed your judgment. I'm grooming you to take over a multi-billion-dollar corporation. If I want to know what you are up to in your personal life, that's my business."

His grandfather's stare launched arrows wrapped in disgust and disappointment at an intimidated and overwhelmed Rocky.

Chastised and unnerved, Rocky answered, "You're right, Grandfather. I apologize." He gulped down what was left in his glass and sat back in the chair.

"Now, as far as flight school goes, go for it. I wish you well. In the meantime, I'll continue to send you reports and financial info. I'll also be forwarding the minutes from board meetings. You'll have to sign a confidentiality agreement. "Now," holding an envelope in one hand, "I'd planned on giving you fifty-thousand shares in Chambers Enterprises. You screwed up. Your attitude today and impulsive behavior makes me question if you are up to the task." He returned the envelope to his inside jacket pocket.

Rocky sat up straight, "What, what do you mean?"

"Exactly what I said. Grow up. Get your act together! I won't wait forever." Rudolph stood up and looked down at his stunned grandson. Rocky's eyes were on fire, jaw clenched. Rudolph pulling out his wallet, tossed Rocky two twenties. "Pay the bill." He turned and walked out of the restaurant.

Rocky, frozen in place, sat watching his grandfather disappear. His mind was blank as he felt his chest cave. Moments later he slumped into the chair. *That man scares me.*

* * *

It was late fall in their senior year. Rocky and Henry were in the locker room following one of the few remaining games. They pulled on sweats and hoodies and headed for the canteen. Locating a seat among the after-game crowd, they ordered double malted shakes.

"Henry, decent job out there today. Thanks for saving my ass. We came close to losing that one."

"No problem, bud. These past two years playing catch on national TV has been a lot of fun. We've pulled quite a few out of our asses. In a couple of weeks, it'll be over. And in five months, we'll have graduated and be outta here! Wanna go out on the town tonight?"

"You know, I'd like that. But it makes me nervous."

"What do you mean?"

"You know what I mean. Don't be such a jerk. You know exactly what I'm saying. We can't keep our eyes off each other in the shower. And I'm not the only one who uses cold water to make sure no one notices."

"So?"

"Well, it just makes me nervous."

"Good. I'll meet you in front of the Mother B at 7:00. Or do you want to meet in the tower?"

Rocky looked at Henry, eyes wide, chin low. "Are you crazy?" He thought for a minute fumbling with his shake. "I'll meet you out front. No funny business. Christ!"

Henry chuckled, "Watch out, mister, 'cause I got some funny business comin' at ya! Yeah!"

"Go on, get out of here."

Later that night as he got ready to meet Henry, Rocky thought, *I'm an idiot. I have no business hooking up with Henry. But he is hot, and I'm horny. It's been a long time. Okay, so all I have to do is play it cool. If we stay out in the open, nothing will happen. Okay, that's the plan.* Rocky knew he was bullshitting himself.

It was 7:15 and Henry hadn't shown up. *Maybe it's just as well. I don't need this. Well, maybe I need it, but I should stay away from it. I'm gonna head back inside.* Disappointed and relieved at the same time, Rocky turned and headed to Mother B.

"Hey, old man! Sorry I'm late. I fell asleep and had to shower really fast."

"No problem. Where to?" Rocky sighed.

"I dunno. Tower or tunnels?" cracked Henry.

Rocky didn't miss a beat. "Tunnels. Steam's on, and its warmer down there this time of year."

* * *

Classes and preparation for graduation consumed most of Rocky's time. A month away from graduation, Rocky was waiting to hear if he was headed to flight school. His orders should have been here by now. Flight school (if it was going to happen) would come after The Basic School. All Academy graduates going into the Marine Corps had to go to TBS first to teach them how to be Marine officers. Rocky checked his mailbox four times a day. This was the third time that morning. He looked through the glass in the box door. This time, he thought he saw an official-looking envelope. He tried to put the key in the lock but fumbled and dropped it. "Shit!" Rocky took three deep breaths. He picked up the key, slid it into the lock and turned it. Grabbing the envelope, he thought, *Holy Shit! Orders!*

Rocky tore the envelope open and there it was, in big, bold, black letters. Almost dancing down the hallway, he shot straight for the phones.

"Hey, Dad! Guess what!" Rocky was almost shouting into the phone.

"I bet I can guess but tell me anyway." William Chambers crossed his fingers hoping the news was the news he wanted to hear. "Hold on a minute. Let me get your mom on the phone."

"Sure, hurry up!" Rocky's chest was bursting. *Hurry, hurry, hurry*, he thought to himself.

Consuelo picked up the extension, "Rocky, what's the news? I hope, I hope!"

"Mom, I can't wait to tell you! Dad are you on the line?"

"Yep!"

"OK, are you ready?"

"Oh, Rocky, please hurry up and tell us!" Consuelo chirped.

"I was accepted into the Naval Aviation Program!"

"Oh my! *Gracias Dios*, Rocky! I'm so happy *mi amor*, and so proud of you!" cried his mother.

"That is fantastic, Rocky," echoed his father. "Tell us more!"

"Well, I got the orders today. I don't know a whole lot more. There's going to be some more physical examination stuff once I get to Pensacola. Once that's done, I am good to go!"

"When does it start? Right after graduation, son?" asked his father.

"Nope, everyone going into the Marines has to spend several months back at Quantico. We have to go to The Basic School. You know, learning how to be a grunt. Not that I'm going be a ground pounder. It's just learning about being an Officer of Marines. Sounds cool, doesn't it?" The pride in saying 'Officer of Marines' put a lump in his throat.

"We are so proud of you. Our son, the Officer of Marines," said his father.

Rocky could not see their moistened eyes and the swelling pride in their hearts, but he felt it.

"After that, I'm off to Pensacola."

"*Bien, mi amor*, when we see you at graduation, will you have time for the family? I mean, just the family?"

"Of course, Mamacita."

"*Bueno*! Let's think about a trip to New York. We can shop, go to the shows and have a wonderful time!"

"That sounds good to me. It'll be great to see you both, along with Alejandro and Sophia. I need to carve out a couple of days to see the grandparents and a friend of mine at Harvard, too. It'll work out fine."

"Friend at Harvard? Who is that? Do we know him?" asked his mother.

"Sure, you met him once or twice on campus. He's the upperclassman who coached me when I first got here."

"I don't think we met him." Consuelo's voice sounded suspicious.

"Sure, Mom, he's the guy who helped coach me and the other quarterbacks the first couple of years. Nicky, I mean Nick, Nick Jeffries."

"Nicky, why do you call him Nicky if his name is Nick?"

Rocky's dad interrupted, "You know, dear, just like we call Ricardo Rocky."

"No, that's not the same. What's his real name?" Consuelo's voice said she would not be sidetracked.

"Nicholas, Mom."

"You should call him Nicholas. Nick is okay."

"Mom, okay, Nick."

"Now, tell me about this Nick. Does he have a girlfriend?"

"Yep."

"When are they getting married?"

Rocky's impatience revealed itself, "Christ, Mom, I have no frigging idea!"

"Watch your mouth, Rocky, don't talk to your mother like that," said his father.

"Okay, sorry. Listen, I gotta go."

"One more thing. Is this Nick and you like you and Umberto, God rest his soul?"

Rocky shuddered. There was silence on the phone.

"Sweetheart," chimed in his father, "He's the one that Rocky pointed out when we were picking him up on campus after a game."

Rocky took six deep breaths during the silence and his father's remark. He thought to himself as his tension subsided with each breath. *Good job Dad, thanks for changing the subject.*

"Oh, sorry Mom. My mistake. Maybe you didn't actually meet him. Anyway, he's a nice guy going to law school for the Navy JAG program."

"What is JAG, *mi amor*? Consuelo had backed off the inquisition.

"Judge Advocate General. They're the lawyers for the Navy and Marine Corps."

"Oh."

"This Nick better not be an Umberto, Rocky!" Consuelo would not let go.

"Yeah, Mom. Okay."

Rocky and his parents finished their conversation. He returned the handset to the wall phone. *After all these years, Mom seems to be loosening up. At least we're talking.* He chuckled to himself.

CHAPTER 14
1988: FLIGHT TRAINING

Sitting in their rented Pensacola house, the four flight-school candidates lounged around the kitchen table, enjoying beer and pizza. "Florida beaches are way different than SoCal beaches," Jed Harden, one of Rocky's housemates, said. "You don't have those waves here."

"Heck, when I was in Miami, we had great surf," answered Rocky.

"Yeah, but this is the Gulf, dead-like in more ways than one. The best things goin' on around here are tail and beer. Plenty of both. Chase the tail, drink the beer, dump the tail and take a piss. You're good to go!" chortled Jed.

Fred Taylor interjected, "Jed, you're a real dumbass. Have you considered you might just have to study and train a little bit?"

"Fuck you, Taylor." Jed got up and headed to the fridge.

"Do you know what the fucking wash-out rate is, party boy?" Tim Thomas asked.

"Not worried, chill out," said Jed.

"You better worry, or we'll have to find a new housemate," cracked Rocky.

"Fuck you, Rocky. Fuck all of you." Jed tossed beers at the trio. All three grumbled about shaking up the beers. Each struck the top of the beers with their thumbs before popping the tab.

"Jed, man, you gotta get serious about this," Rocky continued.

"Leave me alone. We're not at the Academy now and you aren't the bigshot quarterback anymore. Fuck off."

"Chill out, man!" Tim said.

Fred changed the subject. "Hey guys, we gotta muster at MATSG121 at 0800 tomorrow. Word has it we'll get our flight gear."

"That's good news. I feel ridiculous showing up in my civvies. It's like not being part of the program," complained Rocky.

"Quit bitching, Rocky. You'll get your pretty uniform soon enough," shot back Jed.

Rocky got up, looked at Jed and shook his head. He grabbed a legal pad and a pen and went out on the back porch, slamming the wooden screen door behind him. Plopping into a rocker in the shade, he began to write.

Hey Nicky,

Flight school is not what I expected. It's been two months and all of us have spent more time sitting around drinking beer than anything else. All we do is wait.

On top of that, you remember that asshole, Jed Harden? He's been crawling up my backside ever since we got here. It started when he drew the short straw and didn't get a room with a bath. I got the last one and he's been pissed ever since. Sometimes I just want to punch him. I'm surprised he made it to Pensacola. He's always been an underachiever. Remember his bragging about his dad being Top Gun? Must have pulled some strings. Wouldn't surprise me if he washes out.

The beaches suck. No real waves to speak of. Rented a board twice. Not so much fun. The ladies are gorgeous, but I guess you know what I'm looking at!

Have been to several strip clubs with the guys. Talk about boring. Gotta do it, though. I noticed one of the other guys, Fred, looking bored, too. I caught him looking at the guys' crotches. Hmm...

My mother's giving me shit about finding a girl. She said I should be married by the time I get out of flight school. She said it would be good for my career. God, what a pain. I don't think she has any idea just how hard this program is.

We have to muster tomorrow. We haven't been on base in weeks. I've been studying manuals and working out. The swim qualifier is said to be tough. I hear a lot of guys don't make it. You know, sink or swim.

Maybe we'll finally get our Aviation Preflight indoctrination soon. Then it's Christmas. No shit. They call it that when they hand out the flight suits, helmets, sunglasses, leather jacket and all that gear. I'm really looking forward to that.

Wish me luck dealing with asshole Jed.

Over and out!

Rocky

* * *

Three months after reporting to Pensacola, Rocky and his housemates headed to the Naval Aerospace Medical Institute for six weeks of water survival and other training.

"Did you hear Ned failed the swim qual?" said Tim.

"No shit!" said Rocky. He didn't drown, did he?" joked Rocky. "Are they giving him another shot at qualifying in the water?"

"Probably. You know his dad's got pull around here," said Tim.

Rocky thought for a moment. "Not being able to keep your ass afloat is usually the end of a lot of guys. If they give him another shot at it, it'll still set his training back. He better get his ass out of the bars and into the pool and the gym."

"Yep. Maybe he'll be so busy he'll back off on you."

"I hope so, but I doubt it. He really has a bug up his ass. The other day I saw him throw my swim gear off the porch into the mud. He said the wind did it. Not only is he a prick, he's a liar. I sure as hell hope I never fly with or anywhere near him. I think he's the one who ripped up one of my manual. Fred found it in the trash."

"He's just jealous, and scared."

"Scared of what?"

"Getting into jets, or maybe not getting in. His old man was a jet jock. When we were hoisting a few the other day, he said his father could be a real asshole. He got beaten up severely a couple of times when he was a kid. Lots of alcohol and mental abuse. The guy's kinda screwed up. His mother divorced his dad when Jed left for the Academy. She blames his dad's behavior on PTSD. Shooting down jets and strafing people on the ground can really screw a guy up. You could say Jed and his mother are collateral damage."

"That's tough. Maybe I can cut him a huss and ignore him. Better yet, I'll see if we can work things out. I don't need this crap."

Jed burst into the kitchen slamming the screen door.

"Hey Jed, sorry to hear about the swim phys. Don't worry about it. Tim and I've been talking, and we want to help. You know, work out with you.'" Rocky said.

"Don't try to pull that shit on me. I heard you fuckers talking. Just keep out of my way and out of my life!"

"What are you talking about? We're trying to help you!" shouted Tim.

"Fuck you! Fuck you both!"

"Hey, wait a minute! What's wrong with you?" Rocky said.

"Listen, assholes, I don't want shit from either of you!"

Rocky stood jabbing his finger toward Jed's face, "Oh yeah? Who's the asshole? You're the jerk that threw my shit off the porch and trashed my manual!"

Jed shoved Rocky. Regaining his balance, Rocky threw a punch, landing his fist square between Jed's eyes, launching Jed through the screen door. Jed landed flat on his back, out cold.

"Fuck! Jed!" said Rocky as he charged out the door, landing on all fours. He shook Jed. "Shit, Jed, wake up! I'm sorry!"

Tim ran out of the house and threw a pitcher of water on Jed's face. They waited a moment as Jed stirred. Rocky reached under him and tried to prop him up. Jed came to and immediately shook loose from Rocky. He rolled away and sat up. Gathering his senses, he got up slowly, wavered, then walked toward the porch stairs leading to the drive. Stepping down, he stumbled navigating the six stairs. Regaining some balance, he wobbled, walking the length of the driveway.

Rocky and Tim watched him head toward the beach. "Shit, I'm glad I didn't kill him. He's really fucked up."

"I'm glad you didn't kill him, too." sighed Tim. "But you sure fucked him up."

* * *

The swim quals were the toughest physical trials for trainees. After that came land survival. At the end of the six weeks, all but Jed had qualified. Two months later, with his father's "pull," Jed re-entered flight training. He was months behind his housemates.

Rocky, Tim and Fred qualified on the T-34 training. Primary training now accomplished and out of the way, Tim and Fred went on leave, escaping the heat and humidity of the Gulf Coast.

Alone with Jed in the house, Rocky decided to head to the beach, ending the day at Flora Bama, a seedy bar near the Florida and Alabama border. Dressed in flip flops, board shorts and a tank top, he was well into a pitcher of beer and missing Nick when someone pulled up a stool next to him. It was one of the primary flight instructors, Captain Al Simms.

"Hey Chambers, mind if I join you?"

Rocky, somewhat inebriated, looked over. "Sure, no problem." Recognizing the senior officer, he sat up. "Oh, sorry sir. Didn't know it was you."

"Not to worry, relax. Congratulations on making it through Primary."

"Thank you, sir."

"I said relax, were not on base. Call me Al."

"Okay, Al."

"So, what are you doing here?"

"Drinking."

"Looks like it."

The two continued to drink and talk aviation. Oblivious to the crowd, they started discussing personal stuff.

"I heard you and five other hot shots made the Commandant's List. Congratulations. Only guys with top grades and real flying skills get that commendation." Al hoisted his beer and toasted Rocky.

"Thanks, Al. I was surprised. I never thought I'd be on that list." Rocky sat a little straighter and smiled broadly. "Are you going to be there tomorrow afternoon when the old man has all of us in his office?"

"Sure, as shit, wouldn't miss it! Al replied, chucking Rocky under the chin and giving it a friendly shove. They finished their beers and ordered another.

"So, are you dating anyone, Rocky?"

"Nope, just trying to study and make it through the program takes all my time."

"Gotta girl at home?"

"Nope."

"Me neither. I haven't dated girls much. I spend my social time with the boys. How 'bout you?" Al smiled and rested his hand on Rocky's knee.

Rocky was caught off guard. *This guy is hitting on me. Definitely good looking. Always thought so during training. This could prove interesting.* Rocky adjusted himself.

Simms also adjusted himself and turned his bar stool, moving his hand off of Rocky's knee and grazing

Rocky's thigh with his own. Simms took a moment to move away. Both men pulled on their beers.

Rocky, testing the water, brushed Simms's thigh with his knee. Simms did not move away. They continued drinking their beers in silence.

"Wanna go for a walk?"

"Yeah, sounds good," said Rocky.

Paying the tab, they walked out of the bar.

"Listen, let's head back to town and go to my place. I've got some more beer. We can take a couple to the beach," said Rocky.

"Sounds good to me, big boy!" Al gave Rocky a pat on the butt.

Simms jumped on his Harley and followed Rocky to the house.

The house was dark. Opening the fridge, Rocky pulled out a couple of beers.

"So, where're your roomies?"

"Two are on leave and the other is probably out partying."

Simms took a step toward Rocky and ran his hands across Rocky's chest.

"Nice pecs."

"Yeah," Rocky said and did the same to Simms.

"Let's skip the beach."

The next morning, Simms was pushed up against Rocky as they lay naked in bed. Rocky wrapped his arms around Simms. "Hey, we better get going. I've got T-2 Simulator time this morning. You fly'n?"

Simms stirred and pressed himself against Rocky. "Yeah, I need to get going too."

Rocky heard movement in the next room. He whispered excitedly, "Shit, Jed's home. If he finds us here we're sunk!"

Just then the door opened. "Chambers, I need a ride to... Oh shit!" Jed stood gawking at the two naked men sitting up in bed. "Look at you two homos! Fuck!" he laughed. Jed turned and left, leaving the door open.

Simms and Rocky could hear him laughing as he came back into the room. "You know that Commandant's List you're on? The next list you'll be on is the one where your ass is drummed out of the Corps! See ya!" He slammed the bedroom door behind him and left the house. Rocky and Simms could hear him laughing as he walked off.

"We're fucked," said Simms.

Rocky stared at the door, "We sure are. He'll definitely report this. That was a short Naval Aviation career," groaned Rocky. He had not taken his eyes off the door. "What can we do?"

"Nothing," said Simms, lying back with his eyes closed. "I've seen this before. They'll quietly discharge us. Hopefully honorably, but more than likely, dishonorably. That would be the end of me either way. Shit. I have nowhere else to go. I'm done."

Rocky didn't move. He didn't see Simms dress and leave. He sat upright in the bed for an hour. His mind was blank. No feeling. No pain. He was numb. The phone rang. He reached over and picked it up.

"Chambers here."

"Chambers, the old man is making the presentation at 1300 hours in his office. Be there."

Rocky didn't respond.

"Chambers, did you hear me?"

"Chambers are you there?"

"Yes, I'll be there."

Rocky sat holding the receiver as the dial tone blared.

Regaining his senses, he headed for the shower. He stood there, water running down his back. *I can deny it. Jed doesn't have any credibility. Everybody thinks he's a fuck-up. The only reason Jed's here is his old man's some kind of hero. Maybe he won't run his mouth.* Rocky shuddered. *That asshole will talk. Why the fuck did I have to knock him out? Sonofabitch!*

Rocky drove to the base and entered the T-2 flight simulator. He concentrated on the training.

* * *

An hour earlier, Jed walked out onto the flight line toward the T-34 trainer. Standing alongside the aircraft, he spied Simms. Jed rendered a salute. "Good morning, sir," Jed smirked as Simms returned the salute.

Jed discarded military courtesy. "Well, we meet again. Did you have a nice night fucking my housemate? Tell me all about it. I'm happy to tell the old man. I'm scheduled to see him later this afternoon." The sarcasm was only eclipsed by his cockiness.

"Shut the fuck up and get in the aircraft."

Ten minutes later, the trainer lifted into the sky. Jed had the controls. "There's been a change in the training schedule today," Simms spoke to Jed through the aircraft intercom as the two helmeted men headed out across the Gulf.

"Okay, sir. What's up? Or maybe I shouldn't use that term."

"We're doing stalls."

* * *

Rocky exited the Turbomentor simulator and headed toward the Commanding Officer's office. He had expected to see the other five awardees waiting in the outer office. He was the only one there. "Excuse me," directing his question to an office clerk. "Am I late? Where is everybody? I thought the ceremony was at 1300 hours. It's 1255."

"Sorry sir, but it's been rescheduled."

"What? I was called this morning and informed it was today at 1300."

"Yes, sir. It was just changed. Are you Lieutenant Chambers?"

"Yes."

"The C.O. said for you to go on in when you got here."

Rocky, bewildered, adjusted his uniform. He took a deep breath and walked over to the door and knocked three times.

"Come in, Lieutenant," roared the Commanding Officer.

Rocky opened the door; marched in and stood at attention. "Lieutenant Chambers reporting as ordered, sir!"

"Sit down, Lieutenant."

Rocky took a seat in the chair opposite the CO. His mind was blank as he looked straight ahead.

"Lieutenant, as you know, we were scheduled to award you and five other men a commendation today." He paused for almost a minute.

The CO adjusted his position, leaned forward, his hands clasped. "I have some terrible news for you. Your friend and housemate, Lieutenant Harden, and his instructor were killed during flight training today." The CO was visibly shaken.

Rocky's eyes grew wide. His head swam as his body recoiled. *Jed gone, OMG! The man who was going to destroy me and Al, gone.*

"Sir, may I ask, who was the instructor? You said he was killed too?"

Rocky had an alarming premonition. *God, no please don't let it be Al.*

"Yes, Lieutenant Harden and Captain Simms are presumed dead. I am sorry to have to tell you this."

Rocky struggled to steel his emotions. He was in a freefall with the agony of the death of two men, one an enemy and the other a newfound lover. He was alone enmeshed in a red-hot searing agony. An agony that he could not share with anyone. No solace. No respite. *Nicky, I need you now, more than ever.*

In the silent room, the ship's clock mounted on the wall struck two bells, startling them both.

"Sir, does anyone know what happened?"

"All we know is that touch and go training was changed to stall recovery. It was out in the Gulf."

"Thank you, sir." Sir, if there is anything I can do to assist the Command or the Lieutenant's family, please let me know."

"Thank you, Lieutenant."

"Yes, sir."

"On another topic, do you know why Lieutenant Harden wanted the three of us to meet later this afternoon?"

Rocky sat in the chair contemplating what he would say next.

"Sir, I didn't know anything about a meeting. When he left the house this morning, he didn't say anything about meeting with you."

"Thank you, Lieutenant. Dismissed."

"Thank you, sir."

Rocky rose out of his chair, came to attention, saluted, did an about-face and exited the office.

"Oh, Lieutenant!" The CO shouted. "I've had orders issued placing you on leave for ten days. When this sinks in, you'll need the time away from here."

Rocky returned to the doorway, saluted, and executed another about-face, departing the CO's office.

Rocky returned to the house and started packing Jed's things. He sat on Jed's bed, his head in his hands, and allowed the enormity of Al's actions to sweep through him.

Taking control of his emotions, he continued to pack Jed's things. Piling the boxes in the corner of the room. He collapsed in front of them. *If Al and I had never met, this never would have happened. Did I kill them? My God, forgive me. Forgive me for being so selfish. Forgive me for my part in this. Jed, I'm sorry. I'm sorry I wasn't a good friend. I'm sorry I wasn't there to help you through your troubles.*

Rocky carried one of Jed's boxes out to the car. His head swimming, he had to put it down. He sat on the box, remembering Al's words. *I've seen this before. They'll quietly discharge us. Hopefully honorably, but more than likely, dishonorably. That would be the end of me either way. Shit. I have nowhere else to go. I'm done.*

Rocky thought out loud, "It wasn't an accident. The stall didn't kill them. Al did."

Rocky loaded several boxes and returned to the house and his room, collapsing on his bed. Rolling over he felt something metal. Reaching underneath his back he retrieved a watch. Al's watch. Rocky remembered taking the watch off his wrist as they made love the night before. Clutching the watch to his chest, Rocky murmured, "You shouldn't have done it."

CHAPTER 15
1992: COMBAT

Rocky completed training in the T-34, Intermediate in the T-2, and advanced training in the A-4. He found himself with orders to Naval Air Station Whiting, and then jet training at Meridian, MS and F-18s at Jacksonville, FL. Three years and the flight-training program finally ended. Rocky was assigned to an aircraft carrier in the South Pacific.

* * *

Dear Dad and Mom,

It looks like our meeting in Singapore will have to wait. The squadron has been reassigned. I can't tell you much more. We're needed elsewhere. It would have been great to see you, but all leaves have been cancelled. The squadron will have flown off the carrier and be on its way to our new duty station before you get this. Use the same address if you write.

The good news is I get to keep flying the F-18. I love that bird. It's the best aircraft in the arsenal. It flies fast and high. I've had plenty of training but believe me, being thrown into the skies off a rocking ship by monster catapults is like no other experience I've ever had. The power and exhilaration of twin engines on the Hornet makes me feel like an astronaut. Unlike the astronauts, I've got missiles and bombs and a Vulcan cannon on board that can destroy anything in my path. It was worth the three-year flight-training grind.

Landing on the deck of a rolling runway at sea is like trying to put down on a postage stamp. But the feeling of the arresting cables grabbing the tail hook when you touch down is a huge relief, knowing you're not going to go rolling off the end of the ship and into the drink.

I don't know if we'll be land-based or carrier-based. I'll miss the carrier landings if it's a land base. Just glad I haven't flown off the end of the ship.

Again, I'm disappointed we won't be seeing each other soon. Love to Sophie and Alejandro.

Semper Fi!

Love,

Rocky

* * *

Two months later, Rocky was sitting in the wardroom aboard the *USS Saratoga*. Flipping through a magazine and drinking coffee, he looked up at the TV monitor. A CNN banner reported:

US F-18 Seen on Russian Video Downing Five Iraqi Aircraft

Rocky shot up out of his chair, upending his coffee. "Shit!"

He caught the attention of several fellow aviators. "Looks like your ass has been caught!" said one.

"You don't know what you're talking about," Rocky said as he tried to clean up the coffee and retrieve the magazine from the floor.

"We know something's up," another aviator quipped. "Yours was the first Winchester I've seen in a long time. Yours is the only aircraft that's come back with no bombs, missiles and no tanks. We haven't seen a Winchester around here in months."

"How would you know that?" one of Rocky's friends said, trying to defend his buddy.

"Everybody on the hangar deck's talking about it."

"Shit, you can't hide anything aboard this ship. Damn it!" said the Squadron Commander entering the room.

"Attention!" Rang out from someone. All present in the wardroom sprang to attention.

"At ease, gentlemen. Captain Chambers, report to my office A.S.A.P.," Squadron Commanding Officer Patel ordered.

"Yes, sir!" Rocky said.

This wasn't the first time Rocky had been summoned to the CO's office. The CO seemed to have a chip on his shoulder and most of the pilots avoided him.

Once inside the stateroom, Rocky closed the hatch behind him and took a seat at the CO's request. The CO sat at his desk and leafed through some official-looking papers. Rocky sat straight up. He was uncomfortable in the metal chair, but he didn't dare move. *I did just as I was ordered. I had a successful mission. What is this about?*

"Chambers remain seated. I'll be right back," the CO said, getting up from his chair.

"Yes, sir!"

Rocky replayed the events of several days ago in his head. The same squadron CO had summoned him to his office. He had told the Marine stationed outside his hatch that under no circumstances was he to be disturbed.

He had started the meeting with, "Captain, I am giving you the chance of a lifetime. You're not my first choice for this mission, but SecDef has requested you. I'm not sure whose ass you kissed or what higher-up you've impressed. Who do you know? Who's your father?"

Shifting in his chair. "William Chambers, sir."

"Never heard of him. Are you related to any government bigwigs or politicians?"

"No, sir."

Rocky felt sweat forming on his brow. Commander Patel, short and round, sat back in his chair and scratched his chin.

"Chambers. Are you related to any of the Chambers Enterprises family?"

Rocky stared. *Crap.*

"I'm waiting, Captain."

"Well, sir, sort of."

"Sort of? You either are or you're not. Which is it?" Patel placed his arms on the desk and leaned forward.

Rocky stared straight ahead and swallowed hard.

"Okay, that's obvious. How are you related?"

Drawing air through his nose and letting it escape through his nose, "The Chairman of the Board and CEO is my grandfather."

Cmdr. Patel sat up straight in his chair and with a contemptuous grin barked, "Well, shit. No wonder. We've got a blueblood. An Annapolis blueblood. Yeah, I remember. Your file said you quarterbacked for the Academy. I think I saw you on TV in an Army-Navy Game. Guess they think just because you can throw pigskins you can drive a plane." Cmdr. Patel sank lower in his chair, agitated. He clenched the paperwork in his hands.

"I've seen pictures of your grandfather with every president I can remember." The CO shifted in his chair. He placed the tortured papers on his desk and made a weak attempt to press out some of the creases he had inflicted. He folded his arms. "If you fuck this up, we're all toast."

The Commander picked up the paperwork and jammed it into a folder. He leaned forward and thrust it at Rocky. The folder was marked Top Secret.

Rocky's orders had been to seek and destroy. It was a solo mission. No support; not even a wingman. He was supposed to bomb the crap out of an Iraqi, Russian-manned air-control facility and, if possible, neutralize any aircraft attempting to escape. Russian intelligence must have known of the attack. Three MIGs got airborne. It was like shooting ducks in a barrel. One, two, three! Then the MIG 25s appeared out of nowhere.

Patel returned to his chair behind the desk.

Rocky's head was still fogged in. He yanked himself back to the present.

"Captain, two days ago, when you were sitting in that same chair, I had misgivings about sending you on that mission. Here we are, two days later. When I was reviewing your report, I was okay with it until you were making the turn to get back to the ship after you nailed those three MIG 23s. It's Iraq's 25s that I'm not so sure about. Give me the details. Start from the beginning."

"Sir, as you know from my report, the aircraft was carrying two A9M Sidewinders, two AMRAAMs on the right outboard station and one AMRAAM on the right cheek station. I also carried a 2,000-pounder and a 500-pounder laser-guided bomb. I had a Single Centerline fuel tank and another tank on the inboard wet station." Rocky waited for the Commander to comment or say something. Patel sat at his desk, hands folded, saying nothing. Rocky thought, *did he hear what I said? Hmm. I'll just keep going.*

"There were no issues getting to the target. When I reached it, I dropped both bombs. While conducting the battle assessment studying the forward-looking infrared, I noticed three MIG 23s on takeoff roll. Immediately I hit the pickle switch and dropped the fuel tanks. I made an immediate hard left bull's eye nose low turn right over the airfield. I pulled right up behind them as the three aircraft lifted off and were just done retracting their gear and joining up when I engaged. Lock-shoot-step, lock-shoot-step, lock-shoot-step. 1-2-3 I took them out. Fox 3 times three and splash three, completely unbelievable!" He paused, noticing that Patel had not moved. He just stared at Rocky.

The CO arched one nostril as his sniffed, "Keep going, Captain."

Rocky continued, "I was banking starboard when the lock on alarms went off. I hadn't noticed two MIG 25s that must have been taxiing for takeoff when I had spotted the 23s earlier. I had to do something. I firewalled to max power, pulled back on the stick and broke hard. I shot straight up, thinking they wouldn't expect it. Frankly, I was scared shitless. I held off unloading the chaff until the incoming missiles got close. It must have worked. It surprised me when the Iraqis didn't follow me. Then it dawned on me, they were running straight for Iran. What the heck, I thought. Those clowns are trying to get away. Air

Interdiction was part of the mission. That's when I got greedy."

Cmdr. Patel kept his attention on Rocky and said nothing.

"At 8,000 feet, I dropped down directly behind them. I thought I'd won the lottery! I went after 'em. They were moving out fast. I wasn't sure I could keep up long enough to knock 'em down. I locked the first one up with tone and fired. I locked up the second one with tone and fired. The friggin' sky lit up as those boys met their maker!"

The Commander continued looking directly at the Captain. He didn't move.

Rocky felt his shirt cling to his back, sweat rushing out of every pore.

"Yeah, Captain, in Iranian airspace. Now we have an international crisis. Someone caught you dead to rights. The fucking Russians! They have it on video. It's plain as day. I'm surprised they don't have a picture of you smiling and flipping them off!"

"Yes, sir! I mean, no sir!" Rocky was now sweating profusely.

"President Tanner is pissed. For Christ's sake! He's just been sworn in, and here you are creating his first international crisis. We're goddamn lucky he's a Republican and supports the military. We're also lucky he gave the Defense Department the go-ahead to do what we need to do. At least we have that in writing. It's still a diplomatic nightmare." As the Commander stood up he said to Rocky, "Stay seated."

"I'm sorry, sir. I had no idea it would come to this."

"Don't be sorry, Captain. You did exactly what I would've done. What anyone would've done. You executed your orders. You sure are a lucky son of a bitch. First of all, you didn't follow procedures and roll up and out when one of those Russians locked on. That sure as shit should go in the record books: F-18 kills three 23s at one time! Then dropping two 25's! You've punched your own ticket. Congrats.

Rocky's pulse thundered and his back ached.

The CO handed several sheets of paper to Rocky. "These are your orders: Report to the Secretary of Defense. Yes, the SecDef himself. You're leaving immediately. Pack your shit and get out of here."

* * *

Rocky entered the Secretary of Defense's office two days later.

"Sit down, Captain," Secretary Nelson said.

"Yes, sir!"

The Secretary came from behind his desk and sat in a chair opposite Rocky.

"Son, we have a problem. You created it. You created it by following orders. Not only did you follow orders, you surpassed them." He paused. "That's the problem. You destroyed an Iraqi Air Control Facility manned by Russians. You shot down three Iraqis." The Secretary paused and sat back in his chair.

"I beg your pardon, sir, but I shot down five," Rocky said, interrupting the Secretary.

"Therein lies the crux of the problem. Entering Iranian airspace, we can deal with. You also shot down two Russians flying Iraqi aircraft."

Rocky heard his pulse pounding in his ears.

"It's your lucky day. The president has decided to change the narrative. In order to make wine out of water President Tanner has decided to award you the Medal of Honor. You are an Air Ace." The Secretary held out his hand.

Rocky sat still, stunned. He didn't notice the secretary's hand.

"Captain, congratulations. Now shake my hand."

"Oh, um, uh, sir. Yes, sir!" Rocky said, taking the secretary's hand and shaking it vigorously.

"Please let go of my hand, son," Secretary Nelson said, smiling.

Rocky did. "Sorry, sir."

"Do me a favor, quit apologizing," the secretary laughed. Captain Chambers, I would like to take a moment to explain why the president is doing what he is doing. First of all, you've earned the medal. So accept it and be proud. Now, let's review the politics. President Tanner is new to the job. He has decided to use this incident to establish himself as a strong military leader. He looks at this as an opportunity to let our adversaries and allies know that we are going to maintain and strengthen our position on the world stage. What better way to do that than fulfill his predecessor's commitment to peace in the Middle East. It doesn't hurt that he gets to tweak the noses of the Russians at the same time."

"It's that simple," Secretary Nelson continued. "Remember, the Constitution tasks the military with advancing the political and economic interests of the United States. You served the nation and our interests. Thank you."

The secretary stood up. Rocky stood up.

"Captain Chambers, it's a pleasure meeting you. I look forward to attending the ceremony at the White House."

"White House?" Rocky mumbled.

"Of course, where else would you do it? The Boy Scouts Jamboree?"

"Yes, sir, I mean, no sir. Thank you, sir."

"Captain don't be surprised if we reach out to you in the near future. We need men like you. Men that think fast and make good decisions."

CHAPTER 16
1992: KIDNAPPED

Following the Medal of Honor ceremony and his assignation with the president, Rocky returned to the Private Residence. The president joined them a few minutes later as if nothing had happened. He was charming and gracious to Rocky's family, as was the first lady

Late the following afternoon, Rocky accompanied his family in the car provided by the White House from Blair House to Joint Forces Andrews Air Force Base. He hugged them all goodbye and returned to the car. Inside the limousine, he found an envelope placed on the console next to his seat. The envelope had not been there when he and his family had exited the vehicle only ten minutes earlier. And there was a new driver.

"Driver, you're not the same guy who drove us here. What's up?"

"Sorry, sir, I was asked by the first lady to take you to your aircraft."

"What do you mean, my aircraft? I am ticketed on a flight back to El Toro in California. What does Mrs. Tanner have to do with this?"

"She asked me to hand deliver the envelope. She requires discretion."

Rocky felt his palms moisten. *Had she found out about him and the president?* Rocky wanted out of the car. This was not the way things were done. Something was wrong. This was not like the Navy or the Marine Corps.

The driver left the tarmac as the jet pulled away. Before the conversation could resume, the limousine was waved through a side gate reserved for VIPs. Rocky was accustomed to controlling whatever vehicle he was in, be it car or jet. How could he stop the car? Get out of the car? Stop the driver?

Toggling a button on the dashboard, the driver raised the privacy screen between the front seat and the rear compartment to three-quarters height. The vehicle was soon bookended by two motorcycles in the front and two in the back. The motorcycle lights were flashing, but there were no sirens. The limousine circled the base's outside perimeter. He was trapped, and he knew it. Rocky loosened his tie, unbuttoning the blouse's top button. It did nothing to relieve the anxiety. Flying at supersonic speeds was exhilarating. This felt like fight or flight.

"Open the envelope, sir."

Rocky stared at the rear-view mirror, into the eyes of the driver looking directly at him. That's when he noticed a second man sitting in the front passenger's seat. Rocky stared at the driver's reflection. Neither of them flinched.

"Sir, open the envelope. It won't bite you."

Rocky reached across the seat and grabbed the envelope. He tore it open only to find another envelope inside, this one crafted from a luxurious heavy cream-colored paper. The upper left side was embossed with gold lettering: FLOTUS. His curiosity gave way to apprehension. She had to know what had transpired in the president's private office. *I guess I can kiss my career and the Medal of Honor goodbye.*

"Sir, open the letter. Now!"

Rocky, startled, tore at the embossed envelope. The top of the first of two pages was also embossed in gold: *FIRST LADY OF THE UNITED STATES.* In a smaller type just below, it read *JOSEPHINE TANNER.* He began to read.

Dear Captain Chambers,

Or should I call you Rocky? I guess it's okay if I address you as Rocky. After all, that's what my husband calls you.

You can call me Mrs. Tanner. Just because you call my husband Hammer, it doesn't mean you can be informal with me. When you've completed reading this letter, the two gentlemen in the car with you will ensure that it is destroyed. These men are in my employ. You will never see them again. Unless, of course, you don't keep your private interview with the president to yourself.

These men cannot be found. You can be found.

Rocky, I am intent on my husband serving two very successful terms. I am my husband's most effective supporter and trusted advisor. Your intimacy with my husband has served him and me well.

Are you surprised that I know? I arranged it. Why did I arrange it?

My husband has needs. When you two first locked eyes on the dais, I knew immediately what must be done. Don't think of me as jaded. Think of me as serving our country. Funny, you probably didn't know you were serving the country as you "serviced" one another. You're a tool. And a tool can be discarded. You will never speak of this to anyone.

Now that you have served my purposes, my husband can concentrate on being president. It has been two years of a long, tiring and dehumanizing campaign. At the end of that grueling journey, he needed to re-establish his equilibrium. You helped him do that.

Do not reach out to either of us. I never want to see or hear from you again.

Josephine Tanner

Rocky sat staring blankly at the letter. Oblivious to his surroundings, he hadn't noticed the limousine had pulled off the road into a remote area. The gentle humming of the adjacent door window being lowered startled him. He looked up and to his right. A nondescript man in a nondescript dark suit stood in a white shirt and colorless tie. Sunglasses covered much of his plain-featured face. His palm was turned upward, inches from Rocky's face.

"Give him the letter and envelopes," the driver said.

Rocky heard the order, muffled by a steady ringing in his ears. He did not move. He sat frozen, staring at the man, the letter resting in his lap, clasped between his hands.

"Captain," the driver said, "we don't have all day, give him the letter and envelopes!"

The man outside the car had not moved.

In slow motion, Rocky lifted his right hand, holding the letter and envelopes toward the large hand reaching in the car window. The hand demanded the words that could destroy the President of the United States. Words that shell-shocked Rocky and could change his life. The large hand took the words, turned his back to the car and stepped away. He appeared to place the letter and envelopes in a small metal container. The smell of charred burning paper soon wafted into the car.

The smoke stimulated Rocky's senses as he surveilled his surroundings. The escort was nowhere to be seen. He contemplated the irony of his environment. He, in his Marine Corps uniform, sat in the back seat of a luxury limousine, surrounded by magnificent trees, a distant babbling brook, chirping birds, burning paper, and gangsters in the employ of the first lady of the United States.

Moments later, the car and its occupants headed back to the main road. Soon they arrived at a private airport, not far from CIA Headquarters in Langley. The limousine pulled into a large hangar. The driver came to a stop alongside an unmarked medium-sized executive jet. A fit young woman dressed in tailored slacks, a white blouse and dark jacket opened Rocky's door. Her hair was short and the cut simple. She, too, wore sunglasses.

Rocky stepped out of the car and walked the few short steps to the aircraft's boarding ramp. His baggage and personal belongings were removed from the trunk of the car as he boarded the jet. The door to the cockpit was secured shut. There were no attendants in the cabin. He took a seat. This was a VIP aircraft. Exquisitely appointed, it could have carried at least twenty passengers. Rocky knew jets. This Gulfstream was fresh off the assembly line. It was customized. It flew high and fast. He heard a thud and a hard close, securing a hatch outside that must lead to the compartment holding his belongings. That felt normal. He would have liked to have his luggage close by, but he would soon have access to it. They would arrive at his base in California in five hours. He assumed that was where they were headed.

Rocky was relieved he was alone. The last twenty-four hours had been a rollercoaster of emotions and strange events. A relaxing flight to California would be nice, hopefully turbulence-free.

The jet's engines fired up. The whispering noise of the ventilation system was comforting alongside the powerful sound and feel of the Pratt & Whitney jet engines. Moments later, the jet slowly emerged from the hangar. The aircraft was no ordinary jet. It was large enough to look ominous, yet small enough to say sophistication and dexterity. Purposely moving along the tarmac toward the end of the runway, the jet accelerated through the turn as the engines powered up for takeoff.

Rocky had located a bottle of scotch and a glass near his seat. He anticipated the gentle but firm G-force that would soon press against his chest, serving as a comfortable blanket, settling him in.

The jet hurtled down the runway, rising powerfully and gracefully into the early afternoon sky. Rocky leaned back in his leather seat as he closed his eyes and savored the comfortable taste of smoky scotch sliding down his throat. He continued to relax as the G-force enveloped him. His eyes remained shut as the jet climbed to its cruising altitude of 40,000 feet. As the aircraft leveled off, he slowly opened his eyes.

On the table opposite his seat were two envelopes.

Rocky didn't have the energy or the will to confront the envelopes at that moment. He leaned back against the seat and closed his eyes, retreating from the obvious.

CHAPTER 17
EUROPEAN ASSIGNMENT

Rocky relaxed, comfortable on the jet following what could only be called his kidnapping.

ᴄaptain Chambers, we have run into some air traffic that has delayed our arrival. We will keep you informed as to our progress," said the First Officer standing next to him.

Rocky, startled, sat up. "Okay, thanks." The First Officer returned to the cockpit. Rocky tried to clear his head. The first lady obviously didn't want him to say anything stupid to the press, so getting him out of DC quickly made sense. He sat in the Gulfstream jet, Scotch in hand, staring at the two envelopes. The larger one looked threatening. There appeared to be another packet inside. The outer envelope was not sealed.

Rocky reached for the mysterious smaller envelope. The dark blue packet measured about eight by five inches. It was constructed of heavy paper and was sealed. The diplomatic- looking casing had "United States Government Official Business" embossed in gold leaf. He broke open the diplomatic seal and pulled out a booklet. The red cover appeared to be some sort of passport. He was familiar with blue passports, but not red ones. He opened the cover. His picture in a civilian coat and tie jumped out at him. *What is this? This looks like a diplomatic passport. That's my picture, but I don't have clothes like that.*

Rocky flipped through the passport. Aside from the diplomatic designation, it had all the characteristics of a normal passport. He gazed out the window and took note of the sun on the port side of the plane. He rose from his chair and went to the starboard side. The ocean was tens of thousands of feet below. Something was wrong. They were headed northeast, not west.

Rocky returned to his seat and picked up the phone. He pressed the button labeled *Cockpit.*

"Yes, Captain Chambers, how can I help you?"

"Are you the pilot?"

"Yes."

"I thought we were headed to California. We're headed north. What's up?"

"That's correct. We'll be landing in ninety minutes. I have been instructed to advise you to review the contents of the envelopes in preparation for our landing."

"Landing where?"

"Boston."

"Why Boston?"

"I am afraid I am not at liberty to discuss that."

Rocky realized the guy was just the pilot and probably didn't know anything. "Okay, thanks." He hung up. *What's in Boston?* He glanced down at the thick envelope. There was a lot of material to get through in ninety minutes.

Rocky turned the large envelope upside down. Out slid an ominous package with "Top Secret Eyes Only" in red across the top. Holding the envelope in both hands, he tried to steady them. Rocky broke the seal on the envelope. He paused, then removed a binder. He opened the cover and began to read the 180-page, double-sided, double-spaced document. *If I'm going to get through this, I better get started.* He finished off the glass of scotch and dove into the material.

* * *

Ninety minutes later, after having completed his first read, he placed the binder on the table in front of him. He gazed out the window, the plane descending, passing through the clouds and revealing the sparkling ocean below.

"We're on our final descent, sir. Please secure your seatbelt," the First Officer announced, standing several feet away. Rocky had not heard anyone approach. Any approaching sound was muffled by the white noise of the Pratt & Whitney engines.

"Okay." He buckled his belt. He returned to the binder and started to review what he had just read. Apparently, he had been assigned orders to NATO.

* * *

Twenty-five minutes later, the aircraft landed and taxied down the tarmac. Rocky returned the top-secret document to its envelope. He placed it in a nearby compartment for safekeeping. He remained seated as the First Officer re-entered the cabin from the cockpit and prepared to open the Gulfstream's door. The jet taxied into a large hangar and came to a stop. The engines wound down as the hatch opened.

The First Officer walked over to Rocky. "Captain, you'll be joined shortly by three individuals."

Rocky didn't say a word. He turned his gaze to the window and into the hangar. Grandfather Chambers' Rolls Royce had just pulled up alongside the plane.

Rocky's heart began to beat faster as he gripped the arms of the leather seat. *So, Grandfather is part of the effort outlined in the document. It wouldn't surprise me if he wrote it. The SecDef and the Tanners must be in on this, too. I've been played ever since I got to Washington! Okay, stay in charge of your emotions. Be respectful, but not cowed.*

Rudolph Chambers exited the car as Harold opened the door. Two other people exited from the far side. One man and one woman retrieved luggage and cases from the trunk of the car. They were too far away for Rocky to identify them. Rocky watched his grandfather make his way to the plane.

Still in uniform, he rose from his seat and made his way to the hatch. "Captain, would you please remain in the aircraft?" Rocky stopped short of the hatch and waited for his grandfather to board. The sound of the cargo bay being opened and loaded reverberated inside the cabin. The old man boarded the aircraft confident, powerful; obviously in charge.

"Grandfather, what a wonderful surprise. One among many, I might add."

"Nice to see you too, son." They shook hands.

Rocky was eyeing the hatch as Nick Jeffries entered the plane in civilian attire. He was carrying a briefcase in one hand with two garment bags draped over the other. Inwardly, Rocky shuddered. His palms began to sweat. The collar of his shirt instantly glued itself with sweat to his neck. He stood staring at the lover he hadn't seen in two years.

"Rocky, you know Lieutenant Commander Jeffries," Grandfather said, gesturing towards the JAG officer.

Nick winked and smiled at Rocky. Rocky managed a smile as he clasped his hands in front of him. "Yes, I do, Grandfather. You know I do. You know I know you do. What's this all about?"

A familiar woman boarded the aircraft.

"Good. And of course, you remember my Executive Assistant, Sonja Abrams," said his grandfather.

"So nice to see you again, Ms. Abrams."

"Nice to see you too, Rocky." She smiled, placing her briefcase on the deck. "You look so handsome in your uniform. Congratulations on being awarded the Medal of Honor."

"Thank you."

"Captain Chambers, we're going to be topping off the fuel on the other side of the field," the First Officer said. "Do you need any of your gear stowed in the baggage compartment before we take off?"

"Thank you, perhaps the small bag containing my toiletries would be helpful."

"Yes sir."

Moments later, his personal effects in hand, the door was closed and secured. The aircraft was towed out of the hangar toward the fueling facility.

"Rocky, these are yours." Nick handed the garment bags to Rocky.

"Rocky, at some point you'll want to change into the clothes we brought you. I had my bespoke tailor put some things together for you. They'll have to do until you can acquire additional items as needed."

"Sure, Grandfather. Thank you." Rocky paused. "When are you going to fill me in?" he asked.

Rudolph Chambers made his way to the large seating area. The area had four comfortable chairs. A small conference table was situated between them. "Everyone, please come over here and take a seat. It'll take some time to bring everyone up to speed."

Rocky got the attention of the First Officer arranging items in the forward cabin. "Excuse me, but isn't it against regulations to fuel this aircraft with passengers aboard?"

"Normally, it would be, but for security reasons that requirement has been waived."

"Aren't we going to change crews? The flight to Europe is too long for the same crew to make the flight without a break."

"That's true. We have taken that into consideration. You can spell the pilot during the crossing."

"But, I'm not checked out in this aircraft."

"According to protocol, it is acceptable for you to pilot the aircraft in flight as long as there is a qualified pilot in the right seat. You can't take off or land the craft, but you can fly it."

"I see. Happy to assist where I can."

The four met for two hours as the jet flew toward Brussels.

"Let's review the purpose of the trip and bring everyone up to speed. But first, Rocky, I'd like to apologize to you for this unexpected change of events. As you know, your grandmother and I would have loved to have been present at your medal presentation. We were told to make our excuses so as not to attract attention to Chambers Enterprises and perhaps compromise our plans. Missing that momentous event distressed your grandmother and me greatly."

Rocky looked solemnly at his grandfather, "Yes, it was a big disappointment for me, too."

"Now, down to business. The purpose of this mission is threefold. I am heading this small delegation on behalf of several corporations and the president. Sonja will be assisting me with administrative duties. Lieutenant Commander Jeffries will be handling contracts and agreements on behalf of the State Department and the Navy. You, Rocky, will serve as the Joint Chiefs of Staff liaison and technical representative."

"Grandfather, I don't understand. I don't carry the rank or have the experience to function in that capacity."

"Don't worry about rank. You will be functioning as an at-large representative of the Department of the Navy. As far as expertise, you are more qualified than you realize."

"While in Europe, we'll be interfacing with the NATO powers and the Israelis. Our primary goal is to ascertain the viability of supplying our allies with sensitive military equipment and technology. As a team, we will review needs and the logistics for meeting those needs. All of us are members of a classified delegation. We report directly to the Department of Defense and the State Department. I have been asked to keep the White House apprised of all developments. Officially, we are on a fact-finding mission. We are exploring opportunities on how NATO can expand its military capabilities with new members."

The First Officer served dinner. Small talk occupied the dinner conversation. Rocky abstained from cocktails and wine served with dinner.

"I'm going to go see if I can spell the captain." Rocky removed his uniform jacket and went forward to the cockpit.

Three hours later the plane's captain took the controls from Rocky and landed the plane in Brussels. The four were met by a nondescript van and transported to the American delegation's compound. Introductions were made. Offices were assigned. From there, they were transported to a boutique hotel on the outskirts of the city.

"When you get settled in your room, Rocky, give me a holler."

"Okay, Nicky."

* * *

"Did you notice that our rooms are adjoined?" grinned Nick as the two enjoyed an afternoon wine on the hotel's terrace.

Rocky welcomed the fresh air after spending nine hours on the jet. The traffic hum was welcome white noise. So much quieter than the jet engines he had endured for hours.

"I was hoping that door went somewhere special," teased Rocky. You know, there are a lot of eyes on us. A significant number in the European espionage community want to know our real purpose."

"Well, maybe not their eyes, but certainly their ears. The rooms are sure to be bugged. We have our assets sanitizing our rooms for bugs daily. The hotel staff is made up of CIA operatives. We just have to assume someone is always listening."

"Good to know," Rocky said. He leaned forward. He whispered, "I was looking for you at the White House ceremony. You said you would be there."

"I am so sorry. I wanted to be there. I was so pissed when your grandfather told me the higher-ups said none of us could go. They said it might attract attention and somehow compromise our mission. I am not sure how it would, but I followed orders."

"Something tells me that you and the old man are a lot closer than I thought."

Nick sat back, looking around to see if anyone could hear them. "Yeah, you're right. We're pretty close. Close enough that he knows about us." Nick shifted in his chair, looking at Rocky.

"Fuck, I knew it. I wished he didn't. But what the hell, he seemed to know I was gay before I did. At least that's what I figure," Rocky said. Did you know he had people watching me at the Academy? He and the Admiral are buddies, for Christ sake."

"Yeah, he told me."

Rocky's face tensed as his eyes pierced Nick's. "So, he knows everything?" Rocky leaned closer, fuming, "Did you kiss and tell?"

"Settle down. He wants to talk to us about it. It's not the end of the world. He knows. So what? What's done is done. Now, listen. He asked me to let you know he knows. He figured if I warned you, you'd have time to get over him knowing about us. You need to be able to concentrate on what he has to say, and he thought you would need time to process the information. Looks like he was right."

"It's not fair that I wasn't in on it from the beginning. I've been treated like shit the last 24 hours. You can't imagine." The veins on Rocky's neck were standing out. His forehead was perspiring, the moisture glistening on the short, wavy tendrils of blond hair hanging off to one side.

"Rocky, I've missed you. I want you."

Rocky coughed, "Bullshit!"

They sat silently, contemplating the hum of the traffic while studying their glasses.

"That ole codger," Rocky complained, "he's always miles ahead of us all. What do you think he wants to talk about?"

"Us."

"Us?"

"Yep."

"Jesus, I can only imagine. When does he want to do that?"

"We're having dinner in his suite in a little while."

"Great." Rocky held up his empty glass. "I think I'll have a couple more of these before *that* powwow."

"Just a couple?" Nick snorted.

* * *

"Come in, gentlemen."

Rocky and Nick, fortified by consuming a bottle of French wine, entered the sitting room of Rudolph Chambers' suite. Wine, cheese, crackers and fruit covered a Louis XIV banquette.

"Nice room, Grandfather."

"Thanks, Rocky. Why don't you two men help yourselves to some wine and *hors d'oeuvres*? I've dismissed the hotel staff until dinner. You'll have to fend for yourselves."

Well provisioned, the three men gathered around a low table, the younger men on a settee, and the older Chambers in a period antique chair across from them. The dimly lit crystal chandelier hung from the twelve-foot ceiling. Light reflected off several gilded mirrors strategically placed throughout the room. "This place feels like a museum," said Nick.

"I feel at home. Louis XIV and I are contemporaries," chuckled the old man.

Nick and Rocky, as if on cue, raised their glasses towards Rudolph. "Here's to our 17th century mentor!" quipped Rocky. Rocky and Nick clinked glasses. Grandfather simply raised his and took a drink. His countenance signaled he was not as amused as the boys.

"Okay, gentlemen. We have a lot to talk about. This isn't business. This is personal. Let's attack the elephant in the room, one bite at a time."

Rocky and Nick exchange "oh shit" glances.

Sitting side by side, they leaned back on the fragile furniture. It creaked. They both sprang back up into a sitting position.

"I know you're lovers. It doesn't bother me. In a weird way, I'm happy for you. I like you both, not just because you're my grandson, Rocky. I respect both of you. You are men of personal and professional integrity."

Rocky and Nick looked at each other, and once again clinked glasses.

Chambers continued, "I'm not going to belabor the fact that if you are discovered to be lovers, your careers are over, your families smeared and embarrassed. You're smart and clever enough to overcome the former and, in time, the latter will heal itself. And, that's that. That's all I have to say about it."

"While you're here in Europe, I want you two to get to know each other better. Enjoy yourselves. Travel and experience life together, and, of course, be discreet."

"Are you serious, Grandfather? How can we do that?"

"Just figure it out, you two are plenty smart. But, there is always a *but.* I want you both to share with one another your long-term goals. What are you going to do when you return to the States? I know what Nick is thinking about doing. I hope that I have a grasp on what you might do, Rocky."

"I don't know what Nicky wants to do. Do I, Nicky? I didn't know you were thinking about anything but the Navy." Rocky was staring at Nick.

"Well, that's not entirely true, Rocky." Nick stood up and walked over to the food to refill his plate. "I shared with you that I was thinking of going into politics."

"Yeah, but I didn't know you were serious."

"I didn't know I was serious at the time. Now, I am."

"Details," Rocky said.

"I don't have details yet, Rocky."

The old man interrupted, "You sure don't. How are you going to do that when you are involved with my grandson? Someone is bound to catch you two at it."

"Shit!" Rocky said as he stood up and headed for the *hors d'oeuvres.* Nick took the long way back to his seat, avoiding Rocky. "What does that mean? Is it one or the other?"

"That's the problem," Nick said.

"And that's one of the reasons I have you two here in Europe together. You've got to sort this out."

"Sort it out?" Rocky started to pace. "What's going on here? Sort what out?"

"My family insists that I get married before I run for office."

Rocky dropped his plate. It crashed onto the parquet floor. The wine glass met the same fate. He stood staring first at Nick, then at his grandfather. He turned, his shoes crunching through the debris on the floor. He walked through the French doors onto the balcony. Grandfather motioned Nick to the balcony, then rang for the staff to clean up the mess.

Rocky leaned forward, his hands grasping the top of the balcony railing. Nick walked up beside him and assumed a similar stance. "Why didn't you tell me?" Rocky murmured.

"Lots of reasons. But I'm sorry. I didn't know how to tell you. I didn't want to tell you. I'm scared."

"That's not good enough."

"I haven't decided. I needed more time to sort it out. I wish your grandfather had left it alone. I was going to tell you."

"When?"

"I'm not sure."

Rocky turned to look at Nick. Nick focused on his hands atop the railing. "Are you making wedding plans?"

"Sheila is."

Rocky felt an emptiness engulf him. "So, what happens now?" he said.

Nick raised his head and turned to look at Rocky. "We enjoy the time we have together."

As they stood staring at each other, Rocky contemplated, *I'm going to have to think about this, but not now. Now I'll do the right thing for Nicky. I'll figure myself out later.* Rocky stuck out his hand. "Congratulations. I'm happy for you both. Now please excuse me." Rocky left the balcony and returned inside.

Nick remained staring out across the city as the sun disappeared over the horizon, and lights illuminated the ancient European city. "This was not how I wanted to spend my first night with him," Nick whispered to himself.

"Where's Rocky?" Nick asked, walking back inside.

"I think he is in the bathroom cleaning the food and wine off his trousers."

The wine and *hors d'oeuvres* had been replaced with a dinner buffet. A table covered with linen, crystal, and silver had been set for three. Champagne rested in an ice bucket close by.

Rocky entered the room, strode over to the ice bucket and yanked out one of three bottles. "Let's celebrate Nicky's news!" hollered Rocky. He tore off the gold foil cap, twisted the wire holding the cork and popped open the bottle. Catching the flowing champagne with one of the crystal flutes. He poured another and served his dinner companions.

* * *

The next morning, Rocky found Nick next to him in bed. He was propped up on one elbow gazing at him. They were both naked. His head ached with a hangover. "Did we finish all three bottles?"

"Yep. Perhaps that is why you were so entertaining."

"Really? What did I do?"

"Well, your most glaring performance was putting on music and insisting you and I dance."

"Did we?"

"Yep."

"Was Grandfather still there?"

"For a while. He disappeared into his room after the first dance. Then we made love."

"There?"

"Yep."

"Oh my God."

"Then we came to your room, and here we are."

"Jesus!" Rocky rubbed his forehead.

They wrapped their arms around one another and fell back to sleep.

CHAPTER 18
SHEILA'S PLAN

Rudolph, Rocky, Nick and Sonya spent the next 17 months going about their business. Per the plan, each focused on their tasks at hand. Nick and Rocky avoided the topic of his impending marriage as best they could.

Sitting on the beach on the Cote d'Azur, Rocky and Nick drank in the sun and several adult beverages. The warm breeze and alcohol relaxed them both.

Nick looked over at Rocky. "I sure hope no one recognizes us here."

"Not likely, we're at the gay end of the beach." Both men were sprawled out on their lounge chairs, sporting speedos and sipping their cocktails.

"Someone might notice that woody you're flying."

"Knock it off. What's that rise in your suit?" Rocky lifted his sunglasses and looked at Nick's crotch. He smiled and laughed.

"Can't help it."

They both reached down into their suits and adjusted themselves.

"This is the life. I could stay here forever," sighed Rocky.

As the afternoon wore on, Rocky began to think about how short their time together as a couple would be. Sooner or later, Rocky would have to face the fact that Nick was marrying Sheila.

Rocky turned to his side and faced Nick. "Well, how'd your trip go back home? Wedding plans coming along?"

Nick took a moment to respond. "Yep, okay."

"I guess you're pretty much situated at the law practice and all that good stuff."

"Yeah, that too."

Rocky sat up in his lounge chair, facing the reclining Nick. "I know we haven't talked about this much, but I'd like to clear a few things up," mumbled Rocky.

"I know this is tough on you. Hell, it's tough on both of us. Even Sheila is having some difficulty with it."

"What kind of difficulty could she be having? She's gets you!"

"She, well," Nick sighed, gathering himself. He sat up and faced away from Rocky. His back to Rocky, he leaned over, his head in his hands.

Rocky eyed Nick hunched over. *I'm the one who should have my head in my hands. He's going off to a happy life that doesn't include me.* Fighting his sadness, Rocky gulped down his drink, stood up and walked toward the water. Nick did not seem to notice his wounded lover walking away.

The bright sun and the effects of several cocktails spun Rocky's head as he walked along the edge of the water. Oblivious to his surroundings, Rocky didn't see the abandoned sandcastle, complete with a deep moat. He tripped and fell onto the ruins of the castle. Shaken, he pulled himself into a sitting position, his feet resting in the disappearing moat. The gentle surf swirled around him covering his lower body in water and undulating sand. Caressed by the warm sand and surf, he stared blankly out over the sparking sea.

The laughter of nearby sun worshippers brought him back. He stood and walked out into the water. He zeroed in on a series of waves and dove under the pounding surf, remaining submerged as long as his lungs allowed. Bursting to the surface gasping for air he collected himself and returned to the shore and Nick.

He took a seat next to Nick on his lounge chair. Rocky wrapped an arm around Nick's shoulder. "So, what did you say?"

Nick placed his hand on Rocky's knee. He removed his sunglasses and reached over and took Rocky's. They looked into one another's eyes. Nick's eyes began to pool.

"We had a long talk. We worked it out. Everything is going to be okay."

"Okay then."

Both men sat looking down the beach, blind to the other beachgoers and beach activities. Half an hour passed. Both men remained silent.

"What did you talk about? Does she know for sure about us?

"We just talked. We're okay."

"No details?" Rocky asked.

"It's no big deal. As you know, she arrives in Brussels next week. You can talk to her. She a special girl, Rocky. I hope you'll like her. She wants to get to know you better. I tried not to encourage it, but she insisted. Nick paused. Turning to Rocky. "I love you, Rocky. I'm very sorry about all this."

"That's the problem. I love you, too."

"Listen, Rocky, I'm doing my best to keep us in each other's lives. I'd like you to be my best man!"

"Yeah, thanks a lot. Great consolation prize!"

* * *

Sheila arrived in Brussels one month before the end of their tour of duty.

"Congrats, Rocky, on your promotion." Sheila sat across from Rocky, dressed in a burgundy Chanel suit. The stylish brimmed hat was cocked to one side *a la* Lauren Bacall in *Casablanca*.

"Thanks, Sheila. I guess all you have to do is shoot down a bunch of enemy jets and they promote you."

Sheila raised her wine glass and toasted the new major.

"Rocky, I'm happy that you and Nick have been able to spend time together in Europe. He's so fond of you. I'm looking forward to getting to know you better." Rocky and Sheila sat in a small bistro in the old city outskirts nursing glasses of Bordeaux.

"Sheila, it's been a great assignment. And yeah, Nicky and I've enjoyed working together. But, we're all looking forward to returning to the States."

Rocky looked down at the table and swallowed hard, fighting back his turbulent emotions. He knew he was supposed to hope things worked out for them, but he wasn't sure he did. She did appear to be a very nice woman.

Sheila reached across the small bistro table. She placed her hand on Rocky's, squeezing it. "I know you're hurting."

He caught himself as he raised his head up and looked into her bright blue eyes.

"What?"

"I know. I know everything," she whispered.

Rocky attempted to pull his hand away. Sheila tightened her grip. "Please, Rocky, listen to me. I'm not here to come between you and Nick."

"What?" He took a sharp inhale and slowly exhaled. His palm began to sweat onto the tablecloth. His heart raced.

Sheila looked into Rocky's eyes. She was calm. She smiled, patted his hand returned hers to her lap. Her bright eyes had turned to cold steel. "I want Nick. I want him bad enough to share him."

"Share him?" Rocky balked internally at the resolve in her gaze and stunning words.

"Share him." Her tone was adamant.

"What do you mean, 'share him?'" His head began to pound. *Does Nicky know about this?*

Sheila sat up straight up. "Nick has told me everything. He loves you. He told me he couldn't marry me because he is in love with you."

Rocky inadvertently brushed his hand against his wine glass. The glass tipped. Sheila's hand flew out from under the table and rescued the Bordeaux from certain death. She placed the wine in front of Rocky.

"You'd better drink this. You appear to need it."

Rocky looked at her, eyes and mouth wide open. "How did you do that?"

Sheila smiled. Sitting back, she laughed and said, "Jujitsu training, I guess."

Rocky drank down the entire glass of wine. "Yes, you're right."

He got the waiter's attention, "*Excusez-moi, serveur, pouvons-nous avoir encore deux verres de vin?*" Rocky turned back toward Sheila. "I hope you don't mind, but I've ordered two more."

"I gathered that," Sheila chuckled.

The waiter returned with two glasses of wine.

"What do you want from me? How does this thing play out? This is crazy!"

Sheila sat back in her chair twirling her glass. Her calm demeanor was disarming. Her head was slightly tilted, eyebrows a bit raised as she said, "Simple, don't change a thing. Continue together as you always have. I want Nick. He wants you. He wants to run for Congress and I'm part of what will make that possible. He can't really run as a single man. Sooner or later he'd be outed." She sipped her wine.

"This makes no sense to me, Sheila." Rocky said, "You're willing to share your husband, for what?"

"I get Nick, a family, and a place in politics and society with influence and power. It's always been my dream. I've wanted Nick since grade school. We get married, we have children, and he gets elected to Congress. Maybe the Senate one day. It'll be an exciting and gratifying life. Not perfect, but who gets perfect?"

Rocky leaned forward. "Let me get this straight. You're telling me to continue with Nicky while you two are married and having a family." He paused and thought a moment. "Are you agreeing to him and me having sex when he's not with you?"

"Well," She giggled and smiled mischievously. "Yes. And perhaps he'll share me with you, too. It's only fair."

"Fuck!" Nearby diners glanced their way as Rocky's voice carried across the room. Rocky, not oblivious to the stares, lowered his voice and leaned forward. "The three of us have sex together? Are you kidding me? Or just you and me? What does Nicky say about this?"

"That's precisely what I am saying. And well, I'll get back to you on what Nick thinks. Once he mulls it over, like I'm sure you will, it might happen."

"Please tell Nicky this is not my idea." Rocky sat back in his chair and looked down at his glass.

"Are you in?" Sheila asked

"Not yet. I need to think about this. Hell, it'd be a good idea to let Nicky in on it, too."

"Don't you worry, I'll take care of that." She began to get out of her seat. "We're headed to Paris this afternoon. I may bring it up then. Who knows, maybe it'll end up his idea. I just might be able to pull that off." Sheila grinned hopefully. "Understand this is not my idea of the best way to live. But I'll do anything to get him and keep him." Sheila stood opposite Rocky seated in his chair.

Rocky said, "I feel like a louse sitting here and even considering this."

"Me, too. Now, please get up and let's go."

"I don't think Nicky will go for it," Rocky said still in his chair.

"As I said, let me worry about that." Sheila reached out and encouraged him out of his chair.

Rocky left 90 euros on the table.

Sheila noticed the extravagant gratuity, "Nice tip."

A mischievous grin and a wink framed his words, "The event and the future it portends warrants it,".

He took Sheila by the arm and headed for the door.

As they were leaving the bistro, Sheila pulled Rocky to her and placed a gentle moist kiss on his lips. Rocky froze. "Maybe there will be more where that came from," Sheila purred.

A gentle rain fell. Rocky held an umbrella as they exited the building. He took Sheila by the hand and escorted her to the curb, flagging a cab and placing her in it.

As he began to close the door, Sheila stopped the door with her hand. "Aren't you coming with me?" Sheila called out.

"Sorry, no. I need some time to think. I'll walk." He closed the door and tapped the roof of the cab. Rocky looked at her as she smiled and winked through the rain-soaked window. He tipped his hat. Waving goodbye, she blew him a kiss.

Rocky, holding the umbrella, walked in the opposite direction. The rain continued to fall. Deep in thought, he didn't notice his shoes absorbing the pooling water. He wandered aimlessly along a cobblestone path bordering an ancient canal.

What the hell was that all about? I'd already made up my mind to let him go when we left Europe. Maybe I won't have to. But how would this play out? 'This is Uncle Rocky, he's fucking your daddy and mommy.' Not a good idea.

A week passed, and Rocky heard nothing from Nick or Sheila. *Either she hadn't said anything to him, or he'd murdered her and dumped her body in the Seine,* thought Rocky. *That would be too easy. Hell, I like her. I could even get to like them married and together. But really, where would I fit in?*

Entering his rooms that afternoon, Rocky found a note on the writing table:

Dear Major Chambers,

Lt. Cmdr. Nicholas Jeffries and Ms. Sheila Hartman request the pleasure of your company for dinner in their rooms this evening, 8:00 p.m. Formal attire requested.
Sincerely,
N & S

Rocky's hands shook as he read the note. *Maybe we're just celebrating? Who else will be there? If it's just me, what does that mean?*

He pulled out his tuxedo. *I never thought I would be wearing a tux in the Navy, but it sure has seen some wear. I hate those boring receptions and dinners.*

He rang the housekeeper to come and have it pressed, then canceled the request and returned his tuxedo to the armoire.

Rocky showered and dressed in his Mess Dress uniform. It was formal attire. He decided to use the hall entrance to Nick's suite. Using the connecting door, which stood ajar, would have been presumptuous, and not worthy of the occasion. Rocky hesitated, then, resplendent in his uniform, knocked twice on the hall door and entered the suite.

Sheila had been transformed into an Art Deco beauty. The plunging neckline brought his progress into the room to a dead stop. She shimmered. She was adorned in a sleek, silver Capelet gown hugging every curve.

Nick wore his White Dress naval uniform. An apparition, a debonair leading man in a steamy romantic film.

The magical couple were pressed against each other. Sheila giggled as she whispered something into Nick's ear. He moaned as she nibbled on his ear lobe.

They turned toward Rocky. The *bête noire* scene had ignited Rocky's imagination. Both holding champagne glasses, their arms wrapped around each other's lower backs. They stood facing the door and watched him enter.

"Oh Rocky! You caught us!" Sheila gleefully said as she handed her glass to Nick. She floated over to Rocky as he closed the door behind him. "We are so glad you're here!" She kissed him squarely on the mouth. She smiled and laughed as she ran her hands down his back. Rocky stood stunned. She took his hand, squeezed it and drew him over to where Nick was standing. Admiring his handsome lover, Nick handed the two glasses to Sheila.

Rocky's lips parted slightly as he faced Nick. Nick took two steps forward, wrapped his arms around Rocky and kissed him. Feeling Nick's tongue in his mouth, Rocky threw his hands around Nick's head and drew him closer.

"Okay, boys. That's enough for now. Join me for some champagne."

The men slowly separated, holding hands as they walked over to Sheila. She leaned toward them, accepting a kiss on her cheeks from both men.

Rocky placed one of Sheila's hands in both his hands. "Thank you, Sheila."

"No, thank you Rocky," Sheila smiled at him. Her steel blue eyes had returned to their bright-blue luster.

"Yes, thank you, Sheila," echoed Nick.

"Don't be silly." Sheila patted Nick on his arm.

She poured Rocky a glass of bubbly. "Now, gentlemen, let's toast our "*marriage!*"

The next morning, Sheila used the now-open adjoining door to return Rocky's uniform. The door remained ajar for the duration of Sheila's stay in Brussels.

CHAPTER 19
PATERNITY

A month later, Rocky and Nick flew from Brussels to Dulles International Airport. Sheila waited for them outside Customs.

"Hey, boys!" Sheila called, waving at them both.

Rocky waved at her as Nick picked up his pace, heading for Sheila. The betrothed coupled embraced and kissed messily.

Only Rocky appeared to notice the overt public display of affection. It set off an aching pressure in his chest, reminding him that Nick would soon be married, but not to me.

Rocky tried to bury his emotions. He walked up to Sheila and gave her a peck on the cheek. "Hey, girl! So glad to see you." His stomach somersaulted as his eyes glistened. He hugged Sheila, whispering in her ear, "Take good care of him." He pulled away without looking at her.

A brittle smile on his face, Rocky turned and hugged Nick.

"So, Rocky, see you at the wedding in a couple of weeks," Nick said, hugging Rocky goodbye.

"Yeah," Rocky murmured. "In a couple of weeks."

Rocky picked up his bags and walked away stoop-shouldered. Nick and Sheila looked at one another perplexed.

"Is he okay?" Sheila quietly asked Nick.

"No," Nick sighed.

He took Sheila's hand and headed toward the exit.

* * *

Rocky was alone in his new townhouse. The home was large, and Rocky had no idea how to furnish and decorate it. Maybe Sheila would help once he told her about his plan. Rocky sat at the only table in the one chair in the four-story, Georgian-style home. Suddenly, the only phone in the house rang. A startled Rocky grabbed the receiver.

"How was the honeymoon, Nick?" Rocky blurted.

"How'd you know it was me?"

"I just got my phone today and left the number on your answering machine. No one else has it."

"It was great! We had a good time. Wish you'd been there!" Nick chuckled.

"Funny!" Rocky laughed

"No, really!"

For a moment, neither of them spoke.

"Well, you've been in DC five weeks. What's new?" Nick asked.

"Oh, I've been busy settling into the new assignment. But I've got a surprise," Rocky said.

"What, another surprise, Rocky? You overdid it with the car you bought for our wedding gift. Maybe you ought to hold off on the surprises."

"That was nothing. Wait till you hear this!" Rocky had jumped out of the chair and was pacing, his hands gesturing aimlessly. "I just bought a large townhouse in Alexandria. There's plenty of room in it for you two to stay here when you're visiting or working in DC. That way, you won't have to drive all the way back to Charlottesville. It will keep us all close. Isn't that great? Do you think Sheila would go for it?"

Rocky looked at the receiver with a wide grin and anticipation. He had not expected the pause on the other end of the line.

"I don't know," Nick responded, his voice suddenly deflated. "Here, ask her. She has her own surprise." Nick handed the phone to Sheila.

"Hey there, handsome! We've got some great news! I'm pregnant. We're having twins!"

"What?"

"Really, we're having twins!"

"Wow, um, uh, that's great," he shivered. "When's the big date? I mean, when are you due?"

"I'm not sure, maybe seven months or so. The doctor will let me know next week."

Rocky felt as if he had been hit by a ton of bricks. "Super! I'm so happy for you! Listen, I have to go. Early day tomorrow. Tell Nick congrats and call me when you hear from the doctor. Bye!"

He hung up, not waiting for Sheila to respond. He looked down at the phone. He gave his head a mental shake.

Rocky sat back down in the chair, head in his hands and elbows on the table. *Seven months?*

* * *

A week later, Rocky was sitting at the same kitchen table devouring a TV dinner. He answered the phone on the first ring. "Chambers here."

"Hey Rocky, Sheila and I went to the doctor today."

"Oh, yeah."

"Remember last week you asked us to get back to you?"

"Yep, I've been waiting for your call."

"Anyway, it's a little early to tell the sex or sexes, but Sheila guessed right, it'll be about seven months."

Rocky shivered as he had a week earlier. He felt his stomach churn. Moments passed.

"Rocky? Are you there? Did you hear me?"

"Oh, sorry. I was just thinking," Trying to sound upbeat.

Rocky felt a surge of energy. "If one's a boy, you could name him after me!"

"Right!" Nick took aim. "We'll call him *dumbass!*" Nick chided.

The remark caught Rocky off guard, but they were both soon laughing. Anything to avoid addressing the elephant in the room.

"So, how are things going with the new law practice? Oh, and yeah, tell Sheila I am so happy for you both."

"Oh, the practice. Um, It's okay. Thanks for asking. Yeah, I'll tell her."

"By the way, I told her about the house. She's keen on the idea. We thought we'd drive up next Saturday to take a look. Does that work for you?"

"Sure does! I bought two beds. One for me and one for the guest room. I don't have much. Maybe Sheila could help me get this place in shape."

"No doubt! She had our place in Charlottesville all put together before she came to Brussels. She even had the nursery done. We weren't even married."

"Yeah, I remember. That used to be the guest room. I had to stay in the nursery when I came for the wedding. Remember, you came to visit me one night? Rocky grinned.

"How could I forget christening the nursery, lover boy?" Nick purred.

* * *

Nick and Sheila arrived late the following Friday evening. They entered the kitchen from the back of the house. As Rocky opened the door, Sheila entered appearing irate, talking to whoever might listen.

"I know I'm not that far along, but I sure am getting tired these days. That car ride wore me out. Nick only stopped three times for me to pee. I'm sleeping all night and take a nap in the afternoon." She plopped into a chair by the dining room table and drank the glass of water Rocky handed her.

"Gee, Sheila, I'm so sorry and surprised. You sure don't look pregnant."

"Whoa, Rocky! Don't go there!" Nick said entering the kitchen carrying their bags.

"Rocky!" Sheila scowled. "I'm only a little over two months into this pregnant thing. What are you expecting? A whale?" Sheila looked at him as if he was an idiot. "Wait a couple of months; I'll get there." She shook her head.

"Sorry, Sheila, just trying to be nice," Rocky said grimacing.

"Try another approach 'Uncle Rocky,'" Nick said. He chuckled as he raised Sheila's feet and placed them on the chair seat next to her.

"Okay, boys. Don't worry about me. Just let me catch my breath and then let's take a look at this monstrous house," Sheila huffed.

"How did you swing this place?" Nick asked. He handed Sheila the bowl of ice cream Rocky had prepared.

"Hey, Sheila?" Rocky stood in front of the refrigerator holding a large glass jar of dill pickles. "Do you also want a couple of these? He sported a large grin and burst out laughing. "I understand ladies in your condition love 'em!"

Nick joined in on the sarcasm, laughing softly.

Sheila swallowed a mouthful of ice cream.

She wagged the spoon, pointing it, alternating between the two jokesters, "As I understand it, you two know how to put objects like that where the sun doesn't shine!" Her feigned scowl morphed into laughter as she watched the guy's figure out exactly what she'd meant.

"Two points, Sheila!" Rocky said. He and Nick laughed and exchanged knowing looks.

The laughter subsided as Sheila continued to enjoy her ice cream. "Don't think I don't know what's going on." Sheila mused out loud.

Rocky decided to answer the previous question. "Well, as far as the house goes, the corporation lent me the money at a low-interest rate. I put up the shares my grandfather finally gifted me as collateral."

"That's still a pretty big monthly nut to swallow. By the corporation, you mean Chambers Enterprises?" Sheila asked.

"Good deduction mother-to-be. You both were busy with the wedding or I would have told you more. I've been working with Grandfather for the last few years. The corporation is renting part of the house back from me. It doubles as a corporate office and a place for my grandfather to stay when he's in DC. The rent pays the mortgage and most of the utilities." Rocky smiled and patted himself on the back.

"So how do we fit in?" Nick asked.

"This is a big place. There are six bedrooms, a library, den, living room, dining room, two kitchens. It goes on and on. There's plenty of room for all of us."

"Crap!" Nick said.

"I'll second that," Sheila said. "Crap! So, where are you suggesting we camp out?"

"You choose where you want to live in the house. I suggest the third floor. It has three bedrooms, kitchen, and laundry. You decide. We need one bedroom for Grandfather and one for me. I can use the library for my office and Nick might want to use one of the bedrooms on the third floor for his office. Also, on the third floor, you'll see that the central gathering room overlooks the backyard and pool. It has a loggia, too."

Rocky took a breath and continued, "What I need is your help, Sheila. Can you help me get this place furnished and staffed?"

Color returned to Sheila's face. She placed her feet on the floor and hopped out of the chair and said, "Okay! Let's get started. Show me around, Major!"

* * *

"Rocky, what do you think of the house? Will it do?" Sheila asked.

"Will it do? Oh my god! Sheila, it's fantastic. I can't thank you enough."

Panting, Sheila said, "Okay, good. The last four months have been fun. But I'm exhausted. I'm headed back to Charlottesville tomorrow. Nick's coming to get me."

"I'm going to miss you. It's been great having you here," Rocky sighed.

"Well, let's be real. I've spent most of the time by myself, and with designers and workers while you've been traveling all over the country on assignments. Nick's only been here on weekends. But, it's kept me busy. That's the best part."

* * *

Three months later Sheila placed an announcement in her local paper:

Mr. and Mrs. Nicholas Jeffries announce the birth of twins, one boy and one girl. Ricardo and Brooke Jeffries came into this world on... The family has asked their dear family friend, Major Ricardo

Chambers, USMC, of Arlington, VA, to serve as the children's godfather...

* * *

Sheila arrived at the townhouse and joined Rocky in the refurbished library. "That was a very nice article, Sheila," Rocky said. "Thank you for including me as a member of the family. That was sweet."

"You're so very welcome, godfather." Sheila smiled and gave him a playful shove.

"I guess it's been about six months since the babies were born. How're you feeling?"

"Fine. It's not that hard when you have two nurses around the clock. I want to thank you for making that possible. Without your help, I wouldn't be able to focus on Nick's upcoming election. As it is, I am well rested. I get lots of sleep. The nurses do the heavy lifting, and all I do is breastfeed and play mommy. The nice thing about that is I can eat anything I want, as long as it isn't bitter or spicy. The children eat like horses. It's a bit tough shoveling in enough calories to feed the three of us!"

"How can you come here without them? Don't they need you close by?"

"Not always. I use a pump to store up milk, particularly when the little munchkins aren't hungry. Not getting any relief, my breasts are full and ready to let loose. I also supplement. It's not a problem. Would you please excuse me? Now that we've been talking about it, I'm leaking. I'll be back in twenty or so minutes." She got out of the chair. Rocky noticed something had spilled all over her blouse.

Sheila smiled as she saw his mouth drop. "Yes, Rocky. That happens when I even think about nursing." She laughed and went into the other room.

Sheila returned to the library wearing a different blouse. She took a seat near Rocky's desk. Looking up from the material he had been studying, he smiled broadly.

"Please come here and sit next to me," Sheila said.

Rocky rose out of the chair from behind his desk. He joined her, taking a seat in the matching wing chair next to where she was sitting.

Her jaw was clenched, her hands clasped in her lap.

"What's wrong, Sheila?"

Sheila sat up. She inhaled deeply. Her lips thinned, "I have something very important to share with you."

Rocky felt his stomach pitch.

"Nick and I've been ignoring the reality of the relationship the three of us have. We've avoided the ramifications and consequences of our actions." Her face fell. Her eyes teared.

Rocky's heart ached observing her physical pain. He rose out of his chair and knelt in front of her, resting his hands on her knees. "What is it, Sheila? Are the children okay? Is there anything I can do? Are you all right? Is Nicky okay?" He felt her body quiver.

She put her head in her hands and sobbed. Rocky reached up and held her.

"Sheila, what is it? Tell me, please," Rocky asked.

"I can't," she continued to sob and convulse. "It'll kill Nick!"

"I don't think anything could kill Nicky. Take a moment. Let me get you a drink."

"I can't have any alcohol. I'm breastfeeding," Sheila moaned.

Frustrated, but not deterred, he thought for a moment, holding her close.

Rocky cheered up and said, "That's simple, don't express any more milk for the next twelve hours. Really, that'll work, I'm sure." Call me Dr. Rocky!"

Rocky stood up slowly and retrieved a box of tissues. Sheila took the tissues that Rocky offered and pulled herself together. She was still sniffling when Rocky returned with an ice-cold martini.

"Shaken, not stirred," Rocky quipped.

"Thank you, Dr. Rocky. You are indeed a dear," she said as she took her first sip.

"When you're halfway through that fabulous cocktail, we'll pick up where we left off. If you like."

"Okay," Sheila said as she savored her beverage. "I haven't had one of these since I found out I was pregnant. Yum!" She smiled at Rocky with her puffy face and bloodshot eyes and breathed easier.

"I've always wondered." She stopped and put the martini glass on an adjacent table. "I have always wondered since I found out I was pregnant with the babies."

"Wondered what?" Rocky asked.

Shaking, Sheila said, "It's too hard to say out loud."

Rocky went over to her and found a spot on the edge of her chair to sit and hold her. Rocky took a breath and said, "I think you are trying to say you have wondered who the father might be."

Sheila's shriek and sobs were muffled by Rocky holding her to his chest. "Yes!"

Rocky rocked her gently. Sheila trembled as she cried and rocked. Finally, exhausted, she stopped moving or crying.

Rocky got up and retrieved a wool blanket from an adjacent couch. He wrapped it around her. He lowered the lights in the room.

"Rocky, don't leave me. Come over here, hand me that martini and sit down." She had partially unwrapped the cover. She was sitting up.

Rocky, puzzled and surprised, did as she asked.

"I am sorry for my histrionics. I can't seem to forgive myself."

"For what?"

"For placing my husband, children and you in this position."

"I don't hear anyone complaining. Do you?"

"No," she whimpered.

"Okay, so we agree that no one is upset except you, right?"

"What about Nick? When he finds out?"

Rocky thought for a moment. "Sheila, you act like you did something wrong. Is it the sex between the three of us? Is that what's bothering you? I hope not."

Sheila dissolved into tears. Rocky could hardly make out what she said, her words drowning in tears. "I feel so cheap, so wrong. Why wasn't I more careful? What woman would do what I did? What was I thinking? How could Nick love a woman who plotted to sleep with his lover? It's so Borgia! I'm Lucretia Borgia!"

"Sheila, we are all adults. It was the moment. It was love. The passion was overwhelming and magical, and we were willing participants. This sort of thing has gone on throughout history. You were not the first and will certainly not be the last. You wanted Nicky and did what you thought you had to do to get him."

"It's painful to think about," Sheila said.

"Sheila, you were placed in an awful position. There is no blame here. It's just life. Nicky has always loved you. He has loved you since you were kids in high school. He just happened to fall in love with me, too. I want you to know that we both love you for who you are. We're a family." Rocky wrapped his arms around Sheila and held her.

Sheila sat up, pulling away from Rocky. She stared at him. Her jaw tightened as she said, "I know that. I know why I did what I did. That was before we were married and had children."

She paused and looked at Rocky with tears in her eyes. "How can he still feel the same about me? Can he still love me? Men change, Rocky. Their egos get in the way and all hell can break loose. That's what I'm afraid of! Him changing and blaming me, hating me!"

Rocky's body quivered hearing what she said. "Nicky loved you then. He loves you now. You would know by now if he had changed."

"Rocky! You aren't listening! When he finds out, he just might change!" Sheila said.

Rocky attempted to calm her by saying quietly, "He knows."

"He knows what?" Sheila asked, her eyes widening.

Rocky was determined to dodge the question. "How's that martini coming?" He knew little remained in the glass. He also knew she would not back off on the question.

"What does he know? Tell me!" Sheila said.

Rocky held his ground. "Answer my question and then I'll answer yours."

"What? Are you kidding me? I want to know. What does he know?" She stammered.

"You heard me," Rocky said.

"It's about finished," she replied with fire in her eyes.

Rocky headed to the wet bar. Sheila remained seated, nursing what remained of her drink with one hand and drumming the chair with the fingers of the other.

Rocky delivered the second martini. He waited for her to drink a bit. Her rapt attention given to the cocktail provided a breather.

Speaking into her glass, "He knows what?" She repeated.

"He and I both know who the parents are."

Sheila played with the olives strung on the silver toothpick in her glass. She twirled them around playfully. "Well, tell me. Who? Wait! Before you do, tell me how you found out," she said in a stern voice. "DNA?"

He winced and mumbled, "DNA samples from Nicky, the children and me."

Sheila stood up, spilling her martini and screamed, "You bastards tested my babies' DNA without telling me? You sons of bitches!"

She picked up an ashtray and threw it at Rocky. Rocky dodged, allowing the flying heavy crystal to crash into the mirror behind him. Glass shattered in all directions.

Rocky felt pieces of glass hit the back of his head and body.

Sheila gasped, "Rocky, oh Rocky, I'm sorry! Stand still. Don't move!"

He didn't move.

"Sheila, I can do this. I can clean it up."

"No, you can't. Glass is everywhere and all over you. DO NOT MOVE!"

Sheila left the room and returned with a broom, dust pan, and vacuum cleaner. "You stay there. I will get this mess cleaned up. I don't want you cut and I don't want the kids to be cut by glass the next time they're in the room."

Sheila went to work cleaning. No one spoke as she worked feverishly.

Five minutes into her task she continued working and asked, "Why didn't you two tell me?"

"We didn't think it was our place."

"Not your place?"

"Think about it. Ultimately, you are the mother. What difference would it make to you as to how you feel about the children? They're your children. On the other hand, there's no certainty, right, wrong, deserved or undeserved here. How would you react? Would you take offense at who the father was? Why bring the children into it? We're all players, but you are the lynchpin. It all rests on you. Do you want that? Do you need or want that knowledge? Nicky and I weren't sure. We agreed not to divulge what we knew unless you asked us." Rocky decided it was time for him to enjoy his martini. He sat down.

"I see what you mean. I'm so lucky to have you both in my life. I may have been blubbering like a buffoon, but I'm no fool, and I *am* strong. I want to know. Please tell me."

"Do you think Nicky should be here for this?" Rocky asked.

"Yes, you're probably right."

"He'll be here in thirty minutes. I called him when you were in the other room pumping."

This news startled Sheila. In a high-pitched voice, "You did? Why?"

"I'd anticipated things rising to this level. I thought he should be here."

"Thank you, Rocky," she paused. "I suppose the martinis were part of the delay tactic?" she chuckled.

"Oh, Sheila, the martinis have served multiple purposes," he laughed and raised his glass to her.

Twenty minutes later Nick entered the house. "Hey everybody, I'm here."

"Hi honey, we're in the library," Sheila called. She had pulled herself together, having changed clothes and repaired her make-up. Tipsy from the two martinis, she had to hold on to Rocky as she got up to greet Nick. They both took a seat on the leather sofa. Rocky delivered a martini to Nick.

As Nick took the martini, they both turned and looked at Sheila, the source of a squeaky hiccup. She giggled as she covered her mouth. Rocky and Nick chuckled.

"Hey Rocky," Nick asked. "Who's been redecorating? What's up with the mirror?"

"I'll tell you later. Things can get wild around here. You know, gays can party!" Rocky lied.

"That'll be expensive to fix," Sheila said.

"Yep," said Nick.

"Looks like you lost that expensive Swarovski crystal ashtray, too," Sheila sighed.

Nick looked askance at Sheila, a question mark on his face.

"I'm a little drunk and a lot sleepy. Let's get on with it," Sheila said.

Rocky brought Nick up to date, summarizing their previous conversation. He minimized the parts where Sheila was upset.

"Sheila, Rocky's been super caring for you. Thanks, Rocky."

Sheila interrupted, "I don't know what the fuss is all about. I didn't do anything. All I've done is cry and drink." She giggled.

Nick and Rocky looked at Sheila and laughed.

Rocky then pulled up a chair so that he could be near them. "Nicky, you're the husband. Please do the honors."

Nick moved closer to Sheila. He put an arm around her shoulders and placed her hands in his. Sheila looked at Nick and nodded toward Rocky. Nick nodded in agreement.

"Rocky, come over here and join hands with Nick and me," Sheila said softly.

"Sheila, not long after we found out you were pregnant, Rocky and I talked. We were concerned about the obvious, the paternity issue. We decided then that we would establish paternity for a couple of reasons. It's only fair to the children and only fair to the father, whomever that might be. Also, if something should happen to you and me, Rocky was our first choice to care for the children. He had the right to know if he was the father. I could care less either way. In my opinion, I didn't think that it would matter to you. But, it appears you want to know. You have the right to know." He paused. "Are you ready?"

"When did you find out?" asked Sheila, holding her hands to her mouth, her voice trembling.

"Several weeks after they were born."

"You've known that long and didn't tell me?"

"Sweetheart, we were very careful not to alarm anyone or give rise to concern," Nick paused. "It was hard. I for one felt somewhat disingenuous and less than honest. I can't speak for Rocky, but my guess is he did as well." Both looked at Rocky.

Rocky nodded. He looked at Sheila. "It was very difficult, but I felt we had to know."

No one moved. Rocky and Nick waited for Sheila to break the silence.

"Yes, I'm ready. I agree. It doesn't matter. She sat for a couple of minutes looking down at her lap. "But, I still want to know." She sat up, poised for the answer.

Nick pursed his lips, inhaled and blurted out, "I'm Brooke's father. Rocky is Ricardo's father."

Sheila sat with her head down. Her eyes moistened. She reached for the tissues on the table and dabbed her eyes. "Thank you." She turned to Nick and wrapped her arms around him and kissed his cheek. "Thank you, Nick. I love you."

Nick pulled her closer and said, "I love you, too, more than ever."

Rocky observed the couple. His body began to relax for the first time that evening. A weight lifted from his shoulders. His heart felt full. His eyes pooled. "I love you both so much," he said.

Nick and Sheila reached out and pulled Rocky to them. The three embraced.

"Well, Rocky, it appears that we are a real family. Welcome," said Sheila.

A thrill ran through Rocky's body. His soul was filled with love and compassion.

"Yes, welcome Rocky," echoed Nick.

Rocky had not experienced this feeling since before he had shared his love for Umberto with his mother. She had forsaken him then. Now once again, he had a complete family that loved him unconditionally. And he loved them.

CHAPTER 20
1996 – 2007: TRANSITIONS

Two years later, Lieutenant Colonel Ricardo Chambers sat reflecting on the passing of time. The flames in the library fireplace provided the only source of light. As the dance of light and color splashed on the walls, his desire to move forward intensified. It was time to make the move. He had laid the groundwork for Chambers Enterprises. He had the contacts and respect of his peers in industry and government. It was time to make the jump and help his grandfather.

Hell, Nicky's moved on. He's got his seat in the House. The kids are great. Everything's good. It's time. Rocky picked up the phone and dialed.

"Chambers residence," said James, the family butler.

"Hello James, this is Rocky. How are you?"

"I'm fine, thank you, sir."

"Is my grandfather in?"

"Yes, I will see if he is available, sir."

Rocky heard muffled voices on the other end of the line. A click, silence, and someone picked up the line.

"Hello there, Lieutenant Colonel Chambers!" The enthusiasm in his grandfather's voice lifted Rocky's spirits.

"Hi Grandfather, I hope I'm not calling too late."

"Not at all, your grandmother and I just returned home after attending the Boston Pops. As always, it was terrific. Your grandmother has been humming one tune or another all the way home."

Rocky smiled as he absorbed the lighthearted banter. *Time to get to the point.* He braced himself.

"Okay, Grandfather. Do you have a moment? I mean..." He paused. "I mean I have something to talk to you about." He waited for the old man to absorb that there was a reason, a serious reason for the call.

"Sure, Rocky. What is it? Are you okay?"

"Yes, I'm fine. It's just that I thought you and I needed to talk."

"Are you sure everything's okay?"

"Everything's fine."

"So, what's on your mind?"

"My tour of duty is about up. Their getting ready to issue me orders for my next duty station. This might be the time to figure out what's next. I'm thinking about the Naval Reserves. I'm also thinking about hopping on a plane and coming up to Boston to see you. I need to discuss this with you. If I'm going to make the transition to the private sector, it's time to pull the trigger. What do you think?"

"Well, Rocky, I think that's a good idea. When will you arrive?"

"How about this weekend?" asked Rocky.

"Excellent, we'll be at the Cape. I'll send a jet to pick you up Saturday morning."

"Great. Thanks. See you this weekend. Hugs and love to Grandmother."

"You bet! Love you, son."

Rocky heard the phone click on the other end. He placed the handset back on the phone. *Well, I guess that's it. I'm moving on. It seems so normal. I've been doing this Marine thing for almost a decade. I haven't ever done anything for that long. Must be a sign that I'm really ready.* He downed his scotch and put on a jacket, then jumped in his car and drove to a gay rights gala.

* * *

Nick returned one evening to the Alexandria townhouse after a long day on Capitol Hill. "Anybody home?"

"I'm up here, changing. I'll be right down. How 'bout fixing us a drink?" Rocky yelled from upstairs.

"Got it, get your ass down here. I have something to ask you about."

The two found themselves out by the pool; the spring evening light waning. "So, Congressman Jeffries, how was your day?" Rocky teased.

"Fine, dear," Nick teased back. "But I do have something to run by you." He took a deep breath and sat back in his chair. "There's been a lot of chatter about gay rights. It's getting lots of headlines. I'm getting a lot of inquiries on my position. I feel like I'm between a rock and a hard place."

Rocky wanted to continue his teasing. "I've got a hard place for you." Rocky winked as they both laughed.

"Okay, wise guy, I've got to think this through. Save that for later. My constituency leans to the right on this."

"You're a Republican. That was your first mistake. Like you've never heard that from me before."

"Knock it off, flyboy. This is serious." Nick sipped his cocktail as he paced. Returning to his chair, he said, "Rocky, I have a decision to make on the upcoming vote. It could impact the LGBT community."

"So, what's the problem? Vote your conscience and your heart. Do what you know is right," Rocky said, tapping his right index finger on a table.

"If I do that, I'll piss off the right. That'll cost me votes in the upcoming election."

"Find a way to keep those votes. What else do they want more? Change the narrative. Get some sort of three-way deal going. Like a bridge or something. Maybe a statue to some confederate colonel," Rocky said, half sarcastically.

"What do you know about politics?" Nick said returning to his seat.

"Come on, Nicky, what do you think I am doing all day long? I've got politicians, the Defense Department, corporate lobbyists, and the White House to deal with. Often, all at the same time. Give me a break! Jesus!"

"OK, you're right," huffed Nick. "Actually, that's a good idea."

Rocky twirled his glass when he retreated to his sixth sense.

Nick watched and grew impatient, "Why do you always play with your glass?"

Rocky ignored the question. He watched the gentle movement of the water in the pool. He said, "Why don't you let me make a couple of discreet inquiries? Some of my gay political friends might have some ideas. Let's see if they have some way to reframe the narrative. It's a long shot, but it might work. I think you should also consider sucking up to the Log Cabin Republicans. Maybe they can work some magic."

Nick cocked his head as he listened. "You know, there might be something to that. Even if I can't vote in favor of the legislation this time, I can make up for it later."

Rocky lost his patience and fired back, "Don't try to bullshit yourself or me. Sooner or later, you'll have to stand up for something. No, it's time you took it by the balls. You have to drive the narrative, or it will sink you."

"It's tough dealing with some of this. I'm struggling."

"No doubt," said Rocky. His tone becoming softer as he cautioned Nick, "You can't go on like this forever. It'll destroy you. It'll eat right through you. I'm not saying you have to out yourself, but you do have to make some decisions."

The next day, Nick contacted the Log Cabin Republicans.

Rocky set up a meeting with the Human Rights Campaign.

* * *

Weeks later, Sheila and the twins arrived at the house earlier in the afternoon. She had directed the household staff to prepare dinner for the three adults. She made dinner for the six-year-old twins. As she handed them off to the governess, Nick walked in.

Nick squatted down as the kids came running to him. There were big hugs and squeals all around. Sheila prepared two martinis as Nick and the kids wrestled. Nick shook off the kids and reached for one of the martinis. He gave her a peck on the cheek. "Hey, babe, glad you are all here. Thanks for the drink." He took a swig and smiled at Sheila.

"Hey, everybody! I'm home!" Rocky hollered from the mudroom.

"Uncle Rocky!" Uncle Rocky went down on his knees as he opened his arms for the youngsters jumping into his embrace. Squeezing them both then releasing them, he went down on all fours and helped them on to his back. Rocky was now their horse. "Rocket! Giddy up, Rocket! Giddy up!" repeated the children.

Sheila and Nick, having seen this performance before, still laughed uproariously. Nick picked up Rick, and Sheila grabbed Brooke from the horse's back. "We'll be right back, we're taking this cowboy and cowgirl upstairs. Your cocktail is on the bar, Rocket!"

Sheila laughed. "Say goodnight to Uncle Rocky," said Nick. "Good night, Rocket!" the twins chimed in.

The house had quieted down with the children and governess upstairs in their rooms. The three adults had almost finished dinner as Nick opened a second bottle of Cabernet Sauvignon.

Sheila sat back in her chair, hoisted the wine glass as she savored the wine and her children's fathers' company. "I love my darlings, but they do keep me busy. It's nice to have adult company for a change."

Nick reached over and patted her on her hand. "I don't envy you, sweetie. Keeping two households going, the kids, and helping me with the campaign is a lot for anyone. You're the best." He threw her an air kiss. She smiled and returned one to him.

Rocky sat admiring the concern and love they had for one another. *Nicky's so committed to Sheila and the children. He has patience, compassion and genuine love for all of us. And how does Sheila do it? The kids alone are enough to wear anyone out. Even with help. She busts her ass on his perennial campaigns and somehow or other keeps herself and the houses running seamlessly. It's got to be wearing on her. She never shows it. I sure hope he likes my idea.* Rocky crossed his fingers.

"Hey lovebirds, I have something that might be of interest." Rocky shifted in his chair, knowing he had spoiled their moment.

"What is it?" Nick asked, turning toward Rocky.

"Sheila and I actually have something to run by you," Rocky said. He folded his hands on the table.

Nick, confounded, turned his attention from Rocky to Sheila. His quizzical look was returned with a cute "I'm guilty" smile. "Um, okay," Nick murmured as he turned back toward Rocky.

"I've spent some time with a cross-section of my politically active gay friends. First of all, they don't know anything about you and me. All they know is that you and Sheila are gay friendly. So, relax."

"Okay, cool," said Nick. He sat up straight and arched his back. He lifted his chin, and pushed his chest out, releasing tension along his spine. All three heard discs adjust.

"Ow!" Sheila said.

"Feels good," Nick said.

Rocky said, "Since you've set your sites on the Senate, you need to up your game. By that, I mean you need to take your campaign staff to another level." Rocky paused and looked at Nick.

"I'm listening," Nick said adjusting his seat position.

"Sheila and I have a proposition, or an opportunity to discuss." Rocky looked from Nick to Sheila. "Sheila?"

"Rocky's right, Nick. We have something bold for you to consider." She paused and folded her hands as she placed them on the table in front of her.

Nick shifted his weight forward, mimicking his wife's hand position. He smiled at her. "Okay, what is it?"

Sheila pursed her lips and said, "We want you to be the first Republican candidate to hire a gay, transgender campaign manager." Sheila forced a triumphant smile.

Rocky sat pensively, his brow furrowed, chin tucked, staring at Nick.

Nick looked down at the table, clasping his fingers so tight his knuckles were white. His deep breathing was the only sound in the room.

Sheila stood. She leaned forward, her hands on the table supporting her stance. "If I see veins popping out on your forehead, I'm going to douse you with cold water before you have a stroke," Sheila said sternly. "Now, chill out. You're acting like a spoiled child!"

Sheila moved toward the kitchen cabinets and pulled a large bowl from the cupboard. She walked to the sink and filled the bowl with water. She placed it on the table in front of him. "Do you think I'm kidding?" Sheila had softened her tone.

Nick hadn't moved. The pressure on his knuckles had subsided and his color had returned.

Rocky watched the performance, enjoying what was left on his plate and savoring the wine. The theatricality of the moment amused him.

"Go ahead, do it, Sheila!" Rocky laughed, almost choking on his food.

Sheila gave Rocky the evil eye, then a slight grin and a wink.

"Shut the fuck up!" Nick said as he continued to stare at his hands and the table.

Rocky couldn't contain himself any longer and let out a laugh. He smacked his hand on the table. "Listen, Nicky. This is a great opportunity to take charge of a national conversation. Think about it. Headlines, Republican Congressman Jeffries, candidate for the U.S. Senate, hires gay transgender man to lead his campaign!" You might piss off half your constituents, but most Independents and some Democrats will embrace you. With gay marriage legal in several states, there's momentum. You really don't have a choice. You must get the electorates' attention. Get national attention. As it is right now, the incumbent, Senator Horowitz, will kick your ass."

"Who do you have in mind?" Nick said, not moving.

"You know her, I mean him. Gina, now Gene Smithers," said Rocky.

Nick nodded and relaxed his hands. Still staring at the table. "Yeah, I know of her, or him, whatever."

Sheila sat in her chair, running her index finger around the edge of the bowl. "He's the best in the business and needs a job. The gay community will certainly let up on their attacks if you help out one of their own. He's also affordable. Think about it." Sheila said.

"Who's run the numbers?" asked Nick, now looking at Sheila.

"Gene has," she said.

"That's convenient, and certainly no conflict of interest there," Nick snorted.

"Don't be a dick. You know his integrity and reputation. He isn't going to compromise that for a longshot candidate, even if he is starving. And I don't like the way this sounds coming from you. Why do you think we would recommend him or anyone else? Why would we do that if we didn't think it was the right thing to do? You're really pissing me off," Sheila said. She got out of her seat and walked out of the room. "I'll check on the kids," she said from the hall.

"Well, dumbass, you sure set her off," Rocky said. "Maybe you aren't ready to lead." Rocky got up and walked toward the hallway. Turning to speak to Nick, he said, "Think about it. If you can't embrace it, don't do it. But I'll be damned if either Sheila or I can think of another way to make you something other than a footnote in Virginia politics."

* * *

"Gene, I appreciate your taking the time to come and speak to me today. My wife and friend insisted the other night that we talk. You may have guessed, but I'm not so sure about this. This is difficult for me. I know it hasn't been easy for you for a long time," Nick said, as he and Gene Smithers sat alone in his congressional office. "I have huge respect for what you have accomplished as a professional and in your personal life. It's truly amazing and some, including me, would say heroic."

Gene's appearance resembled that of any six-foot, portly, middle-aged man. His conservative dress and genteel manner labeled him a WASP. "Thank you, Congressman. Frankly, I'm surprised to be sitting here. Then again, I'm not really."

"Why is that?"

"You're best friends with one of my favorite people on earth, Rocky Chambers," he said as he smiled and looked knowingly at the congressman.

Nick swallowed.

"He and your wife have done a fantastic job of selling you to my team and me. They believe in you. They believe in your commitment to serving the American people. Rocky is emerging as a leader in the LGBT community. His personal and financial commitments are making a difference. His confidence in you is why I'm here. If Rocky Chambers did not have gravitas, we would not be having this conversation. Just the fact that we are sitting here talking speaks volumes on his belief in you and your ideals. Qualities that can transform campaigns and transcend partisan politics."

Nick sat transfixed, mesmerized as Gene painted a picture of what could be his future.

"All you have to do is embrace the possibilities, Congressman. Senator John F. Kennedy internalized the attributes of those portrayed in his book, *Profiles in Courage*. He thought outside the box and envisioned the dream that was manifested with landing a man on the moon. What is your vision?"

Nick had not shifted his gaze from Gene. He remained transfixed on the now-silent enigma. The intercom buzzed.

"Congressman, your next appointment has been waiting for twenty minutes."

Nick, yanked from his thoughts, pushed the phone intercom button. "I'm sorry, this meeting is a priority and taking longer than expected. I'll need more time. If you have to, please reschedule the meeting. Thank you."

He turned his attention back toward Gene, folding his hands on his desk. "Gene, you have given me a glimpse into something that is far beyond what I initially saw when I decided to run for the Senate." He paused. "I have to take a step back and rethink this. That doesn't mean that I don't embrace what you've laid out. It means that the reality is larger than me. It's larger than life. I can't accomplish anything like what you are espousing without people such as you. Many people like you. People with talent, ability and faith." He rose from his chair, came around and leaned against the front of the desk, his arms folded. "I want to be able to do this, but it's out of my comfort zone."

He moved to the chair next to Gene and looked into Gene's eyes, "I want to talk more about this with you. I want to make this happen. I would like you, Sheila,

Rocky and me to get together. Would you be open to that? Perhaps dinner tomorrow, something informal, a cookout by the pool at the house?"

Gene nodded, stood up and stuck out his hand. "Done. See you tomorrow night. 6:00 p.m.?"

"Sure."

Gene turned toward the door and then back around. "At some point, we'll have to talk about the fact that I'm out and transgender."

Nick stood still. He watched Gene open the door, walk through and close it behind him.

"Yeah, I forgot," Nick muttered to an empty room.

CHAPTER 21
2007 – 2014: PAST AND FUTURE COLLIDE

Gene said, "Nick, thanks for putting this together. There's nothing like breaking bread together to get to know one another."

"Yeah, Gene, it seemed like a good idea to me." Nick looked around Rocky's backyard as the caterer put the finishing touches on the table and fired up the grill. "Sheila and Rocky are running a bit behind. She's headed back from the dentist with the kids. Rocky is stuck on the George Washington Bridge. Some sort of accident a few cars ahead of him. Hopefully, they'll be here soon."

"While it's too bad they are running behind, it'll give us a chance to chat." Gene refreshed his wine glass from a bottle sitting on the outdoor kitchen counter. "Cheers!" Gene raised his glass. Nick raised his martini glass in return.

"Let's talk." He motioned Nick over to chairs several yards from where the catering staff was working. "Bring your drink."

"Nick, there are several things we need to get out of the way."

"Okay, shoot." Nick relaxed in one of the yard rockers.

"I've had this conversation with Rocky and Sheila. I need to have it with you, too."

Nick sat listening, taking an occasional sip from his glass.

Gene continued. "A Republican running for the Senate is always perceived as conservative. They are labeled pro-business, pro-military, anti-taxes and oblivious to social issues. Specifically, religiously inspired issues – gay marriage, trans access to bathrooms and the like. Is that who you are?"

"No!" Nick said, annoyed.

Gene leaned forward in his chair and said, "Who are you? What are you? Where do you stand on these issues? Talk to me."

Nick remained seated. He latched onto Gene's eyes with his own and drilled deep. "I'm a fiscal conservative. I hate waste and corruption. I'm pro-military. I despise unnecessary taxes. I embrace social issues. Racism, misogyny and homophobia are cancers that must be eradicated. I believe in comprehensive immigration reform. I am, above all, a compassionate man who believes in family and individual values. I believe in privacy. I believe elected officials are the representatives of a sovereign people. We are elected to serve and protect, not coerce and subjugate."

"Bravo!" Gene cheered and clapped, as did Rocky, Sheila, and the twins. Everyone had arrived simultaneously.

"Yay, Daddy!" clapped Rick.

"Yippee," chimed in Brooke.

Gene and Nick rose from their chairs. Gene motioned theatrically with both hands toward Nick. Nick took a bow. They all clapped and hollered one more time.

"I think we have the building blocks for a platform," Gene said, smiling at Nick. "Let's hope there's a large constituency that feels that way, too!"

"Here's to that! Welcome home, everyone!" Nick said. "Anybody hungry?"

"I am," Rick said.

"Me, too!" Brooke piped in.

"Okay, then. Follow me into the house and let's wash our hands," Sheila said. The kids ran for the house. Sheila trotted behind them.

Turning to the adults, Sheila said, "We'll be right back! Gene, how about seeing if that husband of mine will fix me a drink?"

"Done!" hollered Gene watching Sheila as she disappeared into the house with the children.

"You heard the lady, Nick. Get to that drink!" Gene ordered.

Rocky sidled up to Gene. "So, Gene. What do you think about our candidate?"

"Well, he's a bit too handsome for a Republican, but he'll have to do."

"That's hysterical! That's the same thing I said when Tanner awarded me the Medal of Honor!"

"Tanner! Have you heard the rumors?" Gene asked.

Nick said, "What rumors?"

"I think I know what you mean," Rocky murmured.

"He's a switch-hitter." Gene said. "He hit on at least one of the Secret Service guys protecting him. At least one we know of. Some say Tanner eventually tired of him. When the first lady got wind of it, the agent was transferred to some dead-end job in the Aleutians. What the fuck they had that poor bastard doing in that God-forsaken place is beyond me."

"Are you kidding me?" Nick said.

Rocky tensed as he was reminded of Tanner and their tryst. He was glad he never shared that experience with anyone. However, he wondered if it might come in handy someday.

Rocky changed the subject. "Speaking of the Tanners, I'm going to a White House dinner tomorrow. This is the first time the Tanners have been back to the White House since the end of their second term. President and Mrs. Nelson are honoring former President Tanner. It has something to do with his and Mrs. Tanner's foundation. I'm sure fundraising for the Tanner's Presidential Library is on the agenda."

Nick and Gene stared at Rocky. "Where did this come from? Since when are you on the A list?" Gene snorted.

Rocky held his chin just a bit higher, "Chambers Enterprises is a big financial supporter. I've donated some of my own money, as well."

"You're kidding!" Gene said. "That's huge. Are you planning on getting some face time with the Tanners?"

"Not so much him, but her. She owes me," Rocky said.

Nick looked at him incredulously.

"I've got some unfinished business."

"Like what?" Gene asked.

"One day, I just might tell you," Rocky smiled. "No more questions now, though."

Nick gave Rocky a '"what the fuck?" look and then turned his attention toward Gene.

"You're not going to tell us what it's about?" Gene asked again, his hands on his hips.

"Not now, maybe never. Here comes Sheila and the kids. Let's eat!"

* * *

"Mr. Chambers, it's a pleasure having you back at the White House again," said the White House butler, Mr. Matthews.

"Thank you. I'm honored to be here," Rocky said.

"I remember, sir, when you were awarded the Medal of Honor. It was a special day. If you will follow me, I will escort you to the East Room. President Nelson, the first lady and the Tanners are hosting a receiving line."

"Thank you." He walked the length of the first-floor main hall alongside his escort.

Once again, he found himself in the East Room. He breathed deeply and joined those waiting in line.

"Mr. President, it's a pleasure to see you again," Rocky said, smiling and shaking the recently elected President Nelson's hand.

"Rocky, it's great to see you as well. I understand this is the first time you've been back at the White House. Do you recall our meeting at that long-ago event? I was a member of the Cabinet then."

"Sir, I do. You were Secretary of Defense. You will recall we first met in your office at the Pentagon." Rocky nodded and moved on to Mrs. Nelson. Rocky could feel the president watching him. He noticed the president speak with an aide. The aide walked behind the receiving line and whispered something in Josephine Tanner's ear.

As Rocky held out his hand for the first lady, he thought to himself, *I know damn well he remembers it. So does Josephine Tanner. I wonder if President Tanner has any clue what happened.*

"Hello, Mrs. Nelson, it is a pleasure seeing you again. It's been many years since we first met in this very room." Mrs. Nelson's smile was the tired diplomatic mask worn by fatigued political spouses. "Thank you for including me in this evening's festivities." They chatted stiffly and a bit longer than anticipated, as President Tanner was engaged in conversation with the former United Nations Ambassador preceding Rocky in the line.

Moving on in the line, Rocky extended his hand. "President Tanner, it's been a while." The former president, caught off guard, hesitated -- clearly not recognizing Rocky. The protocol officer stepped in and introduced the two men. *Awkward and very amusing,* thought Rocky.

"Oh, um, yes! It was Captain Chambers back then! Right? Now it's CEO Chambers, am I right?" Tanner voice stumbled but recovered.

"Yes, sir! You have it right!" Rocky glanced to his left and could tell Mrs. Tanner was aware of who he was. She looked to be eavesdropping as best she could. "Do you by chance recall that evening as vividly as I do, sir?"

Tanner shifted his weight from one foot to the other and back again. "Why of course, Mr. Chambers. It was very special and one of my greatest honors presenting the Medal of Honor to you."

"Anything else about that evening, sir?" Rocky was thoroughly enjoying the banter as he baited the former president.

Tanner's eyes opened wide. He Inhaled deeply. He was still holding on to Rocky's hand, slowly pumping it up and down. "Oh, there was so much going on that evening. Yes, indeed. So much." He handed Rocky off to his wife.

Mrs. Tanner latched on to Rocky and pulled him to her and away from her husband. They stood facing one another for a moment, smiling broadly. She released his hand. "Hello. We meet again," she said.

"Yes, we do." Rocky paused and reached inside his jacket pocket. He removed an envelope. Josephine's eyes had not left Rocky's gaze. He handed it to her. "It's quite different than the one you delivered to me." Rocky held her gaze.

Mrs. Tanner took the envelope and held it with both hands.

"Good evening, ma'am." He nodded, turned and left the reception line.

Familiar with lobbyists, politicians and donors, Rocky mingled easily with the other guests at the reception.

"Mr. Chambers, would you please come with me?" the familiar majordomo asked.

"Sure, what do you need?"

"It's not me, sir. It's Mrs. Tanner. She would like to speak with you."

"Very well."

Josephine Tanner stood near one of the side doors leading from the East Room. "Rocky...may I call you Rocky?" she asked. "It was Captain Chambers years ago. So formal."

"Yes, you may." Rocky observed the once all-powerful woman. *Well, it appears I have her attention.*

"Rocky, my husband and I have been so appreciative of the generous donations Chambers Enterprises has made the last several years to our foundation. Thank you."

"You are very welcome. I believe in supporting worthwhile causes." As he spoke, his disgust and distrust were thinly veiled.

"This check you presented. It's a personal check. It's for my husband's library. It's for a million dollars." She pursed her lips and sucked air between her teeth.

"Yes, ma'am."

"Why? Why would you do this after what happened?"

"I have my reasons."

"Are you going to share them with me?" she asked, in a kinder voice.

"I have two reasons. One is, I believe your husband's administration served the country well. The second is, I want to help support and propagate you and your husband's vision for our country."

"I appreciate that. I know my husband would as well. But I know there's more."

"There is," Rocky said.

"What?" She trembled. "What is it that you want?"

Rocky reached into the opposite inside jacket pocket and pulled out another envelope. "This is a copy of the letter you thought was destroyed. The one that your henchmen took from me after I read it. The one you hand wrote on your official stationery and signed."

Josephine looked at the envelope Rocky held. The color leaked from her face. Her eyes opened wide. She began to falter and reached for the wall to steady herself. She waved off a Secret Service agent. Rocky placed the letter in her hand.

She turned to Rocky. "Follow me," she snapped. She led him out of the room. In the adjoining hallway they seated themselves on a small divan out of earshot. A server presented a tray holding several glasses of champagne. They both helped themselves and sipped the beverages.

"That letter was destroyed," she insisted.

"So, we all thought," Rocky said.

"How did you get this?"

"It appears that one of your trusted boogey men must have switched it. He didn't destroy it. Oh, and for your information, he works for me now," Rocky taunted.

Mrs. Tanner inhaled, her face ironclad. "What do you want?" she demanded.

"Nothing, at the moment."

"What do you think you'll want?"

"Honestly, I don't know."

She looked at the envelope and said, "You know I have to destroy this."

"That's all right, I have the original and copies."

"Why do you feel you have to hold me up to this?" Mrs. Tanner asked.

"Why did you have to kidnap me? Why did you have to set me up with your husband? What did I ever do to be singled out and treated like that?" Rocky then stared at a portrait of a past president on the wall opposite them.

"It wasn't about you. Like I said in the letter. You were a tool, nothing more."

He turned from the painting as he said, "You use people. And when they no longer serve your purpose, you discard them."

"What is your point?" she sneered at him.

Rocky's jaw tightened. "You should never have discarded the secret agent you pimped out to your husband. Just the way you discarded me. You were careless, trusting people you shouldn't have. Obviously, the letter you have a copy of in your hand was not destroyed. Your hired thug screwed you. Switched it out and kept it. Now I've got it."

Rocky cocked his head and laughed. "Funny, it appears the people you fucked are intent on returning the favor."

Josephine pursed her lips and glared at Rocky.

"How did you get this?" she asked.

"Patience. I listened very carefully to an old gentleman, years ago. It was summer at the Cape. And then again, at the Academy, he reminded me of an old saying. He taught me to keep my friends and family very close. And to keep my enemies closer."

"Everyone knows that," She scoffed, wiping the condensation from her glass.

"Mrs. Tanner, there's a third and fourth element."

Josephine gulped down the last of her drink and almost broke the glass as she placed it on the table next to her.

"And what are the third and fourth?" she said, narrowing her eyes.

"Compensate your sources generously and loyalty runs in both directions. You shortchanged your people on both counts."

Mrs. Tanner stood up. She looked down at Rocky. "Do not share this with my husband. He just might do something stupid and out himself and destroy our legacy. Remember, I still have the resources to make your life very miserable. Maybe even end it."

Rocky was caught off guard by the vicious words dripping from her lips. *This bitch plays for keeps. So do I.*

Mrs. Tanner's voice spewed contempt. "Let me, and only me, know what you need and when you need it." She turned and walked back into the East Room.

* * *

Hired to run Nick's campaign, Gene crafted a platform based on Nick's declaration made the night of the backyard cookout. Seasoned politicians scoffed at the idea of boldly appealing across party lines. They said the conservatives would not embrace the left-of-center social elements. Nor would the liberals adopt the right-of-center fiscal agenda. Gene counted on Independents embracing Nick's platform. He knew that many voters on either side of center were looking for commonality. He was correct.

* * *

CONGRESSMAN NICHOLAS JEFFRIES DEFEATS SENATE INCUMBENT

The headlines ran nationally. Op-Eds and columnists nationwide asked how an unknown Republican congressman adopted fundamental elements from an opponent's platform, and how did he rip a Senate seat out from under a time-tested, entrenched liberal Democrat?

As he perused three morning papers, Rocky said to Nick, "The papers and talking heads are claiming you are a flash in the pan. They say you're a charlatan and you don't believe in the platform you ran on." Rocky buried his head in the paper and read on.

Nick sat, coffee cup in hand. He and Rocky were in the family room. Nick looked out onto the fields behind Sheila's and his home in Charlottesville. "I guess that's what you'd expect from entitled party elitists asleep at the wheel."

Rocky looked up from his paper and said, "These are media accounts, not Democrats."

"Really, what's the difference?" Nick grunted.

Turning the pages of the newspaper, Rocky mused, *I don't agree, but why spoil the moment? Let him savor the victory.*

"Well, congratulations, Senator," Rocky said, getting out of his chair. "You know, as one of your constituents, I have needs. Needs that only you can meet."

Facing Nick, Rocky loosened the terry-cloth robe Nick was wearing. He slid his hands inside the robe as

Nick placed his coffee cup on the table. They held each other's gaze.

"Sir, as your newly elected Senator, I feel it is my duty to satisfy your needs." Nick cupped Rocky's face in his hands and kissed him deeply. Rocky moved his hands over Nick's body, rediscovering what lay hidden beneath the robe.

CHAPTER 22
A BRIGHT LIGHT EXTINGUISHED

Rocky and Gene sat in Nick's Charlottesville office, facing the Senator seated at his desk. Gene led off the conversation with, "We have a big, fucking challenge. It appears that someone is floating a rumor that you two are gay. It's getting some traction."

"No shit!!" Nick said, jumping out of his chair His crazed look startled Rocky.

Rocky's stomach turned, and his throat tightened.

Gene, not fazed by Nick's reaction, continued. "With your senate re-election bid next week, it could cause a last-minute glitch."

"Fuck me! That's not a glitch, it a goddamn nuke!" Nick said, now pacing and ringing his hands.

Rocky got up and walked over to Nick. He placed a hand on his shoulder, "Hey Nicky, chill out a little. Everything's okay right now. We'll figure this out."

Gene began again. "We all know this race is too close to call. We can't afford to lose a single vote."

Nick's face was now ashen. He looked at Rocky and said in a strangled voice, "Rocky!"

Rocky pulled Nick to him and held him. He tried to think of what they could do, and how he could comfort his lover.

Gene said, "We don't know where it's coming from. It doesn't look like social media, or it would be viral by now. We have to nip it in the bud before it leaks online. We've got to keep this out of the press until after the election. We only have to get through four days."

Rocky and Nick looked at each other then returned to their chairs.

"I have an idea. I can get together with some of my more politically savvy friends and see if they can come up with an idea to buy us some time," Rocky offered.

"What the hell do you have for currency to buy that kind of help?" Gene scoffed.

Rocky turned in his chair and faced Gene. "How about the fucking millions I've donated to the LGBT community? Why would you ask such a stupid question, Gene? You, of all people?"

Gene glared at Rocky. "You don't need to get personal, Rocky!" He fired back.

"Personal!" Rocky said jabbing his finger inches from Gene's face. "I'll tell you what's personal. It's the accusations that could destroy Nicky, Sheila and the kids! That's personal! It sure as hell is personal to me!"

Nick appeared to have regained his composure. He sat quietly observing the interchange between Gene and Rocky.

"Okay, you two, settle down. It's personal and political. We've got to figure this thing out," Nick said, as he rose from his chair and began to walk around the room. "Hell, my family and I and Rocky live together in DC. He's godfather to my kids. Can't we just say we're like family?"

Gene sat up straight, clearly agitated as he wagged his finger back and forth between Rocky and Nick. "You two have not been smart. This pisses me off. How the hell could you two be so irresponsible? You have facilitated these perceptions leading to this accusation. Perceptions you could have avoided. If this comes out before Election Day, it will blast a hole in this campaign!"

Rocky heard what Gene had said, all the while keeping a close eye on Nick. *I have to help hold him and the family together.* His heart felt as if it could bust.

"You hired me, a gay, transgender campaign manager." Gene paused. "That act took courage. I am grateful you believed in me. People got over my being the campaign manager. But now, it'll look like the campaign is out of control and some sort of orgy is running rampant in the campaign and in your lives. Couple that with Rocky being a prominent gay-rights contributor and activist. For Christ's sake! You two live together! What did you expect to happen? You're either living in some gay fantasy world or you're just plain stupid! I've always suspected and never asked if you guys were fucking each other. It doesn't surprise me that someone else suspects you."

Rocky starred at Gene during the tirade. His jaw had grown firm and his face stone cold. "Like you hadn't figured it out! Ha! Me thinks he protests too much!"

Gene flipped Rocky off and continued focusing on Nick. "Your sex life aside, how did we get where we are politically? Frankly, it's the gays that held their noses and voted for you six years ago. Their support made a difference. You have Rocky and me to thank for that. Independents and gay friendlies brought you over the top. A lot of right-wingers reluctantly went your way. They like you as a person, a f-a-m-i-l-y man, and also because of your strong military and economic-growth positions."

"That's all true. Why can't we keep the same voters this time around?" Nick argued.

"How can you be so naive?" Gene laughed out loud. "Jesus!"

Rocky responded gently to Nick's question. "Nicky, if voters think you and I are having sex, with or without Sheila's knowledge, they'll run in the other direction. It's that simple. You'll catch the same blowback Prince Charles did when he was fucking around with Camilla and dumping on Princess Di. They love Sheila. You can't survive that."

"Christ Almighty!" Nick slammed his fist on the desk, startling Gene and Rocky. He sat back down in his chair and folded his arms. Several minutes passed as Gene stared at his phone. Rocky appeared lost in thought and Nick fumed, looking out the window.

"We need a distraction. How can we hold off the story until after the election?" Rocky asked both men.

Gene rose from his chair and clasped his hands behind his back as he spoke. "The *Washington Post* has asked for a comment. I can hold them off for one day, maybe two, but they won't wait long. This is much too hot. They like you as a candidate for re-election and as a senator, but they are Democrats, through and through." Gene stuck his hands in his pockets. "I also called in a favor with the Human Rights Campaign Director. She used her influence with the *Post*. That's the only reason this hasn't blown up on us yet."

"Yeah," said Rocky, "and they don't want to look a gift horse like me in the mouth. You may not realize how important my activities and financial contributions to the LGBT arena have been. We've accomplished a lot for transgender people. Gene, you might not be here if it weren't for me. Now this campaign is in big trouble. What are you going to do about it?"

Gene glowered at Rocky "Speaking of gift horse, you can get off your high horse. Your being out and high profile are as responsible as anything for where we are at this moment. Defeating a Republican incumbent is a huge trophy, and you may not be as valuable to the Dems as you think you are. If they had a viable Democrat candidate for this seat, they would ditch Nick in a heartbeat."

Rocky sat up straight and shouted back, "Fuck you, asshole. Fix this problem. If Nicky loses, you lose."

Gene ignored Rocky's outburst and picked up his briefcase and overcoat. "This is what we're going to do. I'm going to return to DC to hold back the floodgates. Nick, you and Rocky see if you can come up with a plan to quash these rumors. Maybe Sheila can help. Nick, try to get Sheila to be seen with you 24 hours a day. Rocky, get on the phone and pull in some favors. Get this shit tamped down!"

Gene walked out of the office, slamming the door behind him.

* * *

Nick picked up his cell and called Sheila. "Hi honey, what are the chances you could leave the kids with your folks tonight? Rocky's here. Gene just left. We have a problem and could use your input. I've got several campaign appearances today, so we need to fit it in later tonight," he paused and listened. "Great, see you later at the house. Love you. Bye."

* * *

Later that evening, Nick and Rocky sat in their boxer shorts in Sheila and Nick's kitchen, eating takeout.

"I sure as shit hope Sheila has some ideas. I couldn't keep my mind focused on any of my campaign speeches today. I don't think I can take four days of this kind of stress," Nick said, as he swallowed pizza and chased it with beer.

"Slow down; either eat or drink. Don't do both at the same time," Rocky said.

Sheila walked into the kitchen from the garage. "Hi there, guys! Miss me? Had to have me, huh? Made me leave my folks and the kids to come and spend time with two hot guys just lying around in their underwear!" She laughed as she came up and gave each of them a kiss.

"Did you two boys have fun today while the kids and I were at my folks?" Sheila asked.

Rocky and Nick smiled, but their smiles did not reach their eyes.

"This has been a shitty day, dear," Nick said.

"I guess so. By the looks of things around here all you've done is lounge, eat and drink. Where's mine?" Sheila tossed off her jacket, "Sure is warm in here. No wonder you boys are half naked. She leaned up against a counter and wiped sweat from her forehead. "I'm feeling a little queasy."

"Well, take a break. Here, let me get you some water." Nick got out of his chair, ran a glass of water at the sink and handed it to Sheila.

"That did the trick, thanks," said Sheila as she placed the empty glass on a counter. "So, what's the problem? Why the late-night meeting?" As she spoke she picked up around the family room and kitchen. Wiping her forehead several times, she reached out to an easy chair and fell into it. "I sure feel wobbly." Sheila laid her head back.

Rocky looked up from his pizza. "Sheila, why don't you take a break and eat some of this with us. Maybe you need food. I can clean up the mess."

Sheila didn't stir.

"Sheila, sweetie, did you hear Rocky?"

Sheila still did not answer.

Rocky and Nick exchanged looks, got up from the table and walked over to her.

"Sheila," said Nick. Rocky kneeled on the other side of the chair, grasping one of her hands. She didn't move. Nick shook her gently.

"Rocky, get a damp cloth."

"Hey, honey, what's...? Rocky! Something's really wrong," Nick exclaimed fearfully.

Rocky jumped up, grateful to be doing something. He pulled a dish towel from a drawer and ran it under the refrigerator water dispenser. He wiped the sweat from her forehead and face. She suddenly felt cold to his touch. "Something's really wrong here," Rocky's voice quivered.

The two exchanged looks of panic.

"Check her pulse, Rocky," Nick said. "This isn't like her. I'm worried." Nick's face retreated into a ghostlike trance.

Rocky placed his index finger and middle finger against the side of her neck. "There's a pulse, I think, maybe." Rocky felt his body imploding. "Jesus! Call 911!"

* * *

Sheila lay in a hospital bed hooked up to multiple monitors and i.v. tubes. Her bandaged head was slightly elevated, and her eyes were closed. Nick and Rocky were seated on either side of her bed.

"She's going to want to know what's going on as soon as she wakes up," Rocky said.

"Yeah, I'm praying she wakes up soon," Nick said.

Tests had been run all night. CAT Scans, MRIs and blood work. "Nicky, the doctors have been frank. The test results were bad. We need to think about the next step," Rocky said, as his heart beat heavily in his chest. "We're going to have to reach out to the kids and the rest of the family soon. It's almost noon. I'm surprised they haven't called to see when Sheila's picking them up."

"They're waiting for us to call them. They'd keep the kids as long as we'd let them. They're great that way." Nick's hand was trembling as he held Sheila's. "I just can't believe it." He burst into tears, resting his head on Sheila's thigh. "Please...a miracle. Please!"

Rocky watched Nick, knowing he must be in agony over the possibility of losing Sheila.

"Listen, Nicky. I'm going to go back to your house and go by Sheila's parents to check on Brooke and Ricardo. I need to tell both your folks something about what's going on," Rocky said.

Rocky stood behind Nick, putting his hands on his shoulders. "Hang in there, Nicky," he whispered softly in Nick's ear.

Nick, still holding one of Sheila's hands, answered Rocky in the same tone. "That sounds like a good idea. I know you'll handle it. If you get a chance, call my office and let them know that Sheila's very ill. Tell them I won't be able to campaign for the foreseeable future. Insist they don't say a word to anyone, especially the press."

"Sure, no problem. I think you're going to have to say something to the press. I'll reach out to Gene and let him handle it. Not showing up for appearances three days before an election is going to set off some alarm bells."

"You're right. Forget what I said. You two handle it as you think best. Thanks," Nick said as he stared down at his wife.

"Okay, will do." Rocky paused. "My grandfather and I have already put out feelers for specialists dealing with strokes. I'll let you know if and when I hear something. Can I get anything for you from the house?"

"I'm okay, thanks. Give my love to the kids. Let them know Mom is resting." He paused and wiped a tear. Tell them Mom and Dad love them."

"Do you need anything, clothes, work stuff?"

"No, thanks," Nick said.

Rocky left the hospital. He jumped in his car and called his grandfather. "How are things going with Sheila?" Rudolph Chambers asked immediately.

"Well, she actually woke up for a moment and spoke briefly. Then she nodded off."

"I'm so sorry for all of you, Rocky. I've been making inquiries. We are doing our best to find doctors that might be able to help. As you know, time is of the essence. It doesn't look good. Strokes as serious as hers typically don't end well. Please don't get me wrong, we're on it. I'm just being realistic."

"Grandfather," Rocky said, tears running down his face. "Is there anything out there? Any chance?"

"Son, I don't know. It's devastating. Don't give up hope."

Rocky said, "Thank you for looking. I've got to alert Nick's office and go check on the kids."

"Okay, son. Hang in there and let your grandmother or me know if we can help. Your dad has tried to reach you. So has your mother."

"Yeah, I know. Mom's not cool with Nicky and me. I'd rather not talk to her. I've never told her that Rick's my son. I don't want that to come up just yet. Do you think you could call them, update them and tell them I'm swamped and appreciate their calls?"

"Of course, Rocky. I love you," Grandfather said, his voice shaking with emotion.

* * *

"Call Gene Smithers," Rocky spoke into his phone.

"Gene here, what's up, Rocky? I expected to hear from you hours ago. How did it go with Sheila? Do you guys have a plan?"

"Gene, there's a problem," Rocky paused. "A big one." He used the back of his hand to wipe the tears obscuring his vision.

"What could be worse than the possibility of losing the election, for God's sake?"

In a dead, flat tone, Rocky said, "Sheila's dying."

"What?" Gene coughed. Rocky could hear Gene instruct people to leave his office. He heard a door close. "Rocky, what's going on?"

Rocky gave Gene the details on Sheila's health.

"She's on life support," Rocky sobbed.

"Hey, Rocky. Are you driving? If you are, pull over," Gene insisted.

"Okay."

Rocky turned into a strip-mall parking lot and shut off the engine. He removed a handkerchief from his back pocket and wiped his face, then leaned back into his seat.

"Are you still there?" Gene asked

"Yes, just give me a second." Rocky ran his palms and fingers up and down the front of his face and around his neck. He took a moment to relax, slowing his breathing.

Rocky cleared his throat and said, "The doctor showed up early this morning with another doctor, a specialist. Sheila had a massive stroke. It doesn't appear she'll make it out of the hospital." As his throat constricted and his heart broke, he cried, "Damn it, this just isn't fair!"

"Oh my God, Rocky. I am so sorry. This is unbelievable. This is so horrible for you, Nick and the kids. What can I do?" Gene's voice quaked.

Neither spoke for several moments. Knowing Gene was on the phone and cared for them all helped ease the agony Rocky was feeling. "Gene, I know you want to help, and you can. We need your help. Nicky needs your help. Someone has to focus on the election. What you can do is quash the other story, at least until after the election. That and Sheila on her death bed is unbelievably overwhelming." Rocky took a deep breath and cleared his throat, "Can you do this for us? Can you, Gene?"

Gene's voice sounded as if he was summoning strength to inspire confidence. "Yes, I think we can change the narrative. Let's head the gay accusations off at the pass. We might be able to keep the story buried until after the election." Gene was quiet for a moment. "We'll be totally transparent about Sheila's stroke. Sheila's health and every medical detail will be dripped out to the press hour by hour. We'll play this like a Greek tragedy, detail by detail, emotion by emotion. It's going to be tough for your family and friends to see it and hear it on TV and radio. They'll just have to tune it out. The public loves drama during elections. They love feeling the pain. This could work for us if we can make them feel they are part of the drama. Their empathy should turn into votes!"

Rocky thought it sounded like a cruel circus. He also knew Nick would hate it. But the gay-accusation story was lying in wait He knew it was his call.

"Gene, it's okay. Nicky said you and I should take care of everything. Go for it."

"Will do. Keep me informed on Sheila. We'll need to get medical info right away. I'm on it!" Gene said.

"I will, Gene, but hold everything until I speak with the families. I'll text when you can launch the story. You'll still have time to make the evening news." Rocky abruptly terminated the call, a hollow pit forming in his stomach.

He sat in the car for twenty minutes. *I need to keep going forward. I have to be there for Nicky and the kids.* Rocky seized what energy he could muster and shifted his body into overdrive. He set about his task of informing the children and families.

* * *

Rocky met with Nick's parents and then went to Sheila's family. He asked them to let him meet alone with the children.

Rocky huddled with Brooke and Rick, just the three of them. "Your mother wants you to know she's sorry she didn't pick you up today. She's not feeling well. Your dad and I took her to the hospital last night. She's resting there now."

Brooke asked, "What's wrong? When is she coming home? Can we go see her?"

Rocky, his arms around both of them, said, "I don't know when she's coming home. I will check with the doctor to see if you can visit. Is that okay?"

"That's all right with me. How sick is she?" asked Rick. Brooke nodded.

"I tell you what, I'll see what I can do to get you both into the hospital," Rocky said, getting up.

"Thanks, Uncle Rocky," Rick said.

Brooke nodded and jumped up to hug Rocky. "You look really sad. This is bad, isn't it?"

"It's serious, sweetie. Hang in there, you two! I love you and will be back soon." Rocky smiled and walked out the door, holding back tears.

* * *

Rocky headed back to Nick's office. During the drive, he texted Gene that the families had been brought up to date on Sheila's health. Gene responded with warm wishes to the family and promptly instructed his staff to send out a press release after he gave the go-ahead to the *Washington Post* with an exclusive:

SENATOR JEFFRIES CANCELS ALL CAMPAIGN APPEARANCES
WIFE ON DEATHBED

While Rocky was tying up loose ends with the family, Gene Smithers had offered the exclusive to the *Post* in exchange for burying the expose on Nick and Rocky. That fire would surely smolder and raise its ugly flames again, but for now it was out. In Gene's meeting with the *Post*, the editor said, "You know, Gene, we never wanted to hurt the senator. He's as good as it gets as far as Republicans go. But a story is a story. Out of respect for the senator and his family we'll bury it, but not for long."

"And for the exclusive on Sheila's stroke," Gene harrumphed.

"Yes, that too," the editor said wryly.

"Thanks. Can you give me a heads up on the outing story when you plan to run it?" Gene asked. "I mean, if he loses the election, your story will have little value. If he wins, there'll be six more years of grist for the mill."

The editor started laughing, "Hell, sure. If he wins and the story sticks hard, he might not make it past Christmas! With these crazies in the media and the nut jobs on Capitol Hill, who knows?"

"Who knows," Gene agreed.

* * *

Having shared the news of Sheila's condition with the senator's office and campaign staff, Rocky drove to Sheila and Nick's house. He showered, rested for a couple hours and collected a change of clothes for the kids. He delivered the clothes to them and headed back to the hospital.

"Nicky, don't you think you should take a break? You've been here a long time," Rocky said as he entered the hospital room.

"I want to be here just in case she wakes up again. I can't miss it," Nick sniffed. "If she wakes up, just for a second, I want to be here," he repeated. A moment later he asked, "How're the kids?"

"They're sad. I told them she was very sick and that she was trying to get better. I don't think they totally understand the situation. They're growing up, but they haven't really grasped how serious it is. Maybe it's my fault. Perhaps I should have been more forthcoming with the details. They're agitated and want to see her."

Nick mumbled, "I think they need to see her. I just wonder how they'll handle seeing her lying in this bed. Should they have to deal with something like this at their age? They're barely teenagers. It's tough enough being a teenager. Losing their mother will not make growing up any easier."

Rocky said, "We might be unfairly denying them the right to see their mother one last time." Rocky put his hand on Nick's shoulder. Would you consider allowing them to come? They've asked to see her.

Nick looked up from Sheila, his eyes swollen. "I don't know. What I really don't want them to see is the TV coverage this is getting. The reporters are camped outside our house. They can't go home. If they come here, they could be mobbed by that horde waiting for her to die."

"I think I could get them in here, past the mob outside. Nicky, the press can be assholes, but they're just doing their jobs. This is big news. She's always been popular with the press. Come to think of it, her numbers are higher than yours," Rocky smiled.

"You're right, but I still hate the bastards."

"If you're okay with the kids coming here, I'll get them in without having to run the press gauntlet."

Nick took Rocky's hand and said, "They should be here. They're old enough to deal with it. They might hate us both forever if we kept them from seeing her. Do what you can to keep them away from the press."

Rocky wrapped his arms around Nick and whispered, "You know Sheila loves you with all her might. She knows you're here. She knows you love her. She knows we all love her and are praying for her. You and I both know she would want to see the kids, or at least feel them close by."

Rocky released Nick and patted him on the shoulder. He kissed Sheila on the cheek. "Hey girl, I'm going to get Rick and Brooke. Be back soon."

"Thank you, Rocky," Nick said.

"You got it, buddy. I'll get 'em here the best and fastest way I can," Rocky said as he hurried out of the hospital room, a man on a mission.

Nick looked at his wife lying motionless in the bed. He took one of her hands in his. "Babe, I don't know if you can hear me. Maybe you heard Rocky and me. I hope so. If you did, is it all right if the kids come to see you?"

An electric shock bolted through Nick's body as he felt her press his hand. "Oh my God! Sheila! Was that for real? Was that you saying okay?" She squeezed his hand ever so slightly, twice.

"Oh baby, baby!" He tried to find a way to wrap his arms around her, navigating the tubes and wires. He pressed his cheek against her forehead, his tears running onto her face. She was limp in his arms, but alive and aware.

The door opened. "Senator, what are you doing? Get off those tubes! You might hurt her and mess up the equipment!" the nurse protested. She reached the bed and gently tugged him away from Sheila.

"She just squeezed my hand twice. Two times the second time!"

"That's wonderful, Senator. Try not to crush her when she does that," the nurse admonished kindly.

Nick sat back in his chair and spoke to Sheila nonstop. He went on about the family, the children, his love for her, politics and anything he could think of. "Sheila, you're an international personality. There are reporters and TV crews from all over. You're a star! You have to get well so you can capitalize on all this fame!" Nick said, sounding upbeat.

Twenty-six hours into his bedside vigil, he laid his head face down on the edge of the bed and dozed off.

"Dad? Dad? Are you awake?"

Nick, sound asleep, was roused by Brooke and Rick gently shaking his body.

"Daddy, it's Brooke and Rick. We came to see you and Mom." Nick felt tears welling. He forced himself to sit up and opened his eyes to find Brooke and Rick on either side, holding his hands.

Nick turned and stood, reaching around both of them. He kissed them each several times. The three were glued together. "Thank you for coming, kids," he said. "Your mom let me know she wants to see you."

"Did she talk to you?" Brooke asked.

"No, she squeezed my hand," Nick said, the joy spreading across his face.

"Do you think she will talk to us by squeezing our hands?" Rick asked.

"I don't know. I hope so. Why don't you get on opposite sides of the bed and hold one of her hands? Talk to her and see if she hears you." The two kids scrambled to their mother's side.

Brooke and Rick took turns talking to her. Their speech was animated as they told her how much they loved her and wanted her to get better. They each launched separately into monologues detailing their activities since they had last seen her.

"She squeezed my hand!" Brooke shouted. "Mom! Do it again!" No one spoke.

"She squeezed mine, too!" Rick said. "Do it again!"

All four waited patiently for another squeeze.

Rocky stood at the foot of the bed. "Let's give your mother a chance to rest."

The twins patted their mother's arms and told her they loved her. The four stood or sat, looking at Sheila lying in the hospital bed. Brooke picked at her cuticles. Rick rocked back and forth on his feet, arms folded and face glum. Nick was transfixed on Sheila. Rocky wished someone would say something.

"Dad guess how we sneaked in here," Rick said.

They didn't wait for him to respond. In unison, the twins said, "In an ambulance!"

"Really!" Nick said, doing his best to lift their spirits, acting more surprised than he really was.

Rick grabbed his father's arm and said, "Uncle Rocky had the ambulance come to Grandma's house and put us in it. Then we came here. The lights were flashing, but no sirens. The ambulance guy said they didn't want to attract too much attention. There's a lot of people outside the hospital. Some have cameras and vans with satellite antennas! It's really cool."

"Good job, Rocky. Excellent. Snuck 'em right in, huh?" Nick beamed, his eyes bloodshot and wide.

"Almost. One reporter and cameraman were pretending to be sick or injured, lying in wait in a hallway. They got photos of the kids and me getting out of the ambulance. It's sure to be all over the news any minute. Anyway, they got in here without too much trouble. That was the whole idea."

"Did you see all the flowers?" Brooke asked. "They're everywhere! Outside and inside! How come none are in here?"

Nick put his arm around Brooke. "That's so nice of people to send flowers. I know your mother would like to see them. The nurses and doctors said they can't be in the room because of germs and allergy things." He hugged her and kissed her cheek.

Two days later the headlines read:

SHEILA JEFFRIES DIES AFTER SUFFERING STROKE

CHAPTER 23

2014 – 2018: ONWARD AND OUTED

Heavy snow had brought the Capital city to a standstill. The halls were quiet on Capitol Hill. The newly elected Congress had been seated only days earlier.

"Congratulations, Senator, on your second term. No *Washington Post* article to screw up the swearing-in ceremony, thank God," Gene said, as he and Nick sat in the Senator's D.C. office.

"Yes, thank God. I suppose you're here about something other than electioneering."

"It's a bit more complicated. It depends on if you're ever planning on running for public office again," Gene said in a sarcastic tone.

Nick looked up from his paperwork. Annoyed, he said, "Really, Gene? Give me a break. Sheila's been gone only a couple of months. Congress is getting back in session. We're all concerned about what could be a career-killing expose. I'm just not in the mood for your tiresome games."

Gene shifted uncomfortably in his chair and hung his head slightly. "Sorry, I'll get right to it. I had a conversation with Rocky three weeks ago. He didn't want me to bring it up until after you'd been sworn in for your second term."

Nick asked, "What did you talk about? The upcoming *Post* piece?"

"Not exactly, though it's the catalyst for this conversation."

"Come on Gene, quit beating about the bush. Get on with it, please."

"I asked him if you two were lovers," Gene said curtly.

Nick looked up from his paperwork. "And what did he say?"

"He said to ask you. You're the politician. The one that stands to get hurt the most."

"That makes sense." He reached down for his briefcase. "Rocky and I talked about this in some detail soon after Sheila's death. I don't suppose he shared the contents of a letter she left?"

Gene perked up. "No, he didn't."

"Let me read it to you." Nick pulled a piece of paper from the worn, leather portfolio and placed it on his desk. He folded his hands and began to read.

Dear Nick and Rocky,

If you are reading this letter, then I am no longer with you. These are the last words I will say to either of you, and so, I want to begin by apologizing. Apologizing for not telling you about my deteriorating health. I have known about this illness for many months. Who knew petit mal seizures could one day be the death of me? My doctors did, apparently. No matter which doctor I spoke to, they said the same thing: "You may only have a few months before a massive stroke will hit you." I wish I could explain to you the terror and relief I felt with every passing day. That's why I couldn't bring myself to tell you, either of you, about my condition. I couldn't see the terror I felt come to life on your faces. And so, I quietly kept taking the blood thinners. I suppose that's why I survived as long as I did. A few months, the doctors said. But with the small seizures that kept breaking through, I doubted I'd live that long.

While I started this letter by tendering an apology, I am not asking for your forgiveness. When I found out about it, I decided that I wanted all of us to have as normal a life as possible. Oddly, I felt a sense of control over life, and I relished it! It's funny, isn't it? A dying woman taking control of her life. Well, at least this small level of control meant that my time with all of you were tear and worry free.

The one way I could ensure that you would never find out about my health was to move away from you, so you wouldn't see me falter. That's why the children and I spent so much time with my parents. I simply did not have the stamina to be a mother, wife and campaigner at the same time. And you were kind not to push me to take on all of those roles. It made me realize how fortunate I truly was to have you both by my side. It was the only way I could maintain my energy and positivity till the very end. And since you didn't push me to choose, I was able to be mother to my children for as long as possible.

Nick, my darling, I truly am glad that the election kept you extremely busy. It may not seem like it to you, but for me it was nothing short of a blessing to know that you weren't spending your time anticipating my death.

My dearest Rocky, I expect you did not leave Nick's side during my last days. I am sorry to have made you suffer so. You have always been there for us – for Nick, me and the children. And for that, I thank you.

Nick, Rocky, I love you both so very much. Almost as much as I love Rick and Brooke. And I know if all four of you stick together, you will heal with time. You are a wonderful family. My family.

I have finally reached the real reason for me to write this letter. Family. I have seen and experienced how much you and Rocky love each other, Nick. You have loved each other ever since the Academy. So, I think it's time for you two to lead a proper life together. I am blessed to have a child from each of you. You are, and always have been, a family. It's time you lived openly like one. This is my challenge to both of you: Get married. Pick any state that will allow you to get married and do it.

Rocky, I hope you will adopt the children when the two of you are married. Nick, as your second campaign is nearing its end, I sincerely hope that you have been re-elected. Your constituency will get over your relationship with Rocky. This would be another step toward our nation accepting diversity and authenticity. Keep this movement alive. Please, make this journey together. Make it in my memory.

Before I say my final goodbye, I want you to honor a request. I have written two letters, one each for Brooke and Rick. I want you to give the letters to them after I'm gone.

Thank you both for letting me be a part of your lives. We have created legacies on so many different levels. My prayer is that you both continue to love one another and that you will love and raise the children together, making a difference in all the lives you touch.

I am with you, always and forever.

All my love,

Sheila

Gene put his head in his hands for several minutes. Rising up, Nick could see tears had stained his shirt and tie. Nick rose from his chair and removed a handkerchief from his pocket and handed it to Gene. Gene made use of the handkerchief.

"I'm not sure if anyone other than Rocky's family knew. We never shared it with anyone else," Nick said. "My guess is there has been a lot of speculation."

Gene sat and asked Nick to reread the letter. As he listened again, he gathered his composure. Nick finished reading and noticed his listener had recouped.

"Nick, thank you for sharing that with me. My heart aches for all of you."

"You are welcome, and thank you for understanding, Gene."

Gene asked gently, "Can we use the letter, or parts of the letter?"

"What do you mean?" Nick grew visibly agitated. "Are we back to exposing my personal life and loss to the media?"

Gene fussed with paper in his lap and cleared his throat. "I really hate this, but I have no choice. I have a job to do, which you hired me to do." Gene wiped his perspiring brow with Nick's handkerchief. "As we have all agreed, it's better to drive the narrative. We have an uphill battle. Maybe we can use the letter to humanize you both. Show Sheila's support and love. There's a Shakespeare-like quality to this that might capture the hearts of the people. Just think about it."

"This sounds Machiavellian, not Shakespearean," Nick grunted.

"What's your point? Of course, it does. It's politics and you're a politician."

"I don't know. I need to think about it and run it by Rocky. As parents, he and I need to tell Rick and Brooke what's about to happen. I don't think we can fully protect them from the fallout, but we've got to try to mitigate it somehow."

"I understand. Obviously, we want to be and *must* be sensitive to the family. That said, if things go right, your situation presented as a modern-family scenario might be embraced by the public. You and the family could be seen as championing a new era that exemplifies family diversity, and so on."

Nick leaned forward and rolled his pen between his fingers. He sat back in his chair.

"That's something I'd have to discuss with Rocky. It would impact the children. One thing's for sure, we're not going to get into the paternity thing. That's a nonstarter," Nick insisted. "I'll talk about it with Rocky and get back to you."

* * *

Two weeks later new headlines shocked the nation:

WIDOWED SENATOR JEFFRIES AND WAR HERO RICARDO CHAMBERS EXPOSED

A day later the headlines took an unusual twist and announced upcoming television interviews:

NETWORK AND CABLE NEWS TO INTERVIEW JEFFRIES AND CHAMBERS

Gene, Rocky and Nick met with their public relations firm's director at their home in Alexandria as another Nor'easter blanketed the city with snow.

"Gentlemen, it appears we have a chance at driving the narrative," the PR director said. "These interviews may be exhausting and painful, but it's the only way for us to take charge and tell your story."

Standing by a roaring fire, Rocky said, "You're right. Laying the groundwork can serve to make the next six years palatable, or at least livable. Also, it just might help pave the way for some open-mindedness. We don't have anything to lose, and lots to gain. Not just for us, but for thousands coming behind us."

"Aren't you the activist, Mr. Chambers?" Gene said sarcastically. Nick came to Rocky's defense. "I agree with Rocky. Let's continue to embrace this. Should we announce our intention to marry?" Nick asked.

The PR director said, "Absolutely. It'll give you credibility and communicate stability in your family life. There are still many people in the world who think that all homosexuals do is participate in orgies or are pedophiles. They have no concept of how the majority of gay people live. They don't realize that other than their sexual preferences, there's little difference between straights and gays. Members of the LGBT community have the same values, hopes and dreams as everyone else. We have to get that message out there."

Rocky said, "Straight people seem to be against us because we're different. How would they like it if we turned the tables? Why don't gays let straight people know they have no right to condemn our sexuality any more than we have a right to attack theirs?" Rocky scoffed. "Let's make a deal with them. We won't hold their being straight against them if they don't attack us for being gay. I just hate all the hazing, bullying and name-calling. It's wrong!" Rocky said.

"*Carpe Diem!*" Gene said. "It's all about driving the story. Make the modern, diverse family the story, not your relationship."

"Well," Rocky quipped, "Don't forget the hate, bullying, violence and other bonuses that go along with being queer. Then there's that tolerance bullshit, deceptive bastards, masking their hate."

Everyone sat for a moment as the reality of what Rocky had spouted set in. Someone had to breath some wind back into the sails that had been deflated by the reality check.

"By showing the example of our loving, committed family, we just might be able to shed some light and normalcy on all gay families," Nick said.

Gene, visibly impatient, turned to the PR director and asked, "If we're all in agreement, can we move forward with the strategy that you've outlined?"

"Absolutely," said the director. "If we have agreement. What say you, gentlemen?"

Rocky and Nick looked at each other.

"Please give us the room for a couple of minutes, guys," Rocky said.

Alone, Rocky and Nick took a seat side by side on the couch. They held each other's hands.

"What do you think, Nicky?" Rocky asked.

Nick looked down for a few seconds, then looked resolutely into Rocky's eyes. "If I'm to stay in public life, I don't think we have a choice." Squeezing Rocky's hands, he continued, "This will publicly expose you right alongside me, a target for ridicule and constant attack. You need to think about yourself and your family. Your mother, your grandparents and Chambers Enterprises."

Rocky grinned, lips closed. "I thought long and hard about all of that. I love you. I want what you want. I have you. I have the kids." Rocky sat closer and said, "Will you marry me?"

Nick smiled as his eyes lit up. "Of course, Rocky. Of course, my love."

They hugged each other. "Of course," repeated Nick, whispering into Rocky's ear.

"Now, that's settled," Rocky beamed. "About the family. You and the kids are my family. My parents, brother and sister are important, but not players in the decision. Most of them will be fine. If not, that's okay with me. Grandfather and Grandmother are one-hundred percent behind me. They want what I want."

"Now, regarding Chambers Enterprises, I've been running the show since Grandfather semi-retired several years ago. If the Board of Directors doesn't like it, too bad. They can fight it if they want, but they'll lose. I *am* Chambers Enterprises!"

"You're talking about a huge multinational corporation, Rocky."

"I'll fight to the end, regardless. Then I'll fight some more until I win. You know me. I win."

"Chambers-Jeffries?"

"Agreed!" Nick and Rocky called the men back into the office. "Gentlemen, Rocky and I would like to present the future Senator Nicholas and Colonel Ricardo Chambers-Jeffries."

* * *

One week had passed following the airing of the interviews. Rocky and Nick sat having breakfast in the Arlington townhouse. Morning papers, two cell phones and two iPads were strewn across the kitchen counter.

"I can't believe all the hate mail, social media and cable-news trashing. On top of that, yesterday some guy screamed at Rick. He hollered, 'Your daddy's a faggy!'" Nick said.

"I've never heard that one before," Rocky quipped.

"As of the last count, we've had twenty-five death threats. The shit never stops."

"It looks like I've got unexpected headwinds at Chambers corporate. Some board members are making noises. Most want to embrace their CEO being gay. They think it helps the company image, like the Apple CEO. Grandfather is leading the charge on my behalf. There are some conservative holdouts who think we're all going straight to hell, but I think they'll come around."

"Jesus, Rocky, I had no idea. How is it that in this day and age anyone sitting on the board of an international conglomerate still behave that way?" Nick marveled.

"It's all about perception. They're afraid our stockholders might react negatively. As luck would have it, I got the board to postpone the vote. I told them you were considering sponsoring legislation that would require preferential treatment of LGBT-owned businesses bidding on government contracts," Rocky chuckled.

"What?" That's news to me!" Nick laughed.

"Me, too."

Cheshire cat grins broke out on both their faces.

"We need to change the topic and get down to business," Nick said.

"And whatever could that be?" Rocky replied.

"We've got to grab our outing by the horns. It's firing up my constituents on the right and not in a good way. We need to embrace our relationship and frame it on our own terms, terms that advance our lives and my service in the Senate.

* * *

That Saturday afternoon, Nick and Rocky were relaxing at home in Charlottesville. Rocky sat in front of the fireplace in the family room, drinking a glass of cabernet. "I love this room. I love this house! It's the nucleus of our family. No city noises. No airplanes in the background. No reporters hanging around outside. Well, most of the time. It helps having a three-hundred-foot drive with a gate at the end," Rocky said.

Nick leaned against the mantle and looked at Rocky. "Hey, fiancé. When and where do you want to get married? The media is all over this. It's been several weeks since we said we'd get back to them."

Rocky sat back on the couch and crossed his legs. "Well, I haven't asked anybody to marry me. And nobody's asked me to get married. Has anyone asked you?" Nick stepped over to where Rocky was sitting and playfully smacked him on the shoulder. "Have you asked anyone?" Rocky was almost falling off the couch with laughter as he teased Nick.

Nick rolled his eyes. "So, what about that sweet proposal in my Senate office?"

"That was just a dry run. That didn't count," Rocky taunted.

Nick grinned slyly at his lover, then stood at military attention and commanded, "So come kiss me and ask me to marry you, Marine!"

"I thought you'd never ask!" Rocky smiled broadly as his heart skipped a beat. He jumped off the couch and over to where Nicky was standing. Then, on bended knee, he took both of Nick's hands in his. Nick relaxed his rigid posture.

"Nicky, you are the love of my life. I can't imagine loving anyone as much as I love you. Would you do me the honor of marrying me and spending the rest of our lives together?"

Nick knelt so their eyes were at the same level. "Rocky, yes, with all my heart. I love you and so desperately want to spend the rest of my life with you."

They each leaned forward, crossing the inches that separated them. Wrapping their arms around each other, they kissed and sank onto the hearth rug.

"When do the kids get home?" Nick murmured.

"They're on fall break in Mexico, remember?" Rocky moaned.

There was no more talking.

* * *

"This was a great idea. Martin's in Georgetown. Really romantic," Nick said later that evening as they entered the restaurant and bar.

Rocky had reserved a particular table. They sat side by side against the wall, facing out across the restaurant and to the windows beyond. The street lamps illuminated the gently falling snow.

"They say this is the table where Jack Kennedy proposed to Jackie. It's like one of those 'Washington slept here' places."

"Well, Jack slept in a lot of places," Nick quipped.

Rocky laughed as they toasted one another.

"I think Boston also has a restaurant that claims Kennedy proposed there. Who knows? It doesn't matter. It'll be fun celebrating our engagement here," Rocky looked into Nick's eyes and said, "I love you."

Nick smiled and retuned the look, "I love you, too."

"No politics tonight, please," Nick begged.

Rocky's phone beeped. He looked down and read the text message, then looked at Nick, inhaling and exhaling through his teeth.

"I agree, and let's keep it cool while we're here. No public displays of affection other than sitting side by side," he said pressing his knee against Nick's under the table.

"Sure, but why did you say that?"

"I think someone let the cat out of the bag," Rocky said.

"You're kidding!"

"Nope, that was a text from Gene."

"What's it say?" Nick asked in an apprehensive tone.

Rocky read the text, "'The press may have been tipped off to your dinner and its location.'" Rocky paused looking at his phone and returned it to his jacket pocket. "My guess is someone on the restaurant staff leaked it. They're the only people I've talked to. Do you want to leave? We can go somewhere else."

"No, if they know where we are, they may already be outside." At that moment a flash went off near the restaurant's entrance, followed by a figure quickly exiting through the door.

The noise around them promptly ceased. The other guests directed their attention to Rocky and Nick sitting side by side in the booth. Patrons started whispering among themselves. Both men directed their gaze at the figure now passing outside by the restaurant windows.

"Looks like someone got a good picture for tomorrow's papers," Rocky said slamming his napkin on the table.

"Damn! I hope that's the last of it for tonight," Nick said, fumbling with his glass. "Okay, let's go with the flow and try to enjoy our engagement dinner."

Rocky sat with his back pressed against the banquette. Slowly drawing air through his nose, expanding his chest, he exhaled quickly through his mouth. "I'd really like to kiss you about now."

The corners of Nick's mouth curled into a subtle smile.

"Yeah, I'd like that, too." Nick squeezed Rocky's hand under the table.

Someone bursting loudly through the front door shattered the magic of the moment. The intruder scanned the room, his eyes soon landing on Nick and Rocky at their table 15 yards from the door.

Startled, Nick and Rocky looked to see the fast-moving figure barreling through the room toward them. The restaurant again became silent. Only the stranger's boots hitting the bare, oak floor could be heard. As the stranger stopped in front of them, both men jumped out of their seats, overturning the table. They gasped as the large intruder slamming the overturned table up against them, pinned both to the back of the banquette.

"Hey Senator, you faggot! You're going to meet your maker tonight!" The intruder was large and burly, dressed in worn jeans and a brown, plaid shirt. A bright-red hat emblazoned with "REPENT!" in black letters sat squarely on his shaggy brown hair. A course, splotchy beard failed to cover his pockmarked face. A large pistol was visible in his right hand.

As if on cue, the sound of falling tables, glass and china competed with screams as patrons dove to the floor for cover. Several people escaped out the door as others crawled under tables and behind the bar as the big man held his gun on Rocky and Nick.

"Which one of you is the homo senator?" Both men, now partially standing, froze. "Answer me, damn it, or I'll shoot you both!"

Lifting his hand above his head, Rocky said, "I am!"

"Bullshit! Now I can see it ain't you. It's that queer next to you! I seen his picture!"

Nick turned toward the assailant as he aimed the gun at him.

"I was wrong, you ain't goin' to meet your maker. God don't want no cocksuckers anywheres near 'im!"

He held the pistol grip with one hand. Rocky heard the piece's action as he cocked the gun with the thumb of his other hand. Focused on the 45, Rocky's keen vision allowed him to see him wrap his index finger around the trigger.

Flight gave way to fight as Rocky spun toward Nick, shielding him from the bullet now traveling towards them. The sound of the gun discharging the bullet splintered the hearing of everyone in the small bistro.

The bartender, a former football quarterback, also heard the gun being cocked and had forcefully thrown a full bottle of gin. The bottle crashed into the back of the lunatic's left shoulder as he squeezed the trigger. The liquor bottle's strike threw off the shooter's aim.

The bullet pierced Rocky's upper right shoulder positioned just above Nick's forward-facing left shoulder. Blood flew in every direction, coating Nick's face, the table and the wall behind them. Rocky slumped down, laying half on the half on the upturned table and half on Nick.

The screaming grew louder as more patrons fled out the front door and others out through the kitchen.

The shooter, stunned with having missed the senator, stood contemplating his next move. A guest behind him took advantage of the hesitation and raised a chair high in the air, driving it down on the shooter's head. As he fell to the floor, the gun fell out of his hand and slid across the dining room.

Four patrons pounced on the sprawled attacker, pinning him to the oak floor.

Nick had reflexively caught Rocky when he fell against him, pushing them both against the wall and down onto the booth bench. Nick now held the semi-conscious Rocky, cradling him as best he could. "Hang in there, babe. An ambulance will be here soon."

Rocky's breathing grew increasingly shallow as the pain increased and his vision fogged. The ringing in his ears obscured the screams around him.

"Help me get him up!" Nick shouted.

A man and a woman rushed to Nick's side. The three hoisted Rocky off the overturned table and laid him on the floor.

The sound of the shot still ringing in their ears, the other patrons were now milling around slowly, saying little and quietly checking on one another.

"I'm a nurse. Get me as many napkins as you can. We've got to stop this bleeding!" the woman said.

Those close by tossed a shower of napkins at her. Snagging several midair she handed them to Nick. "Put your hand under the wound and hold these in place." He reached under Rocky's shoulder and held several against the wound. Nick jerked up as he saw blood on Rocky's chest.

"The bullet went through him!" he shouted to the nurse.

"I know!" she said. "That's why you have blood on your face!"

Pointing her finger at the man who helped place Rocky on the floor, the nurse shouted "You! Hold these napkins on the exit wound. Not too much pressure, just enough to slow the bleeding."

She ripped tablecloths off nearby upturned tables and rolled them into a thick pad, positioning them under the middle of Rocky's upper back and head. "You two keep him raised up a little to stem the blood flow. Remember, not too much pressure; he's got to breathe."

Rocky's eyes were dilated, his breathing shallow

"Hold on, Rocky, help is on the way," Nick whispered into his ear. "I love you. Hang on. Please, hang on!"

The ambulance and police cars' sirens and flashing lights grew louder and brighter as they drew closer.

"Is anyone else hurt?" hollered the restaurant owner. No answer was heard above the low keening of the patrons. The restaurateur repeated himself three times. "Okay, I guess not. Please stay calm and try not to disturb anything. The police will want to talk to all of us." He paused for a moment, looking in the direction of the now prostrate shooter. "An' you guys!" pointing to the four men straddling the shooter, "Don't suffocate the SOB, we want to see the bastard hang legal-style!"

The nurse, the man helping them, and Nick replaced the pack of blood-soaked napkins with clean ones.

As the police and ambulance attendants thundered through the front door of the restaurant, some patrons began to sob again while others shouted into their cell phones. Four paramedics rushed over to Rocky. The woman who had been helping them identified herself as a nurse and updated the medical team.

The police carted the semi-conscious shooter out of the restaurant, ignoring the parameds entreaties to examine the attacker.

Nick struggled to stay close as the paramedics worked on Rocky. "We need room, please move back," insisted one of the paramedics. "Anybody know this guy?"

"I do, he's Ricardo Chambers," Nick said.

Someone in the growing crowd said, "You mean the senator's lover?"

"Yes, he's my fiancé," Nick said in a strong voice.

"You're Senator Jeffries?" asked a paramedic looking up at Nick.

Nick nodded.

"Okay, then. When we get him in the ambulance, jump in."

The room hushed for a moment, and then came alive with conversations and another flurry of cell-phone activity.

* * *

Nick, still in his bloodstained clothes, sat next to Rocky's hospital bed. He held one of Rocky's hands in both of his. As he stared at Rocky, he saw a languid movement in his eyelids as he slowly opened them, revealing the blue eyes Nick loved so much.

Nick gasped and leaned forward to within inches of his lover's face.

"Where am I?" Rocky murmured through parched lips.

"George Washington Hospital."

Rocky rolled his lips together as he tried to lubricate them with his tongue.

"Wow, my head weird...good meds...how long been here?" Rocky stumbled through his words.

"Five or six hours. They've kept you sedated. You lost a lot of blood. Mostly on me," He said gently, smiling at Rocky. "They need to get some of that blood back into you and you're not being very cooperative. You keep trying to get up all the time." Nick patted him on his thigh. "I told the docs the only way to keep you in one place was to knock you out with some powerful drugs!"

Rocky chuckled. He turned his head slowly to the right and then to the left. "Don't feel much."

"You're very, very heavily sedated." Nick patted the patient's thigh again.

Rocky scanned the hospital room as if surveying the heavens. He then focused on Nick.

"You good husband an' wear blood stained clothes to hospital? You my Jackie?" Rocky tried to kid Nick.

"Bad joke, bad taste. Glad to know you haven't lost your sick sense of humor, dear."

Rocky strained to look at Nick. "You okay? Get hit?"

"Nope. Relax. You took it all. The bullet exited your shoulder. Without all those muscles it would have hit me. It carved you up a bit, hit your clavicle and ricocheted into the wall behind us."

"Glad to be of service," Rocky said, forcing a grin, sensing nausea.

Nick rose out of his chair. He leaned over and put a kiss on Rocky's parched lips. "In case I forget to tell you, thanks for saving my life." He then kissed Rocky on the forehead. "My macho Marine saved my life," he laughed. "I think I'll marry him."

Rocky grinned. His eyes glazed over, saying, "Where was I hit? Back?"

"More the shoulder. Relax and get some rest," Nick said, smiling and visibly amused at the effect the drugs were having on Rocky.

"Go home now?" Rocky murmured as he sank into his pillow.

"No, sweetie, not with the drugs you're on," Nick said, patting Rocky's arm.

Rocky dozed off.

CHAPTER 24
POLITICS & MARRIAGE

Gene teased, as he sat with Nick in the hospital room. "Well, Rocky if they gave the Medal of Honor for saving a politician's life, you'd be the first man ever to get awarded the medal twice,"

"He'd get my vote," Nick quipped.

Rocky said, "Thanks, guys, but I think we have something even better." He adjusted the sling holding his arm strapped to his body and winced. "Fuck, that hurts."

"Quit moving around!" Nick said, sensing Rocky's pain.

Gene handed Rocky a glass of water and said, "Let us know what you're thinking."

Rocky took a sip and set the glass on the tray in front of him. "I've had days to sit here in this hospital room listening to the TV and reading the papers. I'm not the political strategist here. Gene is. But I have some ideas."

"We're all ears," said Nick.

Rocky pulled a select stack of newspapers from a pile on a second tray beside his hospital bed. "Here are some of the headlines from the past couple of days. We'll start with my favorite: 'Senator Jeffries's Life Saved by Lover.' There's also, 'Religious Right Attempts Assassination of Gay Senator,' 'Nation's Gays Hunted by Madman,' 'Diversity Slowed By Angry Right,' and 'Family Values Under Assault.' That last one makes no sense. I guess they forgot who was shot. Another good one, 'When Will America Embrace Diversity?'"

"Which one is the strongest?" Gene asked.

"'When Will America Embrace Diversity?'" Nick guessed.

"Right. That's it. Seize this headline and craft it into a narrative. A mantra that could galvanize gays, blacks, Hispanics, women and others," Rocky said.

"How so?" Gene asked

"Use the assassination attempt as a rallying cry to bring the disenfranchised together. I know that sounds vague, but I have a plan that can energize the message. Nicky, I apologize for not asking you about this first, but I've been doped up. My mind is all over the place. I guess I didn't think about not talking to you first until now."

"That's okay. What have you got?"

"Are you sure? It involves our wedding."

"As long as we're still getting married, I really don't care. If it will help bring people together, that's all the better," Nick said.

"It's not a very Republican idea or strategy."

Nick said, "Please, Rocky, just say it."

"Let's set a wedding date for May of next year at the National Cathedral."

"Next May? That's a long time from now. The National Cathedral? I thought we wanted a small, intimate ceremony?"

"I know, I know, but let me finish. The wedding needs to be delayed so we can prepare for what comes together before the wedding. The wedding will be the grand finale. It will be a unification ceremony of not just us, but everyone fighting for equality for all!"

"That sounds terrific!" Gene said as he jumped out of his chair.

The furrows in Nick's brow deepened as his eyes flashed wide and his jaw sagged.

Gene continued, "Are you talking about some sort of rally, parade, a protest leading up to the big wedding?" Gene stood pensive, waiting for Rocky to respond.

"Nicky are you okay?" Rocky asked as he noticed the look on his lover's face.

"I don't know. What exactly are you saying? Make a circus out of our wedding?"

"No, not a circus. That's why I should have spoken with you first. I'm sorry. He rose off his pillows to comfort Nick. Lightning pain shot through his shoulder. "Ow! Damn it, that hurts!"

Nick jumped up and took Rocky's hand. "For crying out loud, Rocky, stay still. You'll never get out of here if you don't let your shoulder heal. Stay still!"

Nick's face was lined with fear, alerting Rocky to how difficult this all was on his fiancé. "You're right. I'll be okay. He placed his left palm on the side of Nick's cheek. "I'm sorry. I'll be careful." Rocky settled back against the pillows.

Gene, strumming his fingers, interjected, "Can you be specific? What do you see happening leading up to the wedding?"

"Is it okay if we keep talking about this?" Rocky asked Nick.

Nick smiled and said, "Sure! Why not? Just stay still!"

Rocky sighed and winced, trying to stay still. "Okay, the idea is to get national support from all those that would like to participate in creating a unified narrative on equality. We should spend the next six months organizing. We have to organize our thoughts and spell out our goals first, then launch in April of next year. We focus all of April on holding rallies, conferences, town-hall meetings and canvassing state legislatures. The first two weeks in May, we get as many people as we can to come to Washington and repeat the process. By the time we're finished, we'll have gained local and national support. This could possibly lead to passing legislation in all fifty states, the territories and the House and Senate, creating a law that has teeth, guaranteeing equality for all Americans."

Nick stood up. Gene and Rocky followed his movement as Nick paced the private hospital room. "So, what you are proposing is that we politicize our wedding. Am I right?"

"I am," Rocky asserted with conviction.

Nick walked over to Rocky and took his hand. He paused for a moment and looked into Rocky's eyes. "You're amazing. I'm supposed to be the politician, Gene the strategist and tactician. Look at you. What you propose makes sense. It could change the lives of millions."

Rocky exhaled and squeezed Nick's hand. "I'm happy you're okay with it."

"I'm more than okay with it."

"I'm curious about the National Cathedral component," Gene said resting his chin on his clenched fist. "You want to invite supporters to the wedding?"

"That's part of it. And I have a grander plan. I want to invite every senator, member of congress, the president and cabinet. We should invite the Joint Chiefs, the Supreme Court, governors, church leaders, state party heads. We should include anyone who can lend a hand in unifying this country by avowing equality, including haters. Publicize the invitation list. Put pressure on everyone -- haters, too. Pressure them to attend and by doing so, empower equality. Our marriage is not just about love between two men. It symbolizes the love between men and women, men and men, women and women, all races and all diverse peoples."

Gene clapped his hands together and exclaimed, "It's like our very own royal wedding!"

"You're so gay!" Rocky laughed.

Gene stood up and pontificated, "Look at the Brits. When they have their royal weddings, they bring the people together. There is, for a time, unity and oneness. We need to do the same thing but make it last!"

"You're right. That's it!" Rocky stopped for a moment, then looked solemnly at the two men. "I hope the nation gets it, too."

* * *

After months of planning and organizing, April was upon them. Nick and Gene huddled in his Capitol Hill Senate office.

"As planned, April has proven to be a banner month. I'm not sure how the conservatives feel, but they're giving a lot of lip service to equality. My guess is they can't wait to get this whole thing over with. They're running scared. Looming midterms are spooking them," Gene said.

Nick was pacing the room. "One of the concerns I have is that the Republicans will wait and try to get rid of me when I'm up for re-election. Rocky's sources say they're looking for someone to run against me in the primary. With all the focus on diversity, I think a lot of Republicans are feeling left out of the conversation. Oddly enough, the Republicans' dislike of the equality issue strengthens the Democrats' support. But I'm a Republican! The Dems wouldn't hesitate to support someone from either party who brings the momentum I bring. Will the Republicans? Or are they fair-weather friends? I'm afraid it's all about power."

"Now you're thinking in the long term, like a seasoned politician," Gene said.

"I'm not so sure I like the sound of that, Gene." I've always despised those so-called 'seasoned politicians,' wanting power for power's sake. Why is it that Democrats have ideas that touch people's hearts and Republicans are seen as the party that craves power? Where is the Republican politician who has a heart and craves fiscal responsibility and a strong military?"

"That would be you, Nick. You just need to find some Republicans who aren't afraid to vote with their heart on social issues and their gut on fiscal ones," Gene said.

"Well, maybe our efforts will cull out self-serving power mongers. The national debate seems to have rattled conservatives and liberals alike. Some of the more seasoned Dems have been complaining that I'm co-opting their agenda. Since when did equality belong to one party? As I recall, it was the Republicans who freed the slaves. When did we lose our moral compass?"

Gene countered back at Nick, "But the Civil War was about more than just slavery. The North and the South were also at loggerheads over trade and agriculture. The northerners were smarter. They marshaled the hatred of slavery to get the upper hand and gain power. It wasn't then, and it isn't now, just one issue.

And, remember, the winning side writes the history," Gene continued.

"That's true. It was about power. But good did win out over evil. I'm not naive, but some things never change. We can still fight for good and human rights. We should always fight for what is right. This doesn't and shouldn't be an issue that pits party against party. Everyone should fight for what is right," insisted Nick, breaking a sweat.

"The only way we'll have equality is if we convince the people, the electorate. To hell with the politicians! Remember what it says in the Constitution. The people are sovereign. It's the politicians who are elected to serve the people, not the other way around," reminded Gene.

"I know the theory, but it's not the reality. Why does Washington have all the power? Because the politicians have given their power to the bureaucracy. They form agencies and hire people to staff them who are insulated from the will of the people. Then the elected officials grow lazy and don't look out for the electorate. They don't protect them."

"Jesus, Nick! You can't talk like that in public. You'll be nailed to the cross alongside other defeated politicians who were never heard from again."

"You're right," Nick said in a defeated tone. "That's the problem with all of us once we're elected and serving the people. We get complacent on our pedestals. We lose our will, our integrity and then our independence. We just go along with our party's talking points and think we're telling our constituents what they want to hear. All we're really doing is parroting what those in power want us to say. Most of us are cowards, pawns in the hands of even bigger, more ruthless cowards. Then there's the right-wing and left-wing media."

"Why don't you forget about running for the Senate again and run for president? You have passion. Unleash your ardor on the country!" Gene's zeal was aroused. "Besides, I charge a lot more for running presidential campaigns!"

CHAPTER 25
TURNERS TURNED

Rocky and Nick sat holding each other's hands as the limousine carried them to the National Cathedral in Washington, DC.

"Are you ready to tie the knot?" Rocky asked, kissing Nick's freshly shaven face.

"Yes, absolutely," a gleaming Nick responded.

"I can't believe our plan worked. We've filled the Cathedral. Four-thousand people! It sure feels like a royal wedding to me. I'm surprised we're not more nervous."

"I'm nervous. Talk about a Big Fat Gay Wedding!" Nick chided.

"I don't think many people had the courage to decline the invite. However, I think those who declined to attend the wedding due to a doctor's appointment were a bit disingenuous.

Seems like a lot of people go to the doctor on a Sunday." Nick and Rocky both laughed.

"Word has it there is a 'designated survivor'," Nick said. Just like they have during the State of the Union address when everyone in government is on Capitol Hill for the speech. If the place gets blown up, they have to have a cabinet member tucked away to run the country in the aftermath. The survivor would take over as president," Nick said.

"Yes, I know that. Do you know who our designated survivor is? I hope it's a Democrat," Rocky taunted his soon-to-be-Republican husband

Nick squeezed Rocky's hand hard. "I have no idea. So much for you thinking about unity!"

"One more thing before show time." Rocky gently tugged on Nick's hand and engaged him eye to eye. "I'd like to honor Sheila's wish. I want to adopt Brooke and Rick as soon as I can."

Nick covered Rocky's hand with his own. "I have the papers waiting for your signature whenever you're ready. Also, the paperwork legally changing all our names to Chambers-Jeffries is ready."

"Thank you," Rocky said, choked with emotion.

"Now, let's get hitched!" Nick said.

"I sure am glad I have a handkerchief!" Rocky declared, sharing his with Nick.

The sun shone brightly as the two men arrived at the Cathedral Church of Saint Peter and Saint Paul, better known as the Washington National Cathedral. Blaring trumpets announced their arrival.

An hour prior, choirs had serenaded guests arriving from all over the country. Several heads of state had been accorded special seating. Only the president, first lady, vice president and his wife, Senate and House leaders, and the two grooms' family members had reserved seating. Those with tickets had no assigned seats and had arrived hours earlier.

Midterm elections were around the corner. Those standing for re-election had to be seen supporting diversity and national unity. The 57 acres that made up the Cathedral grounds were filled to capacity with security personnel, spectators and press from around the world. Large outdoor screens had been erected throughout the cathedral grounds to provide those outside with a birds-eye view of the marriage ceremony.

Inside the cathedral, the mood was upbeat and festive. The sound from the 10,647 organ pipes regaled the attendees with classic Bach and Handel pieces performed by the cathedral's organ master. Modern pieces by Pepping and Wunderlich rounded out the performance.

The wedding ceremony was simple and traditional, or as traditional as a gay wedding could be. The newlywed couple held hands as they turned and faced their guests, Nick dressed in white tie and tails, Rocky festooned in his full Marine Corps dress whites. The Episcopal Bishop of Washington announced, "Mr. President, Your Majesties, Excellences, Honorables, ladies and gentlemen, I present Senator Nicholas and Colonel Ricardo Chambers-Jeffries."

Rocky and Nick lifted their joined hands above their head, smiling broadly at the four-thousand guests who rose as one and applauded their union. Trumpets heralded the introduction to Felix Mendelsohn's "Wedding March" and the cathedral organ thundered the remainder of the piece.

As they walked down the aisle smiling at friends, family and dignitaries, Rocky and Nick hoped the message of unity and equality they had promoted with their wedding would continue, long after this momentous day.

* * *

The midterms were over, and Rocky was on another mission, another clandestine one. He arrived at the Plaza Hotel in New York City. A Secret Service agent met him in the lobby and escorted him to the Vanderbilt suite.

"Good afternoon, Mrs. Tanner," Rocky said as he entered one of the parlors in the 2,500-square-foot suite.

She stood arms to her side dressed in a crisp red form fitting Chanel skirt and jacket.

"Good afternoon." She did not offer her hand. Rocky knew better than to offer his. He stood and waited for her to speak.

She turned and moved toward the center of the room, motioning him to sit.

He sat in what looked to be a replica of a Louis XVI chair. It creaked as he took his seat. *She always makes her adversaries uncomfortable*, Rocky thought.

Josephine remained standing. "What do you want?" Turning to the butler, she said, "You may go. We'll serve ourselves." The butler nodded and left the two alone.

"Again, what do you want? Let me guess. You're here to ask a favor. The senator is going to announce his candidacy for president, and you expect us to endorse him," Mrs. Tanner said in her infamous icy tone.

Rocky smiled at the iron lady who had dominated him in the past.

"Yes."

"I'm afraid that's impossible," she said through her teeth.

Rocky steeled himself inwardly and stated confidently, "You will do it. You will both join other prominent Republicans and make at least a dozen enthusiastic speeches at whatever venues the campaign selects. You will help us gather endorsements. We will provide you with a list."

Josephine cocked her head as she put her hands on her hips facing him and leaned forward. "Are you deaf? I said that is impossible." In a frantic voice she said, "No way in hell are we going to put our reputation and legacy on the line by endorsing a gay man for the White House. This is nuts!"

Rocky rose from his chair and walked over to the large window overlooking Central Park. He waited a moment and turned back toward her.

"Listen very carefully. This is not a request. And believe me, it can only improve your so-called legacy." He walked over to the butler's table and poured himself a scotch. "What you can gain is an unblemished legacy for you and President Tanner. A legacy that will continue to grow, expanding your and your husband's place in our nation's history. Do you follow me?"

"No, I do not. Make your point so I can show you the door." She folded her arms across her chest.

"You will understand, soon enough." He returned to the uncomfortable chair.

"We will tell the nation that years ago, we established a bond when your husband awarded me the Medal of Honor. That day you met and fell in love with my family and me. We'll regale the public with stories of the mentoring and guidance you provided Nick through the years."

Mrs. Tanner was curious, but annoyed. "Why on earth would we bother? We don't need you. We're done with politics. We want nothing to do with the 'odd couple.'"

"Odd couple? Really? Is what you and President Tanner have as a couple -- normal? I would say it's quite odd. It's certainly compromising, don't you think? Have you forgotten our last meeting? Of course, you haven't. If you want to keep the Tanner charade intact, I think you must admit I hold all the cards."

Mrs. Tanner clenched her jaw, visibly straining the muscles and tendons in her neck and face. She marched over to the bar and filled a tumbler with vodka. "I'm listening."

"You'll have the opportunity to take credit for helping spearhead the National Unity Campaign. That is our gift to you. As you know, it has gripped the nation and has international gravitas. It will amaze the world to know that former President Lindsey Tanner and First Lady Josephine Tanner continue to exercise leadership from behind -- leading, counseling and mentoring a young and promising senator. Inspiring our nation's next generation of leaders."

Mrs. Tanner stood motionless, her forehead creased with tension. She downed her drink, then turned her back on Rocky and faced the wall. Moments passed before the former first lady pivoted back around and placed her glass on a table. "I need time to think. Show yourself out."

Rocky nonchalantly gulped down the contents of his glass. He stood up and asked, "Do you still have the copy of the letter I gave you?"

Her eyes cut like knives in his direction as her eyelids narrowed and a stone-cold hardness engulfed her face. "Be here tomorrow at noon. You will have my answer then."

* * *

The following day, Josephine met Rocky at the door to the suite. "Come in. Thank you for accepting my invitation." Nonchalance had replaced her icy demeanor, a trait few knew she possessed.

Rocky followed her down a short hallway to the back parlor. "I've asked Lindsey to join us." If they had not been entering the room, this statement would have stopped him in his tracks. He felt beads of sweat emerging on his forehead and on the back of his neck. Rocky's mouth dropped as he spied the former president sitting at a table prepared for lunch.

"Hello there, Rocky!" President Tanner said. "Josephine insisted I cut short my golf trip to Montana and fly here to meet with you. She said it was important. It's nice to see you again."

"Mr. President, it's, uh, good to see you," Rocky stuttered.

"Sit down," Josephine said, directing him to a chair at the table. "You and I both know he doesn't play golf. We both know what he was up to," she said sarcastically. "Some things never change."

The president shrugged his shoulders and poured three glasses of Beaujolais. Handing them their wine, he said, "My wife shared your demands. Initially, I had my doubts. Josephine has assuaged them."

"What Lindsey is saying is, we're on board."

Rocky looked at them both. Internally he fought to tame his churning stomach.

"Well, what do you say, Rocky? Aren't you pleased? Isn't this what you wanted?" the president asked.

"Of course, he's pleased. He wants to know 'what's the catch?'" Josephine said.

Rocky sipped his wine and looked at Josephine, saying, "That's correct. What's the catch? And what do you really want?"

Josephine smirked, "You know what I want."

The president laughed, "She's so clever. She wants the original and all the copies. I want to be relevant again. We can get your husband elected but you have to play by our rules."

Josephine drank half her glass of wine and put it down. "We want a bigger part. We want to be there when the senator announces his candidacy."

"Why?" Rocky asked.

"For this game to play out, we have to be all in. Gene Smithers is good, but he's never run a winning presidential campaign. She, I mean he, is the senator's choice for campaign manager, right?" the president asked.

"Probably. More than probably. Yes, he is."

"Josephine and I are too long in the tooth to risk tarnishing our reputations. We would not be sitting here if we didn't think the senator could win."

Tanner continued, "The party will be thrown into convulsions when we endorse a gay man married to a Democrat."

Josephine interjected, "Don't change your party affiliation. It works for us and the campaign."

"I wasn't planning to. My affiliation and human-rights activism will bring along some Democrats and a lot of Independents."

"We agree," the former first lady said. "You will focus on the HRC and other LGBT organizations, but because they don't have a history of supporting Republicans, we don't think they'll pledge their full support. If you can neutralize them, we won't have to tie up resources combatting outright hostility."

Rocky twirled his glass. "I think you need to adjust your thinking. We're embracing diversity. Diversity appeals to a large swath of our constituency, at least the open-minded." He paused, "But you're right, that will be my focus."

"Good. Now, we'll assemble our team to advise Gene and his staff. Our people can't be out front. Primarily because we want transgender Gene to be front and center. His prominent leadership will facilitate the diversity angle. We like Gene. Always have," the president said as he refilled his glass.

Josephine sat back in her chair and said, "This is an unforeseen opportunity for the American people to support a third-party concept, an amalgam of both parties. That's what this is. It's a party that can embrace financial conservatism and family values. It's a hybrid Libertarian philosophy that has compassion for all people."

Rocky shifted in his chair and placing his arms on the chair arms. "I see where you're going with this. But never mention the word Libertarian again. It scares the crap out of people. This hybrid-party philosophy is not just family values; it encompasses individuals' values. It's as diverse as our citizenry. This hybrid must embrace a dynamic compassion. It must meet the ever-changing needs of the people."

The three sat for a moment. Josephine finished her wine as the president lit a cigarette. Rocky refilled her glass. The three sat quietly for several minutes.

"We welcome input on strategy. But you will have to leave the platform to us," Rocky insisted.

President Tanner said, lifting his cigarette in the air, "We have a major obstacle to confront. That obstacle is one that we have placated from day one -- the far right."

Tanner continued, "Most Americans see themselves as altruistic and believe in their hearts that they have the best interests of the country in mind. Indeed, many do. Middle Americans, those who work hard to support their families and their communities, make up this group. These same people are scared. They feel under attack. They see the liberal left-coast and northeast elitists as attacking their values. It's possible to reach some of them so we must reach out and include as many as we can. They're not really deplorable, just disenfranchised. All we need to do is show them we care about them." Tanner paused and drank from his water glass. "Then, we have the other elements; those misguided people who think and act much like the far left and conversely the far right. Most of these people are crazies. They're fanatics. They're blinded by their hate. Their thinking can't be altered. They're driven and are dangerous and violent. Our confronting them head on will enrage them. They'll feel betrayed. I hope you're ready for it."

Josephine nodded and looked at Rocky. "Have you thought about that? How do you suggest we should deal with that?" she asked. She helped herself to one of the president's cigarettes and lit it. "I know you smoke, so help yourself, relax and enjoy it." Rocky took a cigarette. Josephine extended her lit cigarette. He removed it from her hand and lit his. He handed her cigarette back to her. Rocky sat back taking a long slow drag and exhaling forcefully."

Rocky's lips stretched into a severe line. His eyes glowered. "We started with the unity campaign leading up to our wedding. We have a committed and unified base. Now it's time to change tactics. Fight the cancer; eradicate it. Face it head-on. Challenge it. Expose it for what it is. Use every asset we have to destroy it. Attack with a strong, proactive message and overwhelming outreach."

Both Tanners sat silent. Neither moved.

President Tanner shifted his weight and added, "It's the center of both parties and the Independents that will provide the momentum. It's the center-leaning fringes of the hard left and hard right that will secure victory."

Again, the three sat another time for several minutes, their breathing audible.

Josephine stood up and leaned over as she placed her hands on the table. She looked at her husband and then turned her attention to Rocky. "What about the letter?"

Rocky looked directly into Josephine's eyes. "What letter?" His unexpected response and blank stare caused Josephine to look down at the table.

Her head remained bowed until President Tanner cleared his throat.

Josephine stood up and said, "Thank you."

Rocky pushed back from the table and stood up. He shook the seated president's hand. "Mr. President, all I ask is that you limit your golf. No one needs to hear about your drives."

Josephine covered her mouth with one hand and chuckled.

"Rocky, I understand. Not to worry," replied the president, visibly amused.

Josephine grinned and said, "I'll show you out."

When the two reached the suite entrance, Josephine turned to Rocky and said, "I want to thank you for giving my husband and me the opportunity to participate in reshaping the nation's narrative." She reached up and straightened his tie. "I also want to thank you for giving Lindsey and me a chance to make up for hiding who we are. By that I mean, who he is." She paused and lowered her head.

Taking Rocky's hands and peering into his eyes, "I've always tried to protect my husband. Perhaps I made a lot of bad choices. I have been scared all my married life. Afraid that one day I would either lose him to another man, or he would be outed. Either way, I would lose the man I love and be ruined. Maybe now we can move forward, and I can atone for some of what I've done. Rocky, perhaps now, we can do something to help those who have been forced to hide like we have, in fear."

She placed both hands on his arms as her eyes grew moist. "One day soon, I hope everyone can have freedom from hate and bullying. A chance to live their lives authentically without fear of reprisal." She sniffed, "Let's advance diversity and equality, part of what makes our country great."

Rocky looked at Josephine. He wasn't sure he trusted her yet, but she seemed genuinely moved. She drew Rocky close to her, placing her arms around him and whispering in his ear, "Please forgive me."

Rocky released any animus, real or imagined, he might have felt toward her.

"Done."

CHAPTER 26

2018 - 2020: CAMPAIGN CALAMITY

The east portico of the United States Capitol was festooned in red, white and blue bunting. A cross-section of politicians, the public and the media crowded the steps and terraces. The mid-morning sun lit up the brilliant white-marble façade.

Senator Nicholas Chambers-Jeffries stood at center stage. Rocky, Brooke and Rick stood to one side. On his other side stood President and Mrs. Tanner and the Republican National Committee chairwoman. The Republican House and Senate leadership flanked them. Behind Nick were assembled Nick and Rocky's parents, siblings, grandparents and other extended family members. A uniformed band played patriotic tunes accompanied by a local church choir.

The event began as the band and choir performed the national anthem. Everyone stood at attention -- some with their hands on their hearts while others saluted. Cheering and clapping erupted as the anthem closed.

President Tanner moved forward to a single microphone stand as the band played "Hail to the Chief."

President Tanner began his remarks, "Members of Congress, assembled guests, and the American people. It is a great honor for my wife and me to be invited to participate in this auspicious occasion. I have the privilege to announce the beginning of a new era, a new dawn for our beloved United States of America!"

Encouragement and applause erupted from the crowd.

"Today, we are launching a crusade of epic proportions. A crusade that will transform this great country into an even greater nation. Today we are reaching out to all Americans to embrace this crusade and lead the charge for justice, liberty and equality."

"We are tearing out the pages of a history chronicling horrific examples of hate and bigotry. We are placing these horrific pages on a bonfire that will consume and relegate these hateful ideas and practices that have crippled our nation. They shall be remanded to the sordid ash heap of history. We will no longer tolerate prejudice, bullying and fear mongering!

On cue, the band and choir performed the song "America."

"My fellow Americans, this morning I have the honor of presenting to you a man who embodies all that is great in each of us. A man of courage. A man of integrity. A man with a vision and the ability to lead us forward!"

"Ladies and gentlemen, the next President of the United States, Senator Nicholas Chambers-Jeffries!

Cheers and applause erupted once again, followed by the raising of "Chambers-Jeffries for President" placards and banners throughout the crowd.

An eighteen-gun salute followed as the band and choir rang out "God Bless America."

Nick waved to the crowds as he made his way to the microphone. He and President Tanner shook hands and embraced, then President Tanner walked back to his wife. Nick continued to wave and smile broadly.

When the choir and band had finished, he motioned the cheering crowd to quiet down. It took a while for everyone to respond as spontaneous cheers, applause and air horns filled the air.

"Thank you. Thank you," said Nick. "Thank you, President Tanner, for your enthusiastic and inspiring introduction. It can't get any better than that. I guess we can go home now and get to work!" he laughed.

The crowd joined him in his laughter, applauding and cheering once again.

Nick waited for the crowd to calm down. "Thank you, everyone, for taking time out of your lives to show your support. So, let's get on with it. I hereby announce my candidacy for President of the United States of America!"

The announcement met with thunderous applause. The band launched into a melody of Sousa marching songs.

The presidential candidate gave the crowd a few minutes to enjoy the synergy and music.

"Why am I running for president? Why would you, the sovereign citizens of the United States, want to elect me president? The reasons are many and different for each of you as individuals. Our founding fathers created a roadmap called the Constitution of the United States to serve all those who have the good fortune to be citizens of America."

Applause erupted again.

"The Constitution does not protect us because of our race, religion, gender or identity. It protects us as individuals. Individuals who have the right to life, liberty and the pursuit of happiness. The right to pursue these freedoms as individuals on our own terms. As individuals, you have the right to honor your cultural traditions and heritage. You are entitled to worship as you choose. You have the right to love who you love. Yet, you do not exercise rights of a specific identity, class or ethnicity. People gave their lives to achieve these rights as individuals. We are finished with identity politics. I will serve each of you as individuals -- protected by our Constitution and free to live your lives as you choose. That is what my candidacy stands for. That is why you should elect me President of the United States!"

The throng was silent. As his words sank in, applause started to sound from different corners of the crowd. The applause grew louder and louder as it began to roll through the multitude. Cheering soon eclipsed the applause. Horns blew as American flags and political signs were thrust into the air.

The national media covering the event live used the time afforded by the raucous crowd to summarize what the senator had said. One network anchor postulated, "Senator Chambers-Jeffries is advocating turning the political landscape on its ear. He has tossed out identity politics and replaced it with the rights of the individual." The news anchor repeated himself as if to validate what he had just reported. "He's advocating throwing out identity politics and replacing it with the rights of the individual. This is a fresh style, a groundbreaking platform and a mesmerizing message. Buckle up, America, we're in for a wild ride!"

Senator Chambers-Jeffries went on to outline his platform, line by line. He ended his speech with an appeal. "My fellow Americans, you can see that our platform is one of inclusion. As individuals, we are one. But, we are still individuals with rights guaranteed by our Constitution. I am reaching out to all of you. All citizens. All political parties. All genders. All races. All religions. How else can I say it? Every single American! Come together, embrace your individualism and embrace one another! Let's join hands and work together to strengthen our nation and empower each of us as individuals. Individuals that love and embrace one another! God Bless America!"

* * *

"Well, Senator," said President Tanner on the phone the following day. "It appears as if the campaign got off to a great start."

"Thank you, Mr. President. Thanks to you, Mrs. Tanner, the support of the party and of course, my husband," Nick said.

"Is Rocky nearby?" Tanner inquired.

"Yes, he's right here. Did you want to speak to him?"

"Actually, can you put him on speaker phone?" The former president asked.

"Sure, hold on." Nick pushed a button.

"Hello, Mr. President," Rocky said.

"Hey there, Rocky. Just wanted to congratulate you both on a terrific day yesterday," Tanner said.

"Nicky and I both thank you for your rousing endorsement," Rocky said.

President Tanner cleared his throat. "Boys, I wanted to follow up on some information my staff and I've been gathering. Some of it is public knowledge. Some of it's from my sources and conversations."

"Okay, great. What is it?" Nick said.

"It looks like the media is still trying to sort out what you said yesterday. They're struggling with ways to try and minimize the message. It's not working. People from all over the political map are endorsing different parts of the platform. No side is unanimous in supporting you, but neither are they dismissing you. You've definitely got them talking."

"That's good, right?" Rocky asked.

"That's more than we could have hoped for. Think about it. Only the extreme left and extreme right are taking total issue. That's about twenty to thirty percent of the population. That leaves more than half the populace trying to figure it out," Tanner said.

"So, what does that mean for moving forward?" Nick asked.

"It means we stay on point. Keep them talking. Repeat and repeat what you've said at every opportunity," Tanner stressed.

"We can do that," Nick replied.

"Good. Now we need endorsements. My folks are working on that. What are you doing about the gays and liberals on the left, Rocky?" Tanner asked.

"I've got meetings with the HRC, the Log Cabin Republicans and other organizations. We've scheduled several interviews on some of the big networks for me to speak on Nicky's behalf. Once we have a feel about how receptive they are to Nicky, we'll schedule him where we can," Rocky said.

"Good. Nick, you need to spend some time with the folks on the right. I'm taking the same tact Rocky is with these folks."

"So, Mr. President, let's delve into where we stand right now," Nick suggested.

"I think we'll find our core with the center left and center right. Independents look really good. We've got to work the minority populations hard. A lot of them can be moved center if they trust you. Trust is everything. It's going to take an 'in the trenches' commitment. Ultimately, they will drive this election over the top." President Tanner took a breath.

He continued, "My guess is if the electorate sees the two of you on the road, they'll see unity and substance. Kind of like the 'two for one' thing the Clintons had going for them. Rocky, focus on LGBT and veterans. Your reputation as a war hero just about hands a big chunk of the military and vets to us. Wear that medal when you talk to those groups. They love that sort of stuff. The fact that you are a colonel in the Marine Reserves is huge. Always get introduced as Colonel Chambers-Jeffries. We have to play the family angle. You're a macho guy, so representing the family shouldn't cause you a problem. Get on some of the midday shows that appeal to women. Talk about the kids. Be a proud dad," Tanner counseled.

"Sure, no problem."

"One more thing. Get checked out in the 737. Let's get the press photographing you piloting the campaign plane. I can't imagine anything with more wow factor. Picture this: Nick on the tarmac and you waiving out of the cockpit window. That'll make the women tear up and give half the men a hard on!"

"Yeah, Gene, I know we are out but let's go easy on that message," said Nick. The three laughed.

"Nick, stay presidential out there. Talk about the family a little but let Rocky handle most of that. Also, remind them you have international experience. The European tour you had with NATO helps. Pull out old photos of you as a senator on overseas trips to Asia and the like."

"As far as the economy goes, I know that's also your expertise. Rocky, don't get into it too deep. Let Nick work through that. We don't want the voters to think you are going to be too involved in the West Wing. Okay, guys. I've gotta go. Meetings all over the place today. See you later!"

The phone conversation ended, and Nick turned to Rocky. "That was one hell of a set of marching orders," said Nick.

"Yeah, but he sure as hell knows what he's talking about. Seems like he's really embraced this race. It's in his blood," Rocky mused.

"What do you hear from your grandfather? Is he greasing the skids for me to reach out to the Dems?"

"Yep, he and I spoke this morning. He knows we need Wall Street. Contrary to what Tanner said, he feels I need to be out there working those guys. I know them, and they respect me. My grandfather has huge influence. He is setting up small group discussions with all the proverbial titans of industry. I don't see it as a problem and it could be an advantage for the campaign, financially and otherwise. And the good news is the market is up since you announced!"

* * *

Late that July, the Republican National Convention was in a fevered frenzy. The National Committee Chairwoman stood at the podium. "Ladies and gentlemen, it is my pleasure to introduce the Republican Party's nominee for President of the United States, Senator Nicholas Chambers-Jeffries!"

The convention hall was hit with a blizzard of red, white and blue confetti, balloons and thunderous applause. Chanting and music added to the cacophony. Nick, Rocky, Brooke and Rick entered the hall and walked to the center of the platform. The twins, in their early twenties, joined their parents, smiling and waving enthusiastically. The foursome projected the epitome of the modern family.

Nick hugged and kissed his family. As they walked off center stage and took their seats, he moved behind the massive podium, looking out into the crowd, waving and smiling. He brandished the victory sign with both hands. The hall, eventually exhausted from cheering and applauding, settled down.

"That sure felt good! Thank you!" the nominee said.

"Four months from now, we will have won the White House!"

The noise meter hit ten as the crowd roared their unified approval. The race was on!

* * *

Two months later, Rocky and Nick were having breakfast in their Los Angeles hotel suite. Gene burst into the room. "Turn on the fucking TV! You're not going to believe this shit!"

"It's on!" Rocky said.

"Well, look at it!" Gene hollered.

Nick and Rocky dropped the newspapers they had been reviewing. They had the sound on mute and were ignoring the TV. They had not noticed the news flashing across the screen.

Former President and Mrs. Tanner Gun Downed by Extremists

"Oh, my God!" Nick said. "Oh no!" He sat with his mouth open and eyes popping.

Rocky shot out of his chair and knelt in front of the giant TV screen. He stared at the screen. His jaw tightened; the taste of copper filled his mouth.

Secret agents entering the suite followed the sound of pounding and doors crashing open. Stunned, Nick and Rocky followed their movements with their eyes. "Sir, we're securing the suite and the entire hotel. Stay down and stay away from the windows and doors!" the head of security barked.

Nick moved to the center of the room. Two agents raced out onto each of the three expansive penthouse terraces. Three more agents closed and locked the glass doors and shut the heavy curtains.

"Sir, former president and Mrs. Tanner are dead. We're required to take every precaution to secure you and your family. We have increased the protection on the children in Charlottesville."

"Thank you," Rocky said, picking up his cell phone. "Nicky, I'm calling them now."

"Good. I want to talk to them when you reach them."

"What about my VP? Where is he? Is he safe?" Nick asked the agent.

"We're on it, sir. His security team just sent a text to confirm that the governor and his family have been secured."

Nick's phone rang. Gene retrieved it from the table where Nick had been breakfasting. "Gene Smithers answering for Senator Chambers-Jeffries." He paused. "Okay. It's the White House, sir." He handed the phone to Nick.

"Senator Cha...Mr. President." He paused. "Yes, sir. We're fine. Yes, the children are secure. Yes, I heard the governor and his family are reported safe. Thank you, sir...yes, sir, it is tragic and frightening...yes, if you would do that sir, it would be helpful and good for the country to hear from you directly. Yes, sir. When you address the nation, would you please express my and my family's condolences to the Tanner family and the country? Thank you, sir."

Nick sat quietly for several moments. He ran his hands through his hair several times. "I guess you all heard that. The president will address the nation as soon as he has more information. It appears the news reports are accurate. It is being classified as a terrorist attack."

"Fuck!" Gene said under his breath.

Nick watched the TV. Rocky sensed he wasn't watching, just staring.

Rocky found a seat next to Nick. "Are you going to be okay?"

"Yes, did you reach the kids? What did they say?"

"They're watching a movie at your parents' house. Rick and Brooke decided to take the folks out for breakfast. Before the four of them could leave the house, the Secret Service locked them down. It's unlikely anyone but the Secret Service knows where they are. They put on a movie when they heard the report and found out we are all right. Check your phone. They sent a text. They wanted to stay out of the way in case you were busy."

"Are you sure they're okay? I asked you to speak with them and let me speak with them!" Nick said, raising his voice.

"Check your text. Then focus on what's happening around here. Everyone is fine." Rocky said calmly.

Rocky's phone buzzed. "Everything's fine. Here's a video your mom just sent. It's a group text so it's on your phone, too."

He played the video for Nick. "See, they're waving at you. See the timestamp? Your mom insisted you pay attention to what's going on here. She said the protection's been doubled at both our parents' homes and our two homes. It'll be all right." Rocky hugged Nick and whispered in his ear, "Take charge, Mr. President."

Nick smiled at Rocky and turned to Gene. "Gene, get the governor on the phone. Contact the media and let them know I will be making a statement following the president's address. Also, reach out to the Tanner children. Find out when it would be appropriate for me to place a call to each of them. In the meantime, have the campaign security team assembled in thirty minutes. I want you personally to contact all campaign division heads and find out what you can. Schedule a videoconference with everyone following the security meeting. Make sure the security team is in that meeting, too."

"I'm on it, sir!" Gene said, swiftly exiting the suite.

The campaign security director entered the suite. "Sir, we have an update on the shooter."

"Okay."

"It appears the shooter may have been an extremist. He was throwing pamphlets around and screaming some religious gibberish as the Secret Service took him down. The ground team seems to believe he was a member of an unknown sect. Material found on the gunman proclaims opposition to individualism. It violates the tenets of their religion."

Rocky asked, "Where were the Tanners when this happened?"

"They were just outside Atlanta at a private airport boarding a plane. They were headed for a campaign fundraiser in Austin. They were both shot in the head. One agent was killed as well."

No one said anything for several minutes. Nick buried his head in his hands. Rocky stood next to him with his hand on his husband's shoulder. Nick looked up at him and Rocky saw his complexion had turned a ghostly gray.

"Don't these people realize that rights for individuals allow them to worship as they please? To preserve their cultural heritage and live their lives as they please?" Nick asked no one in particular.

Rocky went over to the wet bar and filled a tall glass with water. He handed it to Nick. "You look dehydrated. Please drink this."

Nick gulped it down.

"If you want my opinion, sir, it was a splinter group. This is not a mainstream issue," said the director.

Nick grabbed a notepad and a pen. "We have to make a statement before the opposition tries to lay the blame on the campaign or our platform. We can't have the far right and far left fanning the flames of hate. Maybe we can get the Tanner family to echo these sentiments. It's cruel to ask them at a time like this, but it's for the greater good. They said they believed in what their parents were doing. For the first time in their lives, they saw their parents working for the common man."

"The children are being picked up by two of my company's jets. They will be taken to Atlanta to escort their parents' remains to Santa Barbara. That is, if the coroner releases the bodies any time soon," Rocky said as his phone rang. "I'll take this in the other room."

As Rocky closed the door behind him, Nick asked the director, "Do you know anything about the Tanner children's plans?"

"Yes, sir. Your husband texted the arrangements and copied me when you were on the phone with the president."

"Hmm," Nick murmured.

Rocky returned to the room several minutes later. "The Tanner family is on its way here. They should arrive mid-afternoon. They called to say the coroner couldn't release the bodies for at least twenty-four hours. The bullets appeared to have made them both almost unrecognizable. The autopsies are underway now."

"That poor family. It's just devastating," Gene mumbled into his hand covering his mouth.

"Why are they coming here?" Nick asked.

Rocky said, "I stressed how important their father and mother had been to our campaign and your message. I offered them an opportunity to honor their parents' memory."

"What are you talking about, Rocky?" an impatient and perplexed Nick asked.

"I filled them in on what you just said, about making a statement and not fanning the flames of hate."

Nick stood up, "You've got to be shitting me! Did you really say that? And they want to speak?" He paused for a few seconds. "Well, what did they say?"

"They embraced it. Their words were, 'get your people to write it, and we'll say it.'"

"Damn!" Nick's mood elevated "Well done!" Nick walked to toward the terrace door.

"Sir! Stay away from the windows. Please!" an agent shouted

"Sorry," the nominee said.

CHAPTER 27
FIRST SPOUSE

Rocky and Nick decided to wait for the election results with the kids and their families in Charlottesville. The house was surrounded by Secret Service and dozens of media vans. The satellite dishes pointed upward and gave the appearance of a field of metallic poppies reaching for the sky.

The family had allowed the public and media into the fields and pastures surrounding the main house. It was an unseasonable cold and windy day in early November. The twin college grads had come home to be with their dads on the big day. With the security arrangements and crowds outside, they were, by necessity, confined to the house.

"Hey Dad, we're going to make hot apple cider and hot chocolate. Those folks are probably freezing outside. It's cold as crap out there!" said Rick.

"Yeah," said Brooke. "We've started warming the milk and heating the water."

"Why don't we make some cookies, too?" volunteered Consuelo.

"Sounds good to me," Nick said, joining in.

"Me, too. Let's all help. But just you kids will take it out to them. I'm staying inside where it's warm," Rocky said.

"You know, we aren't kids anymore, remember? We've graduated from college. I think we can handle this," Brooke said.

Rocky wrapped an arm around his daughter. "Now Brooke, you two will always be kids to us. Besides, we want to help," he said, heading to the pantry.

"Me, too! Rocky's right. We want to help, but you two can make the deliveries," smiled Nick.

The kitchen was soon filled with volunteers looking for ways to escape the TV following hours of election speculation.

A couple of hours later, Rocky and Nick helped the kids load a barn cart with plastic containers of cookies and several large containers of steaming-hot apple cider and hot chocolate. "How many dozen cookies did we make?" Nick queried.

Brooke smiled and said, "At last count, twenty-four!"

"We could feed a battalion of Marines with that!" crowed Rick.

"We are!" Nick and Rocky chimed in together.

"Okay, off you go! See you when you get back. Say hi to the folks out there from us. Don't tell them we helped make the cookies. They might not eat them!" Rocky laughed, slapping Nick on the back.

Alone in the kitchen, Rocky pulled Nick close. "Just think, in a few hours we may be calling you Mr. President Elect." Hugging Nick closer, he kissed him. They placed their heads side by side on each other's shoulders.

"Can you believe it? Look how far we've come since that day at the Academy when we first met," Nick said.

Rocky laughed, "Yeah, and I'll still be calling you sir or Mr. President! Shit

* * *

The large oak grandfather's clock standing in the entrance hall struck 9 p.m.

"West Coast polls are closing. We'll be getting some numbers soon," said Gene.

"Finally," seemed to erupt from everyone's lips in the room. The fire jointly built sixteen hours earlier by Rocky and Nick overheated the room. The large stones surrounding the fireplace and flue had heated up all day as the well-tended fire helped entertain the constant flow of visitors.

"Open some windows," Nick's mother said. "I'm burning up!"

"You're just anxious, Mom," Nick said.

"She's right," said Consuelo. "It's burning up in here. Let's let some of the icy cold weather in to cool things off."

Rocky went to open the French doors leading to the terrace. Consuelo followed him. "Rocky, I'm so proud of you both. No matter what happens, I wish you two the best."

"Thanks, Mom. What brought that on? I thought you didn't like Nick and I together."

"I suppose I got over that a long time ago. I just haven't had the *cajones* to tell you."

"*Cajones*?" Really, Mamacita? When did you start talking like that?" Rocky laughed.

"Well, at least we have one thing in common, we both like men." Consuelo grinned and gave Rocky a kiss on the cheek.

"*Madre de Dios*, Mamacita! You never cease to amaze me." Rocky gratefully hugged his mother.

"So. Are you going to be a first lady?" Consuelo raised her eyebrows mischievously.

Rocky decided to tease her. "Why yes, of course. In fact, I need you to help me pick out a ball gown. Low cut, revealing. You know what I mean."

"Ricardo! Shame on you!" They both laughed as she swatted him on the arm. She calmly asked him again, "Seriously, what will they call you?"

He took both her hands in his. "First Spouse of the United States."

"Oh! I like that. So, when we get two ladies in the White House one day, they can be First Spouse of the United States too! *Sì*, I like that *mucho gusto!*"

From the other side of the room, "Numbers coming in! It's close. East Coast looks like even-steven. Nope, Dems ahead by three electoral seats. We got Florida. We're ahead! Oh crap, West Virginia, Georgia, Alabama and South Carolina not looking so good."

Someone else chimed in, "Look, we got Ohio. And Pennsylvania. New York's too close to call. Who would've thought! New York may be going Republican. New England not so good."

The hall clock struck 11 p.m.

Gene said, "Hey, we're ahead in the popular, but not in the electoral. *Déjà vu.* Here come some more numbers. Not much change. Wait a minute. We're pulling seats in the Midwest big time. This is looking good. Look at those numbers! We're ahead in the electoral and down in the popular. Shit, I mean that's okay."

"This is unlike any election I've ever seen," said a staffer.

Gene piped in, "It's because the platform's appeal crosses party lines. We just don't know where the lines are!"

"Hold on! Hold on! NBC predicting the election for the Democrats. Fuck!"

"CNN won't call it yet."

"FOX usually has good insight, but they're not saying shit. Maybe that means we're winning? Yeah, maybe. That FOX group is split down the middle."

The clock struck 12:30 a.m.

"California's in! We got Cali! Whoo-hoo!"

Nick and Rocky exchanged glances and held hands tighter. They noticed each other's eyes pooling.

"Holy Mary Mother of God! NBC, CBS and FOX just called it for us! We got it!" Gene squealed at the top of his lungs.

Nick and Rocky turned to each other and hugged tightly. Rocky whispered, "Congratulations, Mr. President."

Nick took Rocky's face in his hands and kissed him. "Congratulations, First Spouse. Without you, this never would have happened."

"I know," quipped Rocky and kissed his husband again.

* * *

Inauguration Day was perfect. The sun shone brightly. A gentle breeze floated thousands of flags and banners in the air. Temperatures were moderate and spirits high. The president-elect had won by enough popular votes and electoral college delegates to claim victory. Not a mandate, but victory nonetheless.

Nicholas Chambers-Jeffries was sworn in by the Chief Justice of the United States. Ricardo Chambers-Jeffries held the Jeffries' family Bible as his husband took the oath.

"I do solemnly swear that I will faithfully execute the Office of President of the United States, and will to the best of my ability, preserve, protect and defend the Constitution of the United States, so help me God."

President Chambers-Jeffries hugged his husband and their children. He accepted congratulations from the outgoing president and first lady.

The vice president took his oath.

Military jets flew over the Capitol Building. Bands played, and onlookers cheered.

The president's speech captivated the crowds and those watching on television and a multitude of electronic devices. After lunch in the Capitol Building, the new president escorted former President and Mrs. Nelson to the east portico entrance and watched them depart in the presidential squadron helicopter.

"Rick, Brooke, how would you like to ride with us in the motorcade?" Nick asked.

"I thought we were supposed to go in another car, Dad," Rick said as Brooke nodded.

"Well, we can change that if you like," Nick said.

"Sure! We'd love to! Right, Rick?" Brooke said.

"Yeah! That'd be cool! The president's ride is way better than ours. It's called the Beast," Rick said.

"Okay, then. Let's go together," Nick said waving them toward the car. The family surprised the Secret Service and onlookers as they piled in. "Sir," said the agent in charge, "are you sure?"

"I am," the president said.

The Secret Service scrambled to revise procedures and protocol. No one, not even the president, could fathom all that was involved in modifying presidential security at the last minute. There simply was no contingency plan in place to accommodate this change.

The motorcade was delayed ten minutes as security modifications were instituted. Halfway down

Pennsylvania Avenue, the president ordered the motorcade to stop.

"Kids, we're going to do what many presidents have done. Walk. But we're different. We're going to walk as a family. We're going to show the world, firsthand, our family. Our modern, loving family."

"Sounds like a good idea, Dad. Besides, I know they want to take a closer look at one of the country's most eligible bachelors," Rick crowed.

Brooke patted him on his knee and said, "I pity the poor girl who ends up with you, Mr. Eligible Bachelor."

Brooke then turned her attention to her heels. "I think I have the wrong shoes for this, but okay," Brooke said with trepidation.

"Brooke, it's not that far of a walk. I'll carry you if your feet get sore," teased Rocky.

Brooke looked at her father as if he were an idiot. "Not likely, I'll take my shoes off and walk barefoot before I let anyone see you carrying me!" The four were still laughing as they got out of the armored limousine.

The crowds' cheering ratcheted up several notches when the family exited the Beast and walked down the wide boulevard. Rocky stood on one side, holding Brooke's hand. Brooke and Rick held hands. Nick held

Rick's hand. Occasionally the young adults would let go and wave to the onlookers.

Rick and Brooke heard their names repeatedly shouted from the crowds.

"Rick, I love you!" was often heard. On one occasion, a man said it.

Brooke could not contain herself and laughed, "Apple doesn't fall far from the tree!"

"You're just jealous because everyone wants me," Rick said waving and smiling to the crowds as they continued their walk down Pennsylvania Avenue.

Rocky beamed at Nick and the children, his heart swollen with pride.

Entering the presidential viewing enclosure in front of the White House, the family settled in with the many VIPs to watch the parade. Two hours later, making their way through the crowds, they crossed the broad lawn accompanied by a phalanx of Secret Service agents. The family walked together toward the White House.

"Brooke are you excited about living in the White House?" Rocky asked.

"I'm not sure. Everything I've read said the White House is just a fancy prison."

Nick and Rocky exchanged "oh shit" looks. "Maybe not, Brooke. I guess it depends on what you make of it," Nick said, trying to sound reassuring.

Rocky took Brooke's hand, "That doesn't mean you won't at least spend the holidays with us, does it? We can go to Camp David or the Charlottesville house if you prefer."

"Not to worry, Dad, of course I'll be wherever you two are on holidays," Brooke said, smiling.

"When do we get our stuff moved in?" Rick asked.

"It's already there," said Rocky.

"What? How did that happen? They haven't moved it from the house," Rick said.

"They started doing it when we left this morning. They've had five hours to pack up, move the boxes on the trucks and unpack and put your things in your rooms. They've also repainted. You'll smell the fresh paint soon enough," Rocky said, smiling.

"Dad," Rick rolled his eyes and turned to Nick, "is he pulling our leg for the hundred-millionth time?"

Nick hooted, "The first spouse knows what he's talking about."

"First spouse!" the twins said in unison, laughing.

"Nick said, "Yeah, I'm POTUS which stands for President of the United States. He's FSOTUS, First Spouse of the United States."

"That's weird," said Rick.

"What do they call us?" asked Brooke

"First Millennials of the United States, FMOTUS," Rocky teased and everyone laughed.

"Just kidding. But you do have code names. Brooke, you are Sunshine, and Rick is Showboat," Rocky teased again.

"No way!" Rick said, a grimace on his face.

Brooke laughed, "You got that right!"

"Just kidding, you're Hollywood. That must have something do with, well, you know." Rocky said redeeming himself.

Rick lifted his chin and the grin on his face signaled approval.

"What about you two, do you have code names?" Brooke asked.

"I'm sure we do. We can talk about it later," Nick said.

"Wow, the White House looks so much bigger when you're close," Rick marveled.

"I'm having so much fun, I know it is totally age inappropriate, but I feel like skipping," Brooke chirped.

"Go ahead, do it!" Nick said.

"I'd love to see that on social media tomorrow!" Rick quipped.

As the family approached the portico, Nick stepped between the twins and put his arms around them. "Thank you both so much for being here and for being so helpful and understanding. It's been a long campaign. He pulled them closer. "I love you both so much!"

A shot rang out.

Nick fell forward, his arms falling from Brooke and Rick's shoulders. He dropped face down on the pavement.

Both Rick and Brooke saw their father fall and screamed, "DAD! DAD!"

"Nicky, no! Nicky!" Rocky hollered as all three of them jumped to the ground surrounding Nick. They all were touching him but didn't know what to do to help him.

Suddenly the Secret Service swept them up and away toward the protection of the White House.

Rocky fought to stay with Nick, but to no avail as three agents successfully subdued him, hauling him toward the White House.

Resisting, Rocky screamed, "Nicky, Nicky!"

"It's for your own good sir, please stop fighting us!"

Overwhelmed by two agents on either side and one behind hm, he craned his head back toward the driveway. His heart ached, and his head felt like it would explode as he saw Nick, face down on the pavement, blood seeping from underneath him.

Secret Agents could be heard on their radios shouting,

"POTUS DOWN!"

AUTHOR'S ACKNOWLEDGEMENT & APPRECIATION

It would not have been possible for me to have finished this book following my having completed the original manuscript without support from some pretty amazing people. I would first like to acknowledge those that steadfastly supported me through the process. You know who you are! Thank you!

I am going to do something rather dangerous and list many of those who have helped in a myriad of ways. They are not listed in any particular order. Perhaps that will assuage any hurt feelings.

Thank you so much to my professional team. Their professionalism, mentoring, expertise, and patience have been invaluable: Trisha Stein: content editor. Jeanne Rawdin: copy editor. Carson McDonagh: cover designer. Larry Nichols and Jim Vann: technical advisors.

Here goes, a random list of folks that have helped me in so many different ways, pushing and shoving to get this book to market: Mike Norton, Elena Bazhenova, Dale Peronteau, Stephanie Burnham , Jan Toon, Anusha Venkatram, Ray Morgan, Peggy Hinaekian, Helen Brahms, Everett Hale, Larry Tritten, Josh Rutherford, Nick Darling, Patty Saenz, Craig and Alex Shaw, Jackie Strayve, Kris Brew, Jae and Travis Barrick, D Maria Trimble, Margaret Bhola, Lane O'Connor, Michelle and David Lowenstein, GW Colvard, Pat Wright, Dan Roper, Mike Vander Griend, Pam Means, Craig McLeod, Ashley Curtis, Johnny Lazootin, and more friends & family that are always there.

ABOUT THE AUTHOR

J.R. Strayve, Jr. has always enjoyed history and political science. A creative streak takes what he has read and jumps into overdrive; unloading compelling and captivating fiction.

A father of three adult children, has enjoyed creating and telling stories to his children and grandchildren. His writings have also been enriched through his experiences as a father of a 'special needs' child, an advocate for diversity, and a Marine Corps officer.

Strayve, a financial advisor and entrepreneur has created and run several businesses. A life as an athlete, sportsman, and adventure seeker have fueled his vivid and 'out of the box' imagination

Made in the USA
Middletown, DE
02 June 2021